making room

by
ELISA POMPILI

Praise for Making Room

"*Making Room* is a gentle love story on two levels; it's a satisfying tale of romantic love but—perhaps more important—it's also a tale of God's love for His people. A touching first novel."

—Ann Tatlock, award-winning author *Promises to Keep* and other books including *Sweet Mercy, Traveler's Rest, A Room of My Own, All the Way Home,* and *I'll Watch the Moon*

making room

a novel

ELISA POMPILI

Ambassador International
GREENVILLE, SOUTH CAROLINA & BELFAST, NORTHERN IRELAND

www.ambassador-international.com

making room

ISBN: 978-1-62020-129-9
eISBN: 978-1-62020-181-7

Cover art, book design and typesetting: Matthew Mulder
E-book conversion: Anna Riebe

AMBASSADOR INTERNATIONAL
Emerald House
427 Wade Hampton Blvd.
Greenville, SC 29609, USA
www.ambassador-international.com

AMBASSADOR BOOKS
The Mount
2 Woodstock Link
Belfast, BT6 8DD, Northern Ireland, UK
www.ambassadormedia.co.uk

The colophon is a trademark of Ambassador

For my grandmothers, who have told me for many years, in no uncertain terms, that I was to write a book. Here you are.

Chapter 1

"The meaning of life? That's easy. The meaning of life is: to be happy, try not to hurt people, and hope that you fall in love."
~ *Mallory Keaton, Family Ties*

A BEAUTIFUL, SUNNY CAROLINA SKY in late June made for calm waters and a perfect morning to spend outside. Elizabeth Tenner stepped outside her rented cottage and strolled barefoot down the ramp to the beach. The wooden planks were cool to the soles of her feet; it was still early, and the sun hadn't warmed them yet.

The sand was another story; it was hot and at first made her jump. She meshed her toes in it, giggling to herself at the way the sand lightly tickled the top of her feet. She was still wearing her cropped white sweatpant pajama bottoms with a black tank top that hugged her torso.

She closed her eyes and raised her head toward the sky, smiling at the sun and raising her hands like she half expected the sky to rain down on her. She felt so lucky; she was relaxing the way she'd always wanted. She had checked in with her family last evening, and everyone was doing fine.

"We miss you, but not enough. RELAX!" her brothers had all told her.

So far, in the first three days of her vacation, Elizabeth had slept until ten or eleven o'clock, laid on the beach, read a book and a half, and ordered Chinese food and pizza for dinner, with ice cream for dessert. She fully enjoyed spoiling herself in all kinds of different ways; her mind was finally beginning to clear after years of one thing after another cluttering it up. She even went running twice, because the beach looked too inviting not to.

Walking along the sand, Elizabeth thought about the stress rolling off her back. She thought about her life back home in Western New York, where the summer weather could be just as warm but lacked this oceanic oasis. It's not that Elizabeth didn't like her life; she loved life. It's just that it was always full of this, that, and the other thing, and it was always for something other than anything she deep-down desired. It had been like that for more than ten years. She had long ago learned to tuck certain things back into her heart, because she knew that if they came to the surface too often and for too long, she'd grow bitter and resentful of the life she led and the young adulthood she never experienced. Elizabeth gave with her whole heart because that's how she believed people should be helped, especially her brothers. She never regretted helping them, not for a second. She only wondered sometimes if she was meant for something else, something easier. But before she could dive too far into details, she once again paid attention to the water.

The ocean waves weren't high, but they still foamed pretty well when they hit the shoreline. Elizabeth stopped walking, turned to face the Atlantic, and let the foamy waves wash over her bare feet. Behind her, there were families all up and down the beach making sand castles, sun bathing, and reading; to the right and left of her were parents chasing their kids into and out of the water, and couples strolling hand in hand. Just to the left, there was a grandfather and his grandson holding hands, just two or three feet into the water, jumping every time a wave came toward them. The little boy giggled loudly, looking up at his grandpa to see if he was having a good time too. They fell into the water a few times, both clearly enjoying this game of tag they seemed to be playing with the ocean. Elizabeth smiled and imagined that would be a favorite memory for both of them.

The affection of the moment, even though it was between a grandson and grandfather, made Elizabeth wonder—again—if her dreams of falling in love, of finding that best friend in a man, would ever happen for her. She tried to push the thought away quickly; it saddened her, and this was her time to relax. The thought saddened her because when she thought of getting married, she thought of two things: having to talk about her parents, which she hated doing, and the possibility of leaving her brothers, which was out of the question for reasons she could and could not control. So instead, Elizabeth's thoughts went to the sunshine. It was shining even brighter now, and she enjoyed the people-watching.

Out of nowhere, a little girl who was staying in the house next to Elizabeth's ran up and hid behind Elizabeth, a tearful expression on her face. A boy followed close behind with a bucket full of water ready to toss in their direction; Elizabeth played right along.

"And what do you think you're going to do with that?" she asked the little boy with mock sternness. His big blue eyes glanced up at her. He couldn't have been more than eight years old.

"She stepped on my castle, so I'm gonna throw some water at her," the little boy said with as much vengeance in his voice as an eight-year-old boy could have. Which, from practically raising her younger brothers, Elizabeth knew could be all too strong.

"I'm not so sure that's a great idea," said Elizabeth gently. "She doesn't look like she really wants to get wet."

"Geez, lady, I'm just playin' around," the little squirt shot back.

Elizabeth laughed; kids could be so honest.

"Well, how about you toss the water on the sand and you both build a castle together? That way, nobody gets wet if they don't want to get wet, and you can build an even bigger one with four hands instead of two."

"That might be fun," said the blond-haired boy. "Will you help us?"

"I would love to," said Elizabeth genuinely. "Where are your parents?"

"They're over there," he said as he pointed about a hundred yards down the beach. "We leave tomorrow, so they said they don't want to do too much on our last day. Will you help us build a sand castle? A real big one with big towers and everything?"

"Sure, sweetie. On one condition," she looked at the boy. "This little girl," she pulled the little girl from behind her, "and I don't get wet until we're all done, and then we will all take a celebration run into the ocean, okay?"

"Deal. Can we start now?" He was impatient but spirited.

After about two hours of going back and forth getting wet and dry sand, digging with various tools—this family had an impressive collection—the two kids and Elizabeth built a sand castle worthy of the admiring glances from passersby. It had four corner towers around a large square middle. There were what passed for stairs, windows, brick detail, and a moat that went around the whole structure. It stood about two feet high because they just kept putting sand pile on top of sand pile. Elizabeth was quite proud of it; she even ran back to her house to get her camera to make sure people believed her when she said she built an amazing sand castle with neighbor kids. But she had a heart for kids who seemed to have to fend for themselves. These two youngsters' parents didn't seem very interested in the kids' desire to build a sand castle, so Elizabeth was happy to take them on for a few hours.

At the end of the afternoon, Elizabeth was tired from being in the sun, but after a short nap and a shower, her energy was renewed. She decided to go into town since she'd been on the beach for three days and had yet to go into more of a real-world setting other than to buy groceries; she just enjoyed the remote relaxing so much.

Deciding on a clean white tank top with a denim skirt, she added pink flip-flops to match the pink bracelet and earrings she wore. Every part of Elizabeth was tan, and she smiled wide in the mirror, proud that she had been able to keep a good shape despite the stress that always found her shoulders tense and her stomach in a knot. She had made healthy eating and exercising part of her daily lifestyle. If nothing else, Elizabeth could control how she felt about her body and herself, and staying healthy made that considerably easier.

Into town she went, taking her purse with only her wallet, cell phone, and lip gloss.

Skipping down the stairs, Elizabeth savored the feel of the balmy night air. The trees were swaying very gently in the early evening breeze, and the sun was beginning to set; orange, pink, purple, and red lit up the sky in the way only a southern sunset could. She took in the sights and sounds of families barbecuing on the porches and balconies of their rented homes, large groups of friends starting their parties early, friends and lovers having dinner at the restaurant patios that lined the streets. Even though each restaurant had twinkle lights attached to its outside decorating, each maintained its own character and personality. Her favorite restaurant was called Shade of the Palm Tree; the atmosphere intrigued her. Each of the four corners of the patio had two palm trees, one small and one large, complete with white twinkling lights wrapped around the trunks. Set up along the white fence surrounding the patio were tiny fake palm tree statues. There had to be at least a hundred of them, just sitting on the ledge. The best part was that under each one was a handmade figurine of a man, woman, or child enjoying the shade of the palm trees. There's beauty to be found in that kind of relaxed environment, and that mood enveloped Elizabeth at this restaurant. She enjoyed every bite of her meal, not saving any of it for leftovers. She had decided that this vacation would not involve being conscious of every detail as she was at home. If she wanted to finish her meal, she would finish her meal, even if that meant going out again the next night. Here on vacation, leftovers didn't need to be saved for lunches and late-night stress-reliever snacks.

During dinner, Elizabeth did more people-watching. She saw a couple in the corner of the patio under one of the palm tree duos, leaning in close, both smiling and gazing into each other's eyes as if they were sharing a great secret. She saw another couple, this one maybe in their sixties, who had almost the same expression as the young couple.

How is that possible, she wondered to herself.

She didn't understand being with somebody that long and still having a great amount of affection for the other.

Elizabeth had been thinking a lot about love lately, not just romantic love but all kinds. Her brothers were the ones who taught her the most about love, because despite all Elizabeth's failings, they seemed to love her unconditionally. She forgot lunch money, missed baseball and football games, lost her temper, and a hundred other things. The oldest brother, Bryce, though younger than she was, had once explained her brothers' forgiving affections: "You didn't leave, Liz. You could have up and left, but you stayed. For that, you…" He had gotten choked up then, being more sensitive than Elizabeth. He finished, "Well, how can we do anything but love you like we do?"

She had appreciated his words and the sentiment behind them. Yet she still often thought about the power of love—if it existed outside her household, outside the bond she and her three brothers maintained. Love was a mystery to her, probably because in her life, with the exception of her brothers, she had known true examples of what she thought love should look like for only a very short time.

Her brothers would want to talk to her about God's love if they were here. *Thank goodness they're not; I don't want to think about that tonight.* Elizabeth allowed her mind to wander into "If only" and "I wonder" lands where she peppered herself with one wishful thought after another: *If only I could let myself be like the woman in that couple at the table. I wonder if they really love each other. I wonder if my brothers will get married. I wonder if I'll get married.*

On went her thoughts until she forced herself to remember that she was on vacation, and she should dwell upon much lighter topics. But one last thought crept its way in: she wondered how long she would have this persona—how long would she be an individual with two sides to offer in any relationship: kind and compassionate but also exceptionally cynical and frustrated much of the time.

The palm trees, real and artificial, the alternating black and natural colored tables and chairs, the twinkle lights, the beautiful weather, all these made Elizabeth imagine what a dream, a pure joy it would be to live permanently in a place like this. Even aside from how serene the weather was, the aura of the place in general was enough to make Elizabeth never want to leave. There was a sense of exhilaration and liveliness it stirred within her, which were unique feelings for Elizabeth. Yet, it was all she truly wanted. What she really wished for was something her heart could be poured into. Something her heart could grab onto and make its own. At twenty-six, she was still searching for her life's passion beyond her family and work.

All this crossed Elizabeth's mind as she sat at her table, long after her food was gone. That's what this place seemed to do to her; she entertained thoughts that she never dared to think at home. She wasn't sure if this would happen at just any old vacation spot. Right now, she was almost certain it wouldn't. The ocean held a dear part of her heart, for reasons she did not understand. Besides, this was her first-ever solo vacation, so it held a great deal of meaning for her. It was natural for profound and complex thoughts to traipse through her mind.

Elizabeth knew that her return home would be met with a huge "WELCOME HOME!" banner and a couple dozen cookies, and all three of her brothers will have stayed home from hanging out with their friends because they'd want to hear about her trip and get their presents. She had spent a total of three weekends away from the boys since becoming their primary caretaker eleven years ago, and upon each return, she received the same warm welcoming even though they were only a weekend at a time. What would it be like after two full weeks?

Elizabeth paid her bill, having decided to walk around town before going home. She still had about forty-five minutes of light, and she wanted to take advantage of it.

In the months and years to come, Elizabeth would wonder whether she would still have taken this walk had she known it would change her life. Sometimes the answer would be yes, sometimes it would be no, and sometimes she just wouldn't know.

Walking south on Market Street, Elizabeth browsed in one of the dress shops, thinking *a woman should buy a new dress every once in a while.* But she couldn't find anything worth spending her money on, so she kept weaving in and out of local shops until an ice cream shop came into view. What she really wanted was a smoothie, which she saw advertised on their outdoor chalkboard. Five minutes later, Elizabeth was walking out the door with a passion fruit smoothie, enjoying the taste of tropical fruits on a summer evening.

In the few steps it took to walk out of the shop, Elizabeth didn't see the dog or its owner coming toward her. She didn't see the yellow lab bound out of his walker's leash grip. She just barely heard the owner scream, "Jax, no!" and she certainly didn't see what the fuss was about until all she saw was a wave of passion fruit smoothie go up over her face and down the pristinely white tank top she had taken much pride in wearing that night. The only one who didn't seem mortified was the dog; he simply licked at her legs where leftover smoothie was dripping, and he stood there wagging his tail, waiting for what, she wasn't sure. Wherever he had been going, he wasn't going anymore. Either he knew he was in trouble—not likely from the look of his wagging tail and sound of excited panting—or he was too entertained to remember his original pursuit. His embarrassed owner stood close by, and Elizabeth wasn't sure how to read his expression either.

Chapter 2

"Some things … arrive on their own mysterious hour, on their own terms and not yours, to be seized or relinquished forever."
~Gail Godwin

I AM SO SORRY," THE owner of the unassuming dog said. "I am so, so incredibly sorry," he said while cautiously trying to wipe the spilled smoothie off Elizabeth. Only, it spilled in awkward places that strangers really shouldn't touch, so his hands just kind of moved around arbitrarily as he handed her napkins that his friend had been holding from what looked to be the end of a messy hot dog.

"Oh that's all right, I was going to dye this shirt anyway," she said with kind sarcasm. She wasn't really upset, only disappointed about her shirt and the smoothie.

"Would you like me to buy you a new drink? How about a new shirt? I feel so bad about this," the stranger said, clearly unsure of what to say or do.

She laughed then, laughed out loud so hard that the stranger seemed unsure of how to handle the embarrassing situation.

"Well, you wouldn't know my size. Besides, it wasn't your fault. You should have your dog buy it for me," joked Elizabeth.

He seemed confused by her good-natured attitude, as if he were expecting her to yell. Instead, Elizabeth just laughed and tried to wipe herself off as best as she could. The pink-orange drink had run from her face all the way down her tank top—inside and out—and down her legs. Good thing it was a warm evening; the smoothie was cold and provided some relief, at least. Her skin, however, would become very sticky if she didn't hurry home and shower soon. The stranger was still trying to offer her another smoothie, but Elizabeth insisted that he didn't have to. Her smile still on her face, she continued wiping pink-orange drink from her skin.

She said, "That's okay, really. I should have known better than to wear white out in public. If I wear white at home, I spill pizza on it. White is not my friend most of the time. I should really learn my lesson."

"I have to do something. I feel just awful," he said.

After this third insistence, Elizabeth started to feel awkward. Sure that the outline of her bra and her tanned skin were both showing through her shirt, she was officially embarrassed and, quite frankly, wanted to get home as quickly as her legs could take her. But the handsome stranger smiled—rather shyly, she noticed—in a way that made her want to see what this man was going to do.

"Wait here," he said, running into a store behind where they were standing, leaving Elizabeth alone with the guilty dog and the stranger's friend, who managed to make the situation more awkward by texting the entire time they stood there alone. But the alone time was short-lived when the stranger emerged from the store with a brand new North Carolina t-shirt.

"I can't accept this! That's ridiculous," said Elizabeth, meaning every word.

"Please? What else can I do? Seriously, I feel awful. I can have Ben here—" he pointed to his texting friend, "take Jax back to the house, you can change your shirt, and we can get ice cream or coffee, or you can pour a smoothie all over me," he joked.

Elizabeth laughed softly at his last comment, but was thinking seriously about the handsome stranger's offer of ice cream.

"Ice cream. Hmm." She paused for a moment, and then continued candidly, "That's not fair; ice cream is my weakness. But I don't know you—you're a perfect stranger. How can I trust you?"

"I have a yellow lab as a pet, one of the gentlest and most loving dogs a pet owner can have. I'll tell you anything you want to know, and ..." he trailed off for a few seconds. "And, I'll just feel so bad if you don't let me do something for you." His eyebrows were raised and his shoulders shrugged, and it didn't seem like he'd let either down until Elizabeth consented to go with him. He continued, "Please. My mom taught me good manners; let me use them."

She agreed because he was persistent, because he was cute, and because he intrigued her. But to him, she insisted it was only because of the ice cream.

So Elizabeth changed into her new shirt and washed off the sticky fruit juice in the bathroom of the smoothie shop, all the while thinking that the situation was crazy. They walked three blocks for what the stranger said was his favorite ice cream shop. The two talked about where each was from—he was from California and had moved out East to teach high school English. Her raised eyebrows caused him to explain that he also had friends in the area and really liked the church he went to, which he knew about before he moved here. But one thing he said made Elizabeth do a double-take.

"Why did you move all the way here from California, just to teach? Couldn't you do that there?"

He thoughtfully considered his answer before responding, "God's grace is more alive to me here."

"God only lives on the East Coast, huh?" said Elizabeth.

He gave a tsk-tsk look. "Ha ha, no. I just love it here, that's all," said Smoothie Spiller.

"Yeah, I do too," she agreed, though distracted. *Church? God's grace is more alive to me here?* She kept that statement in mind the rest of the night, long after she was back at home. But here, she kept up the conversation, talking about the ocean, the peacefulness of the area, the kindness of the people, the tastefulness of the local cuisine.

Elizabeth learned that Smoothie Spiller had gone to school for investment banking and teaching, and he learned she went to school for marketing and English, though she wasn't sure why the English was thrown in there, and that her favorite things were her family, ice cream, chocolate, chocolate, and summer—in that exact order. By the time they were done talking, it was past eleven o'clock. They had been walking around for more than two hours, passing the same street sign at least twice. The information exchanged was nothing profound, just a simple conversation about simple things.

They reached the ice cream/smoothie shop as their evening came to a natural end. "I had a great time tonight. I'm sorry again about your shirt," said Smoothie Spiller sincerely.

She thought he looked rather handsome in the moonlight, but she was thankful he didn't offer to walk her home.

"I had a great time too. Thank you for the new shirt. And for the ice cream, of course," she said.

They stood awkwardly for a moment, not really knowing what to say. He seemed to be acting as if he wanted to ask her if he could see her again but was worried that it would sound too forward.

"Well," Elizabeth filled the silence, "I should be going. Thanks again for the company. Maybe I'll see you around again." She smiled an easy, friendly smile in his direction, met his eyes, and walked away. As she did, Elizabeth pulled out her cell phone and called her brothers, mentioning nothing of the evening she just had but enjoying her younger brother Danny's animated description of his day.

Elizabeth chose to clear her mind of any mixed feelings she was starting to get by having a glass of wine, reading, and falling asleep under a blue-and-white knit afghan in the living room on the plush couch. Her head rested easily on one of the pillows, and she drifted off, dreaming of nothing in particular. Just before she fell asleep, however, she suddenly realized something that amused her: she never got the mystery man's name. Why was this funny? Because she had never felt as free and refreshed by someone's company as she had tonight, and she hadn't even managed to get his name. All she knew was that she went to bed smiling for the fourth night in a row, and she was thoroughly enjoying her vacation.

Chapter 3

"Life is just one silly thing after another."
~Unknown

THE NEXT MORNING, ELIZABETH woke up with the sun shining on her face. It enticed her to rise with its soft, cozy rays of light, warming her instantly; she removed the blanket lying over her body. She realized she hadn't even changed into her pajamas last night when she got home. She looked down.

North Carolina t-shirt. Stained white tank top. From a stranger. From a man with no name. How did I miss that? A man with no name who loves ice cream like I do. Well, not like I do, but to his credit, he still likes it.

The happenings of the previous night gradually came back to her. Elizabeth could be rather slow in the early hours of the morning; she needed breakfast and a couple hours time to be fully awake. The sun was shining brightly for the fourth day in a row. She walked outside, ready for a long walk. There were a few clouds, but nothing too threatening. Halfway down the beach, however, Elizabeth chided herself for her thoughts, because a thunderstorm and pouring rain rolled in from out of nowhere. It came down hard, as if the storm was staking its claim right there. So, after drying off, she spent most of the day in her pajamas, reading, talking briefly on the phone to her brothers, watching movies, cooking, and watching the storm from the screened-in porch.

Glorious. Absolutely glorious.

When the rain finally subsided in the early evening, Elizabeth decided to go grocery shopping. She had cooked some macaroni and cheese earlier, but she was quickly running out of fruit, vegetables, sweets, and the general kitchen staples that she needed if she wanted to cook anything decent the rest of her vacation.

The ten-minute walk to the grocery store was a quick one. On the way, she saw one family of four, a mother, father, and their two children. Both kids were in a green and yellow stroller, the boy in front asking question after question—one answer from his dad not satisfying his drive to find out more about the world he was discovering from his two-foot stature—and the girl in back sleeping soundly. Elizabeth guessed the parents were grateful for the balance. She smiled at the boy's innocence, remembering when her little brothers were fortunate enough to have that and be shielded from the very non-innocent life that surrounded them. She also smiled to herself, thinking that maybe one day she could have a little rugrat like that who asked tons of questions. She hoped she would be the patient parent who answered her kids' questions with a loving, creative, and truthful attitude.

When Elizabeth got to the grocery store, she decided on a cart instead of a basket, just in case. And it was a good thing; either she was really hungry or she felt like her wallet deserved to be aired out, because one hundred dollars of groceries later, her cart was filled. She found chocolate on sale, fresh fruits and vegetables, Italian seasoning to go on some garlic bread she wanted to make, yogurt, and something from almost every aisle, it seemed. She decided it was just because she was used to shopping for a family of four. But really, Elizabeth knew she would eat most if not all of that food between now and the end of her vacation.

The rain had slowly started up again as Elizabeth was about three quarters of the way through shopping. She tried to take a little longer so that the rain had a chance to blow over by the time she wanted to go home. She saw it had dissipated when she was at the checkout counter, but when she realized her cart held a total of ten bags, she stopped dead in her tracks.

I walked, she thought, the dread on her face visible. *I'm such an idiot.* Elizabeth had rented a car for the two weeks, but because it had been such a beautiful night, she had decided to save the gas and enjoy the outdoors.

What in the world was she supposed to do? Could she leave the groceries here, walk home, and come back for them? She'd have to. Or she could take the cart all the way, promising to return it.

Yeah, right, Elizabeth, she chided herself. *That's dumb. Well, I guess there's nothing else I can do but—*

"Miss, are you all right?" the cashier asked her. Elizabeth had her no-car realization after she had paid and therefore had gone into a daydream state, blocking those behind her from being checked out with their own groceries. The cashier startled Elizabeth out of her slight shock. She was mortified; how long had she been standing there?

"Are you okay?" he asked again.

"I'll be fine; thank you very much. Have a nice day!" she said with a nervous smile.

The bags holding Elizabeth's groceries were altogether too heavy for one woman to carry. She went to the service desk to humiliate herself further. Explaining her situation, Elizabeth watched the customer service worker's expression go from indifference to altogether disinterest. The lady behind the counter was about twice Elizabeth's age. With a scowl on her face and a furrow on her brow, the woman promptly rejected Elizabeth's request for understanding and continued on with her business. Even after Elizabeth tried to convince her to please understand, the woman would not budge on her decision. Upon asking to speak with the manager, the rude lady said that she *was* the manager on duty and to please step aside so she could help the next customer.

Down the street Elizabeth went, carrying ten bags of groceries, including fragile things like eggs and bread, heavy things like milk, and a pound of chocolate. She had four bags in one hand, six in the other, about equally weighted. After only three minutes, Elizabeth's hands began to lose circulation, so she sat herself down on the step of an antique shop. She saw purple and red lines on the insides of her fingers and fleetingly wished them to fall off so someone would *have* to help her. After taking a short breather, she picked up the bags again—they seemed heavier this time—and continued walking.

Elizabeth could see her doorstep, so she sped up. She almost tripped on an uprooted sidewalk square, but she quickly caught herself while two little boys on their porch let out a couple of giggles.

She could feel the beads of sweat trailing down her face and arms, and her triceps were burning.

At least I'm getting exercise, she reasoned.

The last twenty steps felt more like six hundred. As soon as she walked in the door, the groceries went to the floor as Elizabeth plopped right down with them. She sat against the back of the door and put her head back, gazing up at the ceiling. Breathing heavily, she wondered aloud if she was crazy and decided no, she wasn't crazy; she just had vacation brain.

All of a sudden, a knock and a bark came from the other side of her front door.

Who in the world could that be?

She brushed off her jeans and stood up, spruced up her hair, looked out the window, and momentarily stopped breathing.

It was Smoothie Spiller with the yellow lab. She ran her fingers through her hair again, nervous, confused, and a little bit excited. She hadn't thought about him since she looked at her new shirt earlier that morning. But suddenly she was very aware of how sweaty and out-of-sorts she was.

Opening the door slowly, she immediately decided how nice he looked in his khaki shorts and white t-shirt that had two thick navy blue stripes across the middle. His dark hair wasn't fixed in any special way, and tan was a good look for him.

"Hi," he said cautiously, going off her disheveled look. Jax, on the other hand, read no social cues whatsoever as he pulled on his leash in an attempt to reunite with Elizabeth. "Jax, sit," Smoothie Spiller said firmly, but quickly bounced back to a smile in Elizabeth's direction.

"Hey, there," she said with a smile; Elizabeth was trying not to look as flustered as she felt. "How are you doing?"

"I'm doing just fine, thank you," said her handsome stranger. He was smiling too. "I just saw you outside, walking with an armload of bags; I wanted to make sure you made it in okay."

"Oh my goodness," she said. She laughed a genuine, hearty laugh. "I think this is where I get really embarrassed."

He paused, waiting for her to explain. His easy grin said that he was at least a little attracted to her, especially as she tried to iron out an explanation for her grocery trip home. There was no escape, was there? He had seen her fumble down the street. He probably heard her collapse against her door, maybe even her sigh of relief. But still, this was a handsome man, and she didn't care to present herself as being this ungraceful.

He's going to find out sooner or later, anyway. Wait! Where did that thought come from?

Regardless of her roaming thoughts, Elizabeth was aware of the raised eyebrows standing at her door, waiting for an answer to a question. And so Elizabeth began describing one of the most embarrassing stories she could ever recall telling about herself.

"Well," Elizabeth started, and then paused. "Wait, first thing's first. My name is Elizabeth Tenner; I'm afraid we neglected that little detail last night."

His smile grew even wider. "I'm Nathan. Nathan Monroe. Nice to meet you, Elizabeth." He was still studying her with a look of amusement on his face, silently inviting her to continue. His left hand was in his pocket, and he rocked slightly on his heels as Jax sat waiting for his next command.

"Right, well," she continued, "I wanted to go grocery shopping. And as soon as I got there, I got pretty excited—as usual—about buying some food. So I grabbed a cart instead of a basket, forgetting I didn't have my car with me. I got all those groceries," she pointed to the pile next to her, "and had no way to get them home! The ridiculous woman at customer service wouldn't let me leave them there so I could get my car, and therefore I had to carry them here by myself. I can't feel my fingers, but I'm sure that's only temporary. I also almost knocked over a kid on his bike. But I made it! I was just about to get out some chocolate and wine to celebrate."

"Celebrate? For getting your groceries home?" Nathan looked at her with a sideways glance this time.

"Well … you know those posters that suggest a reason to party every single day of the year? I have the same kind of idea, but it's reasons for celebrating with chocolate and wine."

Elizabeth invited him into her simple house. It was a cadet blue two-story home with two old wooden rocking chairs on the front porch. The inside was just as charming, with two plush sofas in the front room, hardwood floors, and an antique-beach theme throughout. Once inside, Nathan immediately noticed the warm, light scent that filled the house.

"Wow, it smells really good in here; what is that?"

"Oh," she said as if she didn't notice anything different, "that's a mixture of honeysuckle candle and the cinnamon raisin bread I made earlier. That and the rain. I have most of the windows open."

"Well, it smells great."

"Well, nature and I thank you," said Elizabeth casually.

Nathan smiled, clearly enjoying their easy conversation. He apologized for dropping by unexpectedly and shared his bemusement by the fact that Elizabeth carried all those bags from the market. His eyes were slightly squinted and his eyebrows were somewhat furrowed as he spoke, but he was so good-natured about it that Elizabeth could easily see a combination of amusement and delight on his face. Elizabeth knew she seemed a little out of it, but there was nothing she could do about that. And to his credit, Nathan wasn't making fun of her. He only smiled and said, "I don't have to stay. I can let you get to your groceries. Like I said, I just wanted to make sure you were okay."

That's sweet, she thought. *Say that out loud and ask him to stay.*

"That was very sweet of you, Nathan. Thank you."

Should she ask him to stay? She wasn't sure. Elizabeth was really enjoying the time to herself, but company would be nice, refreshing even, since she rarely entertained company at home. Especially from someone her own age, and of the opposite sex.

Hanging around a good-looking guy never hurt anyone. And she had felt safe with him last night; he ordered cotton candy ice cream, after all. *Harmless,* she thought. She went for it.

"Would you like to stay and help me put groceries away? Then you can have some of the bread I made; I've been told it's pretty good. Though I don't have anything to offer Jax."

Nathan smiled and immediately accepted her offer, stating Jax would be fine with the tennis ball Nathan had taken out of his pocket. He also took eight of the ten grocery bags into the kitchen—Elizabeth managed the other two by herself.

"You rented a nice house," said Nathan.

"Thanks. My brothers pitched in to rent it for me for a couple of weeks," she said.

"That's awesome. The one I'm staying in is a ranch, and the colors are more beige than blue. It's really nice, though; I like it. It has a deck off the kitchen like this one. I've sat out on it almost every night since I moved here, reading or listening to music, or just enjoying the silence."

"What are you reading? Anything good?" asked Elizabeth.

"The Bible," said Nathan with a shrug, as though it was a book everyone read in their spare time. Elizabeth hadn't expected that, but she didn't dwell on it.

"Well, I'm enjoying my porch too. It's so relaxing. It just feels like you've left the crazy and entered the serene. You forget that the real world is just on the other side of the door. You know what I mean?"

"Couldn't have said it better myself."

"So," she asked, "would you like a piece of bread? I can warm it and butter you up—"

Nathan smirked as she corrected herself.

"Butter *it* up, I mean." Oh, how red Elizabeth felt her cheeks get. Good thing they were both smiling.

"I'm telling you, my middle name really should be Grace. I wasn't kidding. It's not just limited to physical movement—it extends to speech."

Nathan laughed. "It's okay, I knew what you meant," he said with a wink in Elizabeth's direction.

He is adorable, she thought. *And fun to be around.*

Elizabeth quickly recovered from her comment and gave Nathan a piece of her cinnamon raisin bread. She was aware that Nathan was watching her as the two talked and as she moved around the kitchen, which was one thing she usually did very easily after more than a decade of preparing meals and lunches for three younger brothers who were always eating. Except just then, she walked right into the counter, bashing her hip and any notions Nathan might have had that she may sometimes be graceful.

Nathan laughed because Elizabeth laughed.

"You'll have to excuse my clumsiness," Elizabeth said nonchalantly. "My grandmother used to say it's because my mind is always racing so I don't think and watch the three-dimensional world in which I'm living."

Nathan was sitting on the counter that divided the dining room and the kitchen. He didn't use the bar stool that was situated at the counter for purposes such as this, but rather he took a more casual approach as they talked about the weather, past pets, favorite ice cream flavors, and driving pet peeves. The content was again nothing intimate, but as the time went on, they became less like strangers and more like friends. The loaf of bread got smaller throughout their conversation; Nathan had enjoyed it so much that he had a second piece, then a third and a fourth. After more than an hour of talking in the kitchen, Elizabeth and Nathan moved into the living room with the wine and chocolate.

"You really do love your sweets, don't you?" asked Nathan, watching her choose her first piece of chocolate carefully.

"Oh, you have no idea. It runs deep," she said.

"If you say so," he said with a grin and that look of delightful amusement. Nathan's eyes were dancing, and he seemed completely at ease. They continued to talk, this time about each other's professions. Elizabeth told Nathan all about her life as a media liaison with a local school district, and he talked about being a teacher. Their professions had some similarities but enough differences to keep the conversation interesting. Elizabeth thought her job to be far less engaging than Nathan's when she saw the passion in his eyes. He didn't just talk about teaching but about the hardships his students faced, how he motivated them with constant encouragement and tough love, how some football coach on TV was his greatest role model for leading teens, and how someday he wanted to work for a big church.

"Why do you want to change from teaching to a church? We need good teachers."

"The way I look at it, they're similar professions. Both involve teaching, molding minds, and helping kids make good choices. And I love doing that as a high school teacher. But, I want to save people in a different way."

"What do you mean?"

"I want to work at a church that goes out and does things, you know? Not just talk about God, but also do things that change people's circumstance or the way they think about their circumstance. You know what I mean?"

"I guess," she said slowly. Inside, she thought this to be a nice idea in theory but tough as the dickens to pull off in real life. People's circumstances sometimes can't be changed; she knew that all too well.

"You seem confused," said Nathan, judging by Elizabeth's creased brow.

"I like your idea of loving people who need love and not just talking to them about God. I just don't get it. Do you think you can just walk away from being a teacher? You seem so passionate about it."

"You know, I'm not sure. I love teaching, and I love ministry. I guess we'll see."

"I don't know about you, Nathan," said Elizabeth skeptically.

Nathan chuckled. "What do you mean?"

She paused and then said, "You talk kind of funny."

Nathan laughed again.

The night breeze flowed into the living room from the front screen door, and Jax was asleep under one of the eight open windows around the room. The wind was blowing just enough that the sweet southern air mixed with salty oceanic breeze. Elizabeth and Nathan were at a place in their conversation when they could either go deeper or cut it off. Elizabeth debated asking him to leave; she could tell an attachment was already starting to grow, and there were too many things to think about and deal with if this continued. Yet, she didn't want to ask him to leave because she so appreciated his company, and before she could get her words out, Nathan got up to get another glass of wine and some more chocolates.

They each drank a second glass of wine and chatted easily about why they loved the beach, the places they each wanted to travel, and a little bit about their families. Elizabeth wasn't ready to share the details of her life and what it was like on a daily basis back home, but as Nathan shared details of various arguments he had had with his father, all of a sudden she found herself telling him the essential pieces of her family's dramatic story.

"You want the short version or the long one?" asked Elizabeth, staring into her empty glass.

"Keeping with the theme of long-windedness this evening, let's go with the long one," said Nathan, in a low tone of voice that made Elizabeth genuinely want to share her story.

Elizabeth started her story by telling Nathan about her grandparents, about how they built the house she lived in but had died when she was fifteen years old. They were great parents and grandparents, but Elizabeth's mother didn't always think so. Elizabeth's mother rebelled in big ways—through alcohol and sleeping around and even doing drugs. She got pregnant at twenty years old, married Elizabeth's father—who was just as worthless as Elizabeth's mother—and moved in with Elizabeth's grandparents.

During the first seven years of Elizabeth's life, it was just Elizabeth, her parents, and her grandparents. But Elizabeth's parents weren't around too much, so it was mainly Elizabeth and her grandparents, which is the way Elizabeth preferred it to be. After those seven years, in a fit of parenthood, her mom and dad started staying home more, drinking less, and had more children; along came Bryce, Mitch, and Danny in the next eight years. But there was still a lot of fighting, long absences by her mother and father— sometimes at the same time—and a general sense of instability.

When Danny was two years old, tragedy struck: a drunk driver hit Elizabeth's grandparents as they were driving home from the grocery store. Elizabeth's parents used the event as an excuse to start drinking again. Her mom kept on as a functioning alcoholic, but she was never home. Her father decided four kids were too much to think about or take care of, so he left.

The house had been paid off long ago, and car insurance and life insurance money went to Elizabeth and the boys, which they split between bills and savings. Any money her mom brought home was used for food and school supplies, things like that. Elizabeth worked a part-time job through high school and put her money toward more groceries and clothes. A kind neighbor watched over Danny for three years until he started school and could ride the bus with Mitch.

Elizabeth shared with Nathan that when she was only fifteen years old, she instinctively knew that she was about to be a full-time mom. When her grandparents were alive, Elizabeth had motherly instincts toward her brothers, but her grandparents did the actual parenting. Left with a feeling of responsibility for her brothers, who after the accident had no grandparents and essentially no parents, Elizabeth took on the burden and learned quickly not to complain about it. She didn't talk to her friends or teachers or a counselor about it, because she thought nobody would understand. She quietly accepted rides from neighbors and sometimes dragged her mom to the store before she had her own driver's license.

For another seven years, Elizabeth's mom was around here and there. Her brothers kept growing up, and Elizabeth did her best as "mom," doing college part-time all year round. And when she was twenty-two years old, three weeks after her college graduation, her mother chose to drive drunk and high —"smart, considering her own parents died from a drunk driver," Elizabeth added with sarcasm—and that was that.

"I was lucky to be offered a full-time job that paid well right out of college," said Elizabeth, completely unassuming of any sympathy Nathan might be feeling for her. She was used to the story. Even though she hadn't told it to anyone in many years—just a college professor who wondered about it during her sophomore year—she said everything as though she fully accepted the cards she had been dealt.

Nathan asked, compassionately and patiently, "Do you like taking care of all of them?"

"It can be trying. I know you're a guy, but you have *no idea* what it is to *raise* one. Let alone three of them. I just instinctively knew what I had to do, I guess. In my situation, I was almost all they had."

"Are they trouble-makers?"

"Actually, no, they are not," answered Elizabeth proudly.

"You must have done a good job," said Nathan.

"Hmm. If my grandparents were here, they would tell you that the reason they are not trouble-makers is because they go to church each week," said Elizabeth with some contempt.

"What do you think?" asked Nathan.

"I think ..." Elizabeth paused, choosing her words carefully because of the church-speak Nathan had used earlier. When she continued, she said, "My brothers fell in with the right crowd. I brought them to youth group because it kept them out of trouble. The leaders brought the boys to their houses countless times over the years. They gave my brothers someone else besides me to talk to, to learn from, and to have fun with."

"It's good you have that attitude. I knew this one guy—his family really needed him. He was one of seven kids, and the dad had passed away. He wasn't the oldest, but he was the second oldest, so his older sister would always ask him to help out and stuff. But he just couldn't do it, or so he said. He bailed one day and didn't show up again until about fifteen years later, after the youngest was killed in a car accident. That totally changed his perspective. But it's really sad that it took him that long."

Elizabeth looked horrified. She asked, "Did his family ever forgive him?"

"They tried. Most did. The mom did first, of course. The younger ones did, the oldest had trouble because she felt he left her high and dry."

"Understandable," she said honestly.

"Yeah, I guess. But their church really helped them put the family back together. A lot of counseling and encouragement," he said.

After a moment he added, "Do you miss being with them? Your brothers, I mean. Do you miss being a mom right now?"

"I miss them, sure. But I've talked to them a few times. There's so much I always want to do at home; I'm hoping that during these two weeks, I can regroup and learn a few tricks to keep the sanity in my life once I get back there."

"Well, you haven't really spent it by yourself. I've been here," said Nathan, with his head down toward his glass but glancing up at Elizabeth.

 She studied him, trying to figure out what to feel.

Attraction? Friendship? Both? Confusion? The last one, definitely.

"Yeah. Well." Elizabeth smirked in Nathan's direction

"What?" he asked with a smile.

Elizabeth was an honest person. And she decided right there that, if Nathan was to be in her life for any period of time, she would have to be completely honest all of the time, and he would understand that. She suspected he would be fine with it.

"Well, you have been good company both nights. But, honestly, I … I have so enjoyed your company, but I still want time to myself." The last words of Elizabeth's statement went up in pitch as though it were a question, as she hoped Nathan would understand and not try to persuade her otherwise. Because if he did, she wasn't sure how to resist. How quickly an attraction could eclipse one's planned moments of solitude.

Nathan looked from the ceiling to Elizabeth's eyes. He seemed genuine when he said, "That's fine. But I will also be honest and say I hope this isn't the last I see of you."

She smiled and against her strongest will—the one that said Nathan was too good to be true and all she needed was her brothers—she said, "I am certain you will still see me around."

He smiled and nodded and stood up to leave. The conversation was winding down, anyway.

"I think I'm going to head home. It's still pretty nice out, but I think I heard it was going to rain overnight, so I'd like to get home before it starts."

Elizabeth put her empty glass on the table next to the chair and stood up to walk Nathan to the door. She noticed that she was sad to see Nathan leave. It even felt like a kissing moment, but Elizabeth didn't want to kiss—well, she might have *wanted* to, but she wasn't ready, especially since she had known Nathan for only two days.

"I had a great time tonight," said Elizabeth.

He smiled at her words, a wide one that let her know he appreciated what he heard. Elizabeth watched him as he strolled down the sidewalk toward his own house with Jax walking tiredly beside him, her mind whirling and her chest feeling something akin to a runner's post-marathon heartbeat.

Uh-oh.

Chapter 4

"Happiness seems made to be shared."
~Jean Racine

ELIZABETH WANDERED BACK TO her chair after Nathan was out of sight, thinking about the evening she just shared with a man she had just met—a man her age who seemed normal and to whom she was most certainly attracted. She was here on vacation for herself, but she was enjoying his company. After talking it through in her mind, Elizabeth decided she would institute the rule she used for shopping: when there was something she really wanted at the store but wasn't sure she should buy, she would wait two or three days. If the item was still on her mind and she still wanted it when she saw it after the waiting period, Elizabeth would buy it. She would do this with Nathan; she would wait a couple days, and if she saw him or was still thinking a lot about him, she would work very hard to run into him, since she didn't have his phone number and didn't know where he lived.

Elizabeth took advantage of the waiting period. She finished another book that had been sitting on her shelf at home for almost a year, went for a two-mile jog each morning, and took a nap the second day. She utilized the surround sound system and had music on almost any time she was in the house, and she took an interest in the families and groups of friends playing on the beach or just outside their beach house. At night, the ocean waves kept her attention with their predictable, soothing, rhythmic song.

The weather was more than agreeable; sometimes, she would stop whatever she was doing just so she could look out over her porch or close her eyes and breathe in the salty ocean air. Sometimes, she'd be lucky enough to smell the food from the restaurants down the street or the jasmine plants that lined the sidewalks. All things considered, Elizabeth couldn't imagine anything but loving exactly where she was. There wasn't one part of this vacation that wasn't pleasant. Not being a mother twenty-four/seven and not feeling like she had to answer to anyone were two distinct pleasures she relished.

Again, not that I am complaining about my life. But I know that some-day I will be a real mom to my own children, and I want some time before that happens to be my own person and know who I am outside of that.

Thoughts like this moved through Elizabeth's mind most often when she was lying in bed or running. They were moments of clarity for her. Five years ago, Elizabeth would have felt guilty about wanting to know who she was outside of being a mom to her brothers, but her heart seemed to have shifted since her first day on the beach. The murky thoughts seemed to be slowly clearing. So far, Elizabeth decided that she had never skimped on giving love to her brothers, not once. But she was only human, and so feelings of wanting to act her age and not wanting mom-level responsibility all the time were natural. She also decided that life wasn't so bad, because she had the love of three wonderful young men back home.

On Friday night, three nights after her wine-and-chocolate evening with Nathan, Elizabeth had a thought that could have been fleeting, but she held onto it and decided to explore it further. She found herself wanting to talk to Nathan. She would think of something he said that was funny or interesting, a cute facial expression, or she'd think of how his deep brown eyes gazed searingly into hers when he was listening to her. Her chest would even almost ramp up to that same post-marathon pace when she let herself daydream about a physical relationship.

I've obeyed my shopping rule, haven't I? She decided it wouldn't be so bad if she ran into him somewhere in town, though she had to decide on an excuse.

Just then, her phone rang, and she was thankful for the interruption as her nerves were growing in intensity as the minutes ticked by.

"Hey, Elizabeth, how's it going?" It was one of her brothers, the youngest, Danny.

"Hey, Danny. I'm all right; how are you doing? How's your day?"

"It's going, you know. I just got back from helping out at the animal shelter all afternoon. One of the dogs was begging me to take him home, I swear."

"Really? He talked to you?" she teased.

"Hardy-har. Noooo, he didn't talk to me," said Danny, obviously frustrated with his older sister's sarcasm. He continued, "I'm not Dr. Doolittle. But I can tell when an animal wants to be near me all the time, and this one definitely does."

"Then it's too bad you can't be at the shelter more, isn't it?" asked Elizabeth, this time seriously.

"You're not even going to let me ask, are you?" asked Danny, this time frustrated for longer than two seconds.

"I'm sorry; go on. Ask away," she said.

Elizabeth heard a little breath from the other end of the phone that let her know he was hopeful, though deep down she was sure he knew the answer. He asked, "Elizabeth, can we adopt Toby?"

"Nope."

Elizabeth didn't offer an explanation because she and Danny had had this conversation multiple times. Elizabeth wanted no more living beings in the house; four was enough.

Six minutes of "Puh-leeeaase" from Danny and "No, I'm sorry. You're going to have to wait until you're on your own" from Elizabeth followed before Danny finally let up.

"Fine," he said with a frown she could hear over the phone.

"Danny, I'm on vacation here. We've gone over this so many times. I really am sorry, bud. You can always go to the shelter more to play with him. Take him for a couple extra walks. Just can't bring him home. Deal?"

Reluctantly, he said, "Deal." She cringed at his clear disappointment, and she thought of Jax. But even if she had been thinking of letting Danny get a dog before her encounter with Jax, she would certainly have had second thoughts after the smoothie incident. *Lucky for me, I already know I don't want a dog.*

Danny was thirteen; his brothers Mitch and Bryce were fifteen and nineteen, respectively. They all looked to Elizabeth as the head of the house, so she wasn't too surprised the "no mom stuff" promise they had made to her before she left didn't last long.

Almost immediately after they hung up, Elizabeth remembered what she was doing before he called. *Trying to think of an excuse to go meander around town so I can run into Nathan.* A number of options passed through her mind, such as jogging (*too sweaty*), out for a walk (*too obvious*), grocery shopping (*remember last time?*). Finally, she landed on going for some ice cream: believable and easy to follow through on if he wanted to join her.

She grabbed her keys, checked her hair and make-up, changed into a cute skirt, and sailed out the door. Not a hundred yards after Elizabeth turned the corner toward the ice cream shop in town, she found out Nathan was right; it certainly was a small community. She saw Nathan looking not unattractive in black basketball shorts and a white t-shirt that said "Backyard BBQ Champs" on it. She guessed he was just about to go for a jog since he had his MP3 player attached to his right arm and his earphones almost in his ears. Almost feeling foolish, she was going to keep walking when Nathan seemed to have a different idea.

"Hey, Elizabeth," said Nathan, unable to hide how happy he was to see her. He was pulling his ear buds out and pressing what she assumed was the "stop" button on his player. Before he did, Elizabeth managed to catch a sneak listen of a soft southern voice.

"Hi, Nathan," said Elizabeth. Her voice was a mixture of uncertainty and genuine happy-to-see-you feelings. She hoped he couldn't tell that her heart was beating hard and her hands were clammy like a fifteen-year-old asking someone to prom.

He was looking at her, waiting for her to say something. He was smiling too, as if he knew she was out looking for him. But she didn't want to give in that easily, so she kept up light, easy conversation until he let out a loaded comment after a small lull: "I was hoping to see you again."

She nodded slowly. Not one given over to romantic feelings often, but not one to keep her opinions to herself, she found a balance: "I think we should have dinner again."

He answered, "I was just about to go for a jog—"

"I see that, and that's fine. I don't want to disturb you. I can wait, or I can just go back home and we can run into each other again tomorrow?" Elizabeth spoke her words quickly in an attempt to end the conversation and diminish the embarrassment she was starting to feel. Even though Nathan seemed to express similar feelings for her, Elizabeth was far out of her comfort zone.

"No, thank you," he said with a slight singsong tone to his voice. "I can jog tomorrow. Let's walk into town and get some ice cream. You were probably headed that way, anyway." Nathan's smile was coy, and Elizabeth knew that he understood she was trying to run into him.

That's okay, she thought to herself.

"So," asked Nathan, "dinner then ice cream, or ice cream then dinner?"

"Oh! Ice cream then dinner," said Elizabeth, because not only was it another perfect night for ice cream, but Elizabeth felt a sense of giddiness at this small breaking-the-rules event the two were about to share. Nathan hurried back outside after changing out of his running gear, and Elizabeth could tell he was more than pleased that she had sought him out. Conversation picked up in line with their easy footsteps. Specifically, Elizabeth wanted more information about this man and his life.

"I have a question. Why are you renting this house? You said you moved here from California."

"I did."

"So why are you renting this house? Aren't these only week-long rentals?"

"They are if you don't know the guy who owns the real estate company that leases them."

"So it's not what you know, it's who you know, huh?" teased Elizabeth.

"Well, I know his son; we went to school together. The guy is a bazillionaire or something like that. He owns a lot of these houses. In a fit of kindness, he said I could stay for a year for much, much less than he normally charges."

"Wow, what made him give you that deal?" She was impressed and curious. "My brothers saved for over a year to rent me my house for just two weeks."

"I'm so charming," said Nathan.

"Mmmhmm. What else?" she asked.

Nathan laughed. "I don't know, really. I had put a feeler out to the people at my church through my pastor before I even got here, and this is what God brought out of that."

"He just decided to be that generous?"

"God or my landlord?"

She blew past his response question, even though she knew he wasn't being sarcastic; he was completely serious. She said, "Your landlord."

"I guess so, Elizabeth. Stranger things have happened," said Nathan. Then he moved onto a new topic. "So, why *do* you like ice cream so much?"

She laughed at what she thought was a silly question. "What do you mean?"

"I mean, it seems to be a true love of yours, just like you said: it runs deep. So I was just wondering why." His honest nature came across in his questions. He had a grin on his face, and she could tell he was teasing her but also testing the waters to see if there was a story there. She enjoyed it, and she certainly—though admittedly uncharacteristically—soaked up the attention.

"Well, I guess it stems back to when my grandparents used to take me to an ice cream parlor when I was five years old. I had the classic vanilla and chocolate twist with sprinkles on top. Then, as I got older, I saw all this potential," she said slowly, wryly. "I saw that I could go for all these different toppings and flavor combinations; the possibilities were endless. And I was hooked."

Nathan looked at Elizabeth sideways and laughed; she could tell he enjoyed the ease with which she spoke back to his teasing.

"You know, I have that same relationship with cookies," joked Nathan.

"Really?"

"Yep, sure do. I started on chocolate chip. Then, my mom introduced me to the rainbow chip cookies. From there, I just moved on up. Peanut butter, macadamia nut. I never looked back."

Elizabeth and Nathan were both laughing, aware of the silliness of their conversation. The kind of silliness that combines first-date jitters with new attraction. They kept walking toward the ice cream shop, talking again about different parts of their lives. They talked more about travel, movies, and music; all these things they had talked about before, but these conversations went into more depth. His favorite place to go was New York City, and her favorite was right here in the Carolinas since she had not travelled to very many places. Both of their biggest travel dreams were about Germany, which she thought was interesting since neither of them was German. They were both movie fanatics and loved watching all different kinds, from horror to comedy to drama. Music was the topic they hadn't yet agreed upon.

"Country?" she asked with disbelief. *Country?* The only man she ever knew to enjoy country music was her father, so she always associated that with older men who drank. Her brothers certainly weren't into it.

"Yeah. Why is that such a surprise?" asked Nathan.

She told him her thoughts. He didn't appreciate it. "Hey, hey, hey," he started, "don't go insulting my music. It's about life and real feelings and God. Men who don't drink can like it too." He playfully nudged her closer to the street with his shoulder. "You don't know what good music is," he teased.

"Just because I like to be classy and listen to music that is relaxing and requires talent, not just picking at your acoustic—" she made the motion with her hands, "that makes me not know good music? I think it's the other way around."

Finally, the two reached town, but they were so engrossed in their conversation that they bypassed the ice cream parlor and kept going toward the beach. They strolled along the water, holding their shoes and splashing each other lightly with their feet. The small waves became warmer on their feet the longer they walked. Eventually, they came to a point where they stood staring out at the sky with their feet at the water's edge. The night had a more romantic feel to it than she had intended, but it also held something else for her that she couldn't quite put her finger on.

Nathan said, "There is something about being at the edge of the world at night. It stirs something inside, something that doesn't come up in regular day-to-day life."

That's what it is. To this, Elizabeth just kept looking straight ahead, wondering what kind of man says deep, thoughtful things like Nathan had just said. She also wondered if the thing it stirred inside her was hope, hope that life wouldn't always be what it currently was for her: a lifetime of picking up the pieces from her broken parents. As profound as her thoughts were and as far as they could carry her, Elizabeth didn't think she was ready to share them with Nathan. Not yet, anyway. So she did something she was good at: making light of something that could turn heavy with people she just met.

She teased, "I told you that you talk funny."

He laughed lightly but kept staring at the sky. Elizabeth and Nathan seemed lost in their own thoughts, and after a while, Elizabeth decided she wanted to hear more of Nathan's God talk. She wondered how it wove into his life story. She had hers; he had to have one too. Nobody moved from coast to coast without having a little something to share. So after a little while, Elizabeth spoke again, this time with a serious tone of voice.

"So, can I ask you something?"

"As long as it doesn't involve country music," said Nathan wryly.

"No, smart aleck. It's about God."

"Oh, okay. Shoot." Nathan looked from the sky to Elizabeth.

"Well, it's just that you talk about it so easily," said Elizabeth.

"Yes," answered Nathan simply.

"Why is that?" She was genuinely interested.

"You really want to know?"

"I told you my story. Tell me yours," said Elizabeth.

He obliged. In the spirit of being as open as Elizabeth had been the other night, Nathan told her how as an only child, his life had started off as something akin to every kid's dream: being doted on with every toy he wanted, getting all of Mom and Dad's attention, not having to worry about a kid brother or sister taking his stuff. But at fifteen—the same time Elizabeth's life changed so dramatically, he noted—his dad cheated on his mom. Their family was torn apart, and the attention that was once doting and loving turned to constant fighting and putting Nathan in the middle.

"The only place I found peace and quiet was at church," he said.

He joined sports and youth group, both of which kept him away from home at least six nights out of the week. Nathan learned a lot about God and the Bible, believing in and taking solace in what it offered.

"That was more than ten years ago, and I felt like I'd been in the same place with God for a while. And for the last year, I have been wanting to escalate my faith and my relationship with Him, so I knew I needed a change—something that would completely challenge me."

"Hmm."

"What?"

She didn't hesitate in sharing her opinion. "It's nothing, just … you and I come from very different places. We took opposite approaches to our situations."

Nathan only nodded.

"And you really moved across the country to get closer to 'God'?" Elizabeth was obviously unsure of what Nathan was saying. She'd experienced the loneliness that came with a broken family, the pain caused by selfish parents. At least she helped herself at home, though; in her eyes, he seemed to be running away. But according to his words, he just wanted a new challenge and a new, bigger way to trust God. Elizabeth wasn't sure what to believe. And Nathan didn't help her question when he only nodded again. But he also said, "No quotation marks. He's real."

"I don't know," she said slowly.

"About what?"

"All this God-talking you do." Elizabeth's face was scrunched up with confusion, but she didn't know what else to say.

"What?" Nathan asked.

Elizabeth wriggled. Her arms were folded, and her face wore an expression of not only discomfort but also uncertainty. Nathan's open and honest expression made her even more uncomfortable and unsure if she should be having this conversation at all. If her brothers were here, they would keep it going. She remembered a moment not unlike this one when her brothers were trying to talk to her about a weekend retreat they had just come back from. They had learned a bunch of new Bible verses and wanted to share them with her. The clammy hands and restless legs were all too familiar. So, in a moment of fear and paralysis of the heart, Elizabeth switched topics by asking Nathan if he wanted to get tacos for dinner. He seemed disappointed but obliged nonetheless.

Deciding on take-out, the two made their way back to Nathan's rental. This was the first time Elizabeth had been to Nathan's house, and even with Jax's spirited welcome causing an orange smoothie flashback the moment she walked in the door, she liked his home. The walls were tan with some palm trees painted on them. It was all earth tones, and not a lot popped out at her while she was walking through and looking around. Most walls had some variation of a palm tree photograph or illustration; there was a beautiful one in the hallway next to the bathroom.

It was a simple milepost leading up to the beach, but the houses on either side were elegant family homes, and the sky was a deep purple, lit up here and there by a few stars. Off the kitchen was the deck he had told her he loved. She noticed only one chair was set up, and a blanket was draped over it.

The spacious living room housed two huge beige couches that matched the walls, with green trimming around the edges of the frame and cushions, complimented by matching chairs kitty-corner to each couch. There were mini palm tree-like plants in the corner, and end tables were sandwiched between the chairs and couches. There was also a big screen television with surround sound speakers. When Elizabeth saw the setup, she teasingly asked if it was the reason Nathan picked that house.

"Of course," he said dryly. He swooshed his hand in the air and had a crooked smile on his face.

"That's what I figured," she teased back. They both smiled, though hers was plagued by thoughts that wouldn't calm down:

Again, it's not that I hate my life back home, she quickly reprimanded herself, *but this is so … so far from reality. I have no responsibilities, no kids to look after, no mother to be. I'm allowed to enjoy this. I'm allowed to let myself enjoy the company of a man who is interested in me.*

In the next breath, she reminded herself, *Back to the conversation. Television setup.*

Nathan added, "No, I picked it because it was the only one the owner would rent me for a year. I definitely didn't complain, though, when I first saw it."

They went into the kitchen, and he asked her if she wanted anything to drink.

"Whatcha got?" she asked.

"I have … not too much," he said matter-of-factly. "I have wine, water, lemonade, and milk."

"That's actually a decent variety for a guy living by himself," she said. "I'll have some lemonade."

After a moment, Elizabeth gave Nathan another small peek into her heart when she said, "When I was growing up, my grandparents made the best lemonade. I thought it was super special, that only they could make it that great. When I was twenty-one, I found out it was just the sugar-water stuff. But I swear it was better tasting when my grandparents made it. I'd play outside for hours, come in for lunch and lemonade, and then go back out. Summer still isn't summer to me without it."

They shared more stories like that one. Nathan had moved another chair outside, and he kept it close to Elizabeth. Once more stars came out, they stretched out on a blanket on the deck and watched the sky, talking about life and its surprises and secrets each had figured out, and the ones each hadn't. Nathan talked more about arguments with his father. He took a deep breath before recounting what he described as one of the worst days of his life: the day he ran into his father's mistress at the grocery store.

"How did you know it was her?"

"She came up to me, said she recognized me from pictures." Nathan's story clearly brought him back to his teenage years. He went on to tell Elizabeth how he told the woman that she ruined his family, then how he ran home to yell at his dad.

"You know what the worst thing was? He just let me yell. I hit him in the chest, I screamed in his face, and he just stood there and took it. I had respected my dad because he was a fighter, but not that day. That day, I saw that he wasn't fighting for anything—not his family, not himself. My hero."

Nodding in understanding, Elizabeth was beginning to see more similarities between her and Nathan than she originally thought. The dramatic family stories, the parents who made selfish, destructive choices, and the determination to be nothing like that. One major difference, however, was the way they chose to deal with their anger. Elizabeth had chosen caring for her brothers; Nathan chose going to church. In that way, their hearts and outlooks on life were worlds apart. Even so, in talking, Nathan coaxed Elizabeth into sharing one of the reasons she so often held back emotionally from others. Her description of the scene brought Elizabeth back to when she was ten years old.

Elizabeth was showing her three-year-old brother Bryce how to dribble a basketball in their backyard, when she heard yelling from inside. She gave her brother the basketball but scooted closer to the house to better hear the nasty words being exchanged between her parents.

"You're pregnant again?! Are you kidding me?" It was her father's voice.

"Why would I be kidding? Of course I'm not kidding, you S.O.B.!" Elizabeth wasn't surprised at her mother's tone; she rarely sounded happy when she talked to Elizabeth's father.

"What are you calling me that for? I bought the condoms."

"They don't work for us when you use them with other women, dummy. I'm the stupid one who keeps sleeping with you."

At this point, Elizabeth had a steady pattern of eye-rolling going on. Yes, her mother was stupid for staying with—and sleeping with—her father. But the point they both failed to recognize was that they drank and smoked often enough that even if there was a condom strapped to their foreheads, the foggy state they were often in would cause them to forget to use it.

Elizabeth heard her father's hands slam onto the dining room table. "Either way, I could barely stand having one child, and right now we have two. How did you think I'd respond to a third?"

"I didn't plan any of them, Joe. You think I want three kids?" Her mother's voice was tense.

"Oh no?" Elizabeth's dad again. "Then why did you force me to come back here? And why didn't you let your mother take care of this more-kids problem after Elizabeth was born? Or better yet, why didn't you let *me* take care of it when we found out about Elizabeth?"

"I didn't want anything more from my mother—you know that." Elizabeth's mom sounded cold, distant, almost hateful.

"And *my* solution when you got pregnant with Elizabeth?" His words were pointed, spiteful.

For a long moment, Elizabeth heard nothing but her brother's clumsy and non-rhythmic dribbling. Then her mother said the sentence Elizabeth had never been able to shake from her memory: "I might not *want* these kids, but I'm not going to *kill* a baby."

"Don't get all Christian on me like your parents."

"That's not getting all 'Christian' on you. It's common decency, you moron."

Elizabeth was brought back to the present by a car alarm sounding in the distance.

She finished quickly. "I didn't fully comprehend that statement until a few years later, but … well, it's pretty clear."

At the end of her story, Nathan reached for Elizabeth's hand. She let him take it because she felt safe and knew his concern was genuine. With their hands interlocked and him stroking her hand with his thumb, they switched to a happier topic: their grandparents. Elizabeth enjoyed listening to Nathan talk about his grandparents; it showed a vulnerable side of him which she liked. She kept coaxing herself to keep talking and not to clam up; sharing details felt incredibly intimate, and she wasn't used to it.

At one point, Nathan called her out on it. "I keep hearing you take very deep breaths, like you're nervous or something."

Elizabeth waited a full ten seconds before responding. "Well, I think it's pretty lame that you figured that out. Yes. I'm nervous," said Elizabeth.

Nathan didn't say anything. She suspected he didn't know what to say. But she preferred silence to empty promises, so she was okay with it.

Toward the end of the night, Elizabeth realized that even though there would be no awkward car ride home, there would be an awkward stand at the door, and when she prepared to leave around two a.m., Nathan (and Jax) offered to walk her home.

They got to her door, and something Elizabeth did not anticipate happened. She was ready for a kiss. He still had one of her hands, and as they stopped at her door, they were still talking. But the conversation quickly halted, because both of them knew what was on the other's mind.

Nathan was the first to speak. "Elizabeth?"

Instead of answering, she kissed him. Quickly, unapologetically, right on the lips.

"Will I see you tomorrow?" Elizabeth asked.

Nathan's eyes opened slowly, and his voice held unmistakable delight when he said, "Yes, ma'am, you will."

"Goodnight, Nathan."

It took all Elizabeth had to fall asleep that night.

Chapter 5

"Life is about not knowing, having to change, taking the moment and making the best of it, without knowing what's going to happen next. Delicious ambiguity."
~Gilda Radner,
It's Always Something

THE NEXT MORNING, ELIZABETH was awakened by a chorus of birds singing to each other outside her window. Though she wanted to think it endearing, she changed her mind after looking at her clock and seeing it was only five hours after she had gotten home and four since she laid down. A groan and a plop of her pillow over her head followed, and she fell soundly asleep for another two hours before, this time, her doorbell was ringing.

"Why is my doorbell ringing?" she asked her empty bedroom.

Groggy, she looked in the mirror once and decided her shorts, tank top, and tousled hair was good enough and walked downstairs. She opened the door to an exceptionally handsome man in his workout clothes and a smile plastered on his face.

"Good morning, sunshine!" he said, almost overly cheerily as he handed her a steaming cup of coffee with the same words written on the side.

She was more than pleased that he had stopped by this early in the day to see her; that meant he was already thinking of her. She smiled as sweetly as she could and thought that maybe she should wonder aloud what he was doing here so early. Instead she said, "Good morning to you, Mr. Bright Eyes," somewhat precociously. "Where's Jax?"

"Home. Mr. Bright Eyes, huh? You're not a big morning person, are you?" He had caught on to her lack of energy and verve with the nickname.

"I am when I have to be. When I don't have to be, no, I definitely am not. I'm a huge fan of meandering and puttering around in the mornings, especially on weekends and vacations." She said her words sweetly and matter-of-factly.

"Well then, even though you are on vacation, either this is a morning for which you *have* to be a morning person, or," he paused and smiled, lifted his eyebrows, and continued, "you let me putter around with you."

Though she thought his tone to be somewhat suggestive for having known each other only a few days, Elizabeth politely said, "Well, since I am still in my pajamas and you came bearing coffee with chocolate in it, I suppose I could let you hang around."

"Good," he said sincerely, "Because I kind of like you."

Elizabeth's face betrayed her calm words, as it displayed shock at his frankness. In her mind, he didn't need to just come out with it as he had. She said coolly, "Nathan, there is such a thing as too much honesty."

"Is that a bad thing? You don't hide many opinions yourself."

"It's intimidating," she said. "It's like you say whatever you're thinking."

Nathan shrugged his shoulders with an expression that said he was unsure of whether this was a good thing or a bad thing.

Elizabeth sighed and said, "I'm just not used to it, I guess. Sorry. Come on in."

They walked inside; Nathan went to shut the front door, but Elizabeth told him to leave it open, as she did as often as possible, taking in every bit of sunshine her house would let in.

Nathan followed Elizabeth into the kitchen. She started reaching for ingredients that together would make French toast, and she even had some strawberries she could wash and cut up for a sweet topping.

"So," she began as she turned on the griddle, "I know *why* you're here, but what brings you here so *early*?"

Elizabeth was keenly aware of how close to her Nathan was standing. Her heart pounded so that she was afraid he might hear it. That or one of her thought streams—sometimes inappropriate ones—might fly out of her mouth with no warning.

Oh my, she thought to herself. *Ohhhhhh my.*

"Well," Nathan said in a low morning voice, "I wanted to see you. Start the day off right."

He smiled at her, and she stopped what she was doing to look up at him. He looked sincere. Elizabeth's heart fluttered at something so simple. He leaned over and gave her a light brush of a kiss on her left cheek; she blushed quite noticeably and then was immediately embarrassed, which only made her cheeks a deeper shade of red.

After enjoying breakfast together, Elizabeth and Nathan decided to go pick up Jax—her affection for him admittedly growing with each interaction—and then they did some fun beach things: playing catch with a football and Frisbee, the latter of which Jax fully enjoyed. They even took advantage of a dolphin tour. As the day progressed, so did the physical closeness, which had Elizabeth's mind running all day. On a pit stop in the bathroom, her inner dialogue started again as she wondered to herself what the heck was happening. She was looking in the mirror, combing her hair.

Am I crazy? Elizabeth thought to herself.

Yes, Elizabeth, you are most definitely insane. This is a guy you just met!

But I'm having such a great time. He's gorgeous and fun to talk to.

That's okay. Just one step at a time. Go. Live. But don't be stupid.

Toward the end of the day, Nathan and Elizabeth weren't ready to let each other go yet. They circled the town twice with Jax pulling them along, altogether walking for more than two hours. Elizabeth told him more of her family history. She revealed some about her relationship with her late mother. Elizabeth never liked talking about her situation, because so many people ended up feeling bad for her. Sympathy made her as uncomfortable as Sunday morning church bells. Even so, she told Nathan; he already knew how she felt about taking care of her brothers, but now she told more of the other side. How tired she got sometimes, especially when they were younger and how she felt when her mom died a few years back.

"I was so angry, but more than that, I was relieved," she said with a biting undertone to her words. "There was no more wondering 'Is Mom gonna be home tonight?' You know, after Gram and Gramps died, she would be gone for days at a time. Three times I called the police to file a missing persons report. There was a lot of pressure when she died, because our dad was already gone and I was left with the boys, but there was a lot of freedom too."

Nathan said he admired her attitude.

"Yeah, well, it took a long time to get to being okay with how I felt. Who's relieved when their mom dies?"

Nathan said he respected how dedicated she was to her family, and he told her it's understandable why Elizabeth would choose to let few people into her life.

"Yeah? Why's that?" Elizabeth hoped he truly understood. She was testing him with this question.

"Because your situation is hard to understand. You don't want to be judged, you don't want sympathy, so you'd rather not explain. And getting to know people, and letting people get to know you, means having to explain," he said.

"In a nutshell. How did you get to be so insightful?" said Elizabeth.

"I'm a teacher; I work with teenagers and their mixed up feelings every day. Plus, I want to be a youth pastor."

Elizabeth barely flinched, but her words came out as though she just crossed over to the defensive side of a conversation. "I feel like you just told me my feelings are on par with a teenager's."

"I didn't mean it that way. I just meant I'm used to trying to figure out feelings."

He sounded sincere, so she quickly let the hiccup go.

When the pair stood again in front of Elizabeth's door at the end of the full day, Nathan wrapped his arms around her like an oversized blanket for a goodbye hug. The moment was quiet, and the silence was comfortable. True to her nature, though, Elizabeth couldn't let it stay that way for too long.

"Okay, Romeo, I've got another question," said Elizabeth without an ounce of subtlety.

"Um, okay. But way to ruin the moment," said Nathan.

She flit her hand like she was swatting at a bug. "You're a Christian, right?"

"Well, I have a relationship with God and believe Jesus Christ is my Savior, yes."

"Oka-a-ay." Her face contorted, asking a completely different question than what her words were asking. "So, usually, and correct me if I'm wrong, but usually Christians move a little slower than this when they have feelings for someone."

"You know what I think?" asked Nathan.

"No, that's why I brought this up," she said with wide eyes.

Nathan sighed. "And I'm the one that just says whatever I'm thinking," he said as he shook his head. "I think I like you. I think you like me. And I think there's nothing wrong with this."

She was comfortable with his answer because it was simple, put no additional responsibility on her shoulders, and he didn't mention God. Pulling back, she looked up into his eyes and gently, slowly kissed him.

"Okay, then," said Nathan.

With that, he kissed her nose and said goodnight.

Elizabeth crawled under the covers once she got into bed. It was late, she was exhausted, and she was excited to think and dream about Nathan and their kisses. And in the still of her heart, she felt like she saw an opening. Whether that was the ocean breeze working its magic or Nathan's kind heart prying into the darkness, she wasn't sure. But whatever it was, for the stillness it offered her, she settled into a deep sleep.

Nathan showed up the next morning with Jax, though not as early. When Elizabeth asked why, Nathan's one-word answer was simply, "Church." Elizabeth was just as unprepared as the day before. She woke from a deep sleep and took some time to fully waken. Their day was not unlike the previous one, either: a lot of conversation and increasing attraction. They walked on the beach and again threw a Frisbee with Nathan's ever-jubilant canine friend, played cards, and went out for lunch. By late afternoon, they sat on Elizabeth's porch, holding hands and talking.

Elizabeth told Nathan again how much the sound of the ocean waves and the feel of the ocean breeze soothed her, saying that she could stay next to it forever.

She saw in his face Nathan trying his luck.

"And you don't think it's anything more than the ocean waves and breeze?"

"What do you mean?" She asked curiously.

"Well, God created the earth, right? He made the ocean waves and breeze just the way they are. Maybe he's trying to get your attention deep down, in an area you've only let the ocean get to."

There it was. The God he didn't mention yesterday. She may be offering more of herself and she may be okay with sharing bits of her life story with Nathan, but God wasn't a topic she wanted to discuss. Not now. Maybe not ever.

Well maybe not never. But definitely not now.

Her decision to sidestep this conversation took all of five seconds to make before she took Nathan's hand and led him into the kitchen, saying, "I am suddenly in the mood to cook with you. What do you say?"

"I say ..." Nathan trailed off, because he moved closer to Elizabeth, looked down at her deep brown eyes, and released a sigh that seemed to come from his toes.

Elizabeth thought she saw a small plea in his eyes—the same plea she saw in Danny's every Sunday when he asked if she was going to church with her brothers. But also like every Sunday with Danny, she felt no need to give in. Her heart stood where it stood; it was a survivor's heart, and she didn't need to explain that she didn't need church or God to make anything better. No, right now all she needed was to cook a pasta and chicken dish while drinking wine and eating chocolate. Nathan looked like he wanted to say more; his eyes held unspoken words she assumed were similar to her brothers' when it came to God, church, and faith. Elizabeth was grateful when he let it settle on his deep sigh. He took a piece of chocolate from the box on the counter—without regard to the flavor of the piece—and popped it in his mouth.

"I think I may have found a soul mate, if for no other reason that you like to drink wine and eat chocolate as much as I do," said Elizabeth.

Nathan smiled. He still looked like he had more on his mind, but he kept quiet. Elizabeth let it go, again keeping with the light mood of the evening. Nathan had plans to unload his thoughts, however, when after dinner he so ominously asked, "Could we talk?"

"Mmm, that sounds heavy," she said. Wasn't this a conversation usually had after more time spent together?

"Well, you leave in six days," said Nathan.

"Yes, I do."

"And?"

"And, I'd prefer not to talk about it because it is quickly approaching and I'm on vacation. Vacation means fun. Vacation means light and breezy," she said, hoping her slightly forceful tone would distract Nathan. Her leaving in six days was something she had thought about but, honestly, not in much depth. She was stuck in the moment, stealing kisses and brief hugs from a man she was coming to adore.

But of course, Nathan wasn't distracted; he said, "I know. So. What do we want to do?"

Nathan wasn't going to back down, that Elizabeth knew. He put energy into being a fighter, and his I've-already-fallen-for-you eyes told her she just made his short list of things to fight for.

"What do you mean?" asked Elizabeth.

"Elizabeth." As he spoke, he again moved closer to her. They had started to clear the dishes, and Elizabeth kept doing so as they talked, but Nathan had stopped. "I want to know what you think we should do about this relationship we're developing."

"I don't know," she said slowly. She truly didn't know. Elizabeth had never been in this situation before. The few dates she had been on were non-winners, by her and her brothers' standards. *But at least they were all in my hometown and not 1,000 miles away.*

"Have you thought about it?" asked Nathan.

Elizabeth stared at him. "Look. I don't know how to do this. It's partly that I'm a mom most of the time, and it's partly my life at home that you know so little about. Clearly I like you, but, well … well … well, I just don't know."

"How about this," Nathan started. He put his arms around her and tipped her chin just so she was looking right up into his face. "How about, we enjoy the time we have left, and once you go back to New York, we write each other and talk on the phone once a week? That'll start it nice and slow for you, and we can get to know each other some more."

"Write each other? Are we in 1935?"

Nathan rolled his eyes and said, "E-mail, smart aleck. Neither one of us does Facebook, and I'd rather not text. Not yet, anyway."

"Why not text?" She seemed confused, since this was how most of the Western world communicated on a daily basis.

"You'll laugh at me," he said.

"Try me."

"I read something once called 'Real Men Don't Text,' and I liked the concept. Old-fashioned courting, kind of. I'd prefer longer conversations over e-mail and phone before we text."

Before she could stop herself, Elizabeth lifted her face and kissed Nathan—their first real, deep kiss. It was long and full of passion. When she pulled back, Nathan asked, with his eyes still closed and his voice down to a whisper, "What in the world was that for?"

"Impulse. Yes, I would love to keep getting to know you through e-mails and phone calls. I can't believe you thought about this," Elizabeth said.

"Trust me, I've been scrambling to find a way to keep on talking past the time you leave," he said.

With that settled, they cuddled up on the couch with Jax relaxing in his favorite spot under one of the windows as Elizabeth and Nathan finished off a carton of ice cream. Elizabeth was pleased that their conversation about her going back to New York lasted less than five minutes, but she surprised herself at how quickly their interaction went from light and flirty to almost cheesy romantic. Even just the cuddling on the couch had taken on a heavier, more serious tone.

At least the conversation included one heck of a kiss.

Finally, after the ice cream was gone and the yawning got to be every thirty seconds, Nathan insisted Elizabeth go to bed. She refused, but as her eyes were closing, Nathan covered her with a blanket and quietly slipped out the door.

Monday morning, Elizabeth woke up a little disoriented.

"Why am I on the couch?" she asked aloud. She didn't remember falling asleep—until all at once the previous night hit Elizabeth, and she immediately smiled, cuddling up to the blanket and couch pillows even more so than she already had been.

Elizabeth lay there thinking about her literal and metaphoric paradise, the former being the beach and the latter being Nathan. She wondered how much of it she could consider reality.

How much of this can I count on to be a part of my regular life?

Elizabeth saw herself and Nathan being terrific at a relationship for the next five days, because nothing else could interfere. What would happen when life got in the way? What would happen when life got too hard as she tried to balance her brothers and a boyfriend?

Boyfriend? Elizabeth thought for a moment. *Hmm. I suppose so.*

Elizabeth smiled from the inside out.

How quickly things can change, she thought. *That's how things go, huh? You're just going about your life, and it can change in a matter of moments.*

So many nights over the years, Elizabeth had wondered what it would be like to have a shoulder to cry on when she got so tired. Sometimes she could use a hand to hold. When Mitch got into a fight at school after Mom died, or when Danny had his first baseball game on the same night as Bryce's Battle of the Bands in middle school. Or when she didn't want to be a mom, when she just wanted to be an untethered twenty-six-year-old woman. Elizabeth rarely let these types of feelings hang around for long, but as Nathan aroused romantic feelings, these thoughts seemed to roll naturally through her mind.

On the other hand, Elizabeth had gotten along on her own for a long time. She had managed by pouring her love into her brothers and retreating into herself when people wanted to get to know her. She was very good at believing nobody could help her; she had done most everything for herself and her family for so long now. What evidence did she have that, by giving in and leaning on anyone or anything else besides herself, it would give way to solid ground?

Only Nathan had gotten a free pass so far, and she wasn't sure why.

Chapter 6

"Hope and fear coexist in many lives, inciting many
contradictions."
~ *G. Oschlager & T. Clinton*

THE REST OF ELIZABETH'S vacation looked pretty much the
same: meet Nathan in the morning, play on the beach most
of the day—sometimes with Jax, his mostly obedient nature surprising Elizabeth with each day. The pair would have seafood for
dinner and then cuddle on the couch and watch a movie or go for
a walk in the evening. Each night ended on a blanket on the beach,
looking up at the expanse of stars before them. Elizabeth took a lot
of deep breaths throughout the week as Nathan kept probing for
more stories from her childhood and her life at home. She shared
some, but not more than a few more. There was a rushing desire in
her heart for Nathan to know all about her and her life, but it was
strongly opposed by a simultaneous and sometimes overwhelming
urge to bolt, out the door, out of this relationship before much else
happened, before her heart got any more involved.

The night before Elizabeth was set to leave, Nathan was holding
her hand and breathing deeply as he looked up at the night sky from
the blanket they had spread out on the sand.

"What are you thinking about?" Elizabeth asked Nathan.

"I'm thinking about a praise and worship song from church.
'You hold the stars in the sky; you hold the mountains up high; and,
yet, you still hold me.'[1] It's one of my favorites."

Elizabeth was quiet, but her hands gave the tiniest flinch. She hoped Nathan didn't realize, but of course he did, and of course he commented on it.

"Does that bother you?" he asked the question in an even tone, neither gentle nor judging, so why was Elizabeth so nervous?

Elizabeth seemed to stutter a little before she said, "I ... I just don't get it. Of all the things I've learned about you this week, your church talk and faith are two things I don't get."

Nathan's response was immediate: "I wish you'd be honest about why it makes you so uncomfortable."

This was one thing Elizabeth hadn't yet shared with Nathan. In all her talk, all her stories, she had left church out because it was the thing she was most uncomfortable thinking about, let alone talking about it. Even so, her response was equally immediate: "I don't want to go. You can go, you can work with your ministries, whatever. My brothers can go; it's better than what they could be doing, fine. But go into a building where people worship a God who left me to my life? No." Elizabeth's words were stoic and final. At the conclusion, she took one short breath and one long one. Then she cleared her throat as if to say, "Enough. New conversation." She pushed aside the God stuff and changed her thoughts to the boys and how they might react to her meeting someone.

Nathan interrupted her quiet: "Okay, your turn. What are you thinking about?"

"About how comfortable I am lying on this soft blanket."

"Deep," said Nathan seriously.

"That's me," responded Elizabeth with a wink.

"And now the serious answer," he said with an almost imperceptible shake of his head.

"Hmm. About the trip home tomorrow and what to tell the boys," she said.

"Want to pray about it?" asked Nathan.

Elizabeth had a feeling Nathan knew the answer to this question before he asked it, but she answered honestly.

"No," she said quickly. Her irritation was back. "What did I *just* tell you?"

"Just checking," he said.

She rolled her eyes. "Whatever."

Nathan was disappointed; Elizabeth could tell even in the dark. But she held her ground; she didn't want to pray. Yet, Elizabeth liked what she thought to be Nathan's atypical Christian behavior. He was careful with his words, and she could tell that was because he was intentional about his relationship with God. He believed in the Bible, and he was open about that, but he was also open about his questions. One of their conversations over the past eleven days had revolved around prayer. Elizabeth didn't initiate this, of course, but Nathan had looked discouraged one morning, and when she asked what was wrong, Nathan talked about his frustration with prayer.

"I feel like it's at the tip of my tongue, and that I almost get it, but it still eludes me. I understand prayer is a way of communicating with God. But, He knows everything in our hearts anyway, right? And we can't always ask for what we want. I mean, we could, but I think that's unrealistic. You know how people use that verse, 'Seek and you will find. Ask and it will be given to you'? Well, it's taken out of context so often that I don't think people really understand. I will not be given everything I ask for, which is ultimately a good thing, I suppose, since God can see the big picture. But when I do ask for them, and certain things aren't given to me, I get very frustrated."

"I wish I had an answer for you. You think about these things far more than I do," said Elizabeth.

"There are just so many questions that sometimes it's hard to grow in my faith because it can feel like I've hit brick wall after brick wall," he said, showing his emotions through his words and wrinkled forehead. For some reason, Nathan seemed compelled to share with her the struggles of his faith even though she had no knowledge—practical or otherwise—of the subject matter. Still, Elizabeth wasn't sure what to say, feeling as though she couldn't offer anything of substance. So she offered what she could, hoping it would be enough. "Nathan, I've always thought God just wants to hear what is in our hearts."

Nathan didn't say much to her response, but he did smile and pat her knees.

Tonight, Elizabeth was looking up at the Carolina sky as she had every other night of her vacation, thinking to herself that there was nothing like the sight before her. She had seen star-filled skies before, but none hit her like this one. She thought how the dome around her was one of the few things in this world that nobody could touch or change; it would always be an amazing display of beauty that every person in the world could appreciate.

She had gotten up and walked to the edge of the water, and Nathan walked up behind her. He slipped his arm around her waist and looked up. They stood in silence for a solid five minutes before either said anything.

"What do you think of this?" asked Elizabeth in a half-whisper.

"What do you mean?"

"I mean," she started, then paused and took a deep breath. She continued, "I mean, what do you think of this beautiful night? Because I was thinking there's nothing like a Carolina sky, and I don't remember the last time I felt this way."

"What way?"

"Peaceful. From the inside out," she answered with serenity in her voice.

The tension from earlier visibly gone, Elizabeth's tone of voice conveyed how much this moment meant to her. She knew that even if this was not a forever-in-your-life kind of relationship, this moment with Nathan would stay in her heart for many years to come. Nathan's response to Elizabeth was a tighter hug around her waist. He pulled her closer to him from the side, and she turned her whole body toward him and wrapped her arms around him in one of the tightest hugs she had ever experienced. But just as quickly as it was initiated, it was over, and she was back to being mesmerized by the star-sprinkled sky.

"What are you thinking?" asked Elizabeth for the second time that evening.

He took longer to answer than she expected, so she said, "You're taking too long. Just tell me what you're thinking right now."

He didn't miss a beat this time. He kept his eyes pointed toward the sky and began, "I'm thinking I really like you. I'm thinking I want to pray. And I'm thinking I agree; there is nothing like a Carolina sky."

Elizabeth asked, "Pray about what?"

"Mmm," Nathan barely stirred. "Thanking God for this." He didn't pause, but his gaze shifted from the sky to Elizabeth's eyes. He said, "I've looked up at this sky so many times before, but the last time I remember it being this distinct, I was five years old. My grandpa took me to a park near our house one night, way past my bedtime. I thought it was *so* cool that it was past my bedtime, by the way. He said there was something special he wanted to show me. We went to the playground, and he said, 'Look up. All those stars are shining for you.' I just remember thinking how incredible it was, how larger than life it was. I guess it made me feel like someone would always be looking out for me."

"That's why you like that song so much," said Elizabeth, encouraging Nathan in his memory.

Elizabeth moved her hand from around his middle to his hand. She gave three of his fingers a squeeze, then brought them to her mouth and kissed them with a very soft touch. Their hearts were focused on something deeper tonight.

———————————

Elizabeth was scheduled to leave North Carolina at one o'clock on Saturday afternoon. She and Nathan spent the morning cooking and eating breakfast, and she snuck in some cuddle time with Jax too, as her heart grew semi-attached to him over the last eleven days. They also set a schedule for communication once Elizabeth was back home. The agreed-upon plan was e-mail as often as each would like, and talk every Tuesday night around eight. She thought about how she was already looking forward to Tuesday.

"Yes, that's the plan. And Elizabeth, I want you to know a few things," said Nathan. His tone frightened her a bit; he sounded so serious. He continued, "I want you to know that, one, you have my word that I will stick to this schedule. And two," he broke into a smile, "I want you to know that I love your kisses, and I most certainly cannot wait for the next one."

She reached up and kissed him quick on the lips.

"And the next one."

She did it again.

Nathan laughed lightly. "And the next one."

This time he surprised her and held her in his arms and pulled back his head so she couldn't give him a quick kiss. Instead, they shared a longer, more passionate kiss.

When they pulled back, Elizabeth held her eyes closed for a few moments and said, "Well, my bags are in the car, so I should get going."

Nathan settled on, "I'll talk to you Tuesday," after looking like he wanted to say more. He kissed her forehead, and off she went. Elizabeth was grateful for the rental car. It would be too much, she thought, if Nathan took her. Bringing someone to the airport had too heavy a feel to it, too much of a relationship task. Even though Elizabeth had admitted to herself and to Nathan that they were in a relationship, and they had already shared a great deal, the offer for a ride to the airport nonetheless felt too substantial for her. She may have been drawing a line in the sand, but at least she was drawing a line.

Elizabeth spent most of the flight home contemplating a way to bring Nathan into her brothers' lives. She knew it would be difficult. They would like Nathan, but they wouldn't like sharing Elizabeth. She had the plan all worked out in her head, and in all the fantasy conversations she had with her brothers, everything went smoothly without one objection from anyone.

"Yeah, right," Elizabeth said aloud when she was in her car on her way home from the airport. She was quite distracted, trying to figure out exactly what she would say to her brothers as she shared-slash-broke the news to them that their big sister "met" somebody. It didn't matter how distracted she was, though; she could have done that drive with her eyes closed, making her way home through semi-urban, mostly suburban roads. The terrain of Western New York suburbs is anything but complicated, and she lived there all her life, driving before she was supposed to, thanks to her "Mother of the Year" being so unreliable. One short stretch of expressway, six separate turns, about twelve stoplights, and she was driving down her used-to-be-country-now-suburban road.

Home by eight o'clock that evening, she pulled into the driveway with a big smile on her face. Elizabeth loved their home. It was familiar, it was comfortable, and it was full of more love than so many others had. Elizabeth had worked hard to erase the destruction and devastation left in her parents' wake; she had done a pretty good job, if she did say so herself.

Honking her arrival, she wasn't surprised that two of her brothers came running out to greet her. At thirteen, Danny almost plowed her over as he gave her a gorilla hug; she was so glad he was not too old for that. The next oldest, Mitch, gave her slightly less than a bear hug. He was fifteen and just at the age where it's not cool to give huge hugs to your sister. But his happy eyes gave away his true feelings: he was glad to have his big sister back home.

"Where's Bryce?" she asked.

Mitch answered, "He's working until ten. He'll be home after that. I think he asked his manager to get off early because you were coming home. But you know how strict they can be.

"You look different, Elizabeth," he added.

Uh-oh, Elizabeth thought. *How can they tell already?*

"What do you mean?" she asked nonchalantly.

Danny answered, "I think you're just tan."

Thankful for the distraction and trying as hard as she could not to convey that anything was unusual, she told the boys of all the beach-time she had and that she'd tell them all about it in a couple of hours when Bryce got home.

"There can't be that much to tell," said Mitch in his teenage I'm-cooler-than-you voice.

"And I can give you your presents," said Elizabeth.

"Now you're talking," said Mitch, this time with a smile.

The two boys each carried a bag into the house for Elizabeth. It was definitely more than she had left with—she had to buy another bag while she was there just to pack the souvenirs, clothes, and extra food she bought in North Carolina.

Bryce got home early from work, just as the boys expected, and Elizabeth was glad because she had just finished putting a second load in the washing machine. His first words to her when he walked in the house were, "Wow, it's good to see your face," as he gave her a hug.

Once everyone had their pajamas on, the four siblings sat in the living room eating the cheesecake the brothers had bought for Elizabeth's homecoming and talking about the past couple weeks of their lives. It had been strange for all of them that, for fourteen days, the brothers didn't know what was going on in Elizabeth's life every day, and vice versa.

In between Danny telling Elizabeth about trying out for the football team next year, and Mitch talking about his summer soccer, and Bryce telling her about his classes for summer semester, she almost forgot to tell them about Nathan. Their time right now was full of jubilant conversation; she almost hated to bring it up for fear of losing the current feel of the room. Yet, the grown-up in her knew it was either now or never. Now meant difficulty but honesty; never meant dishonesty and probably deeper complications. The Tenner siblings had been talking in the living room for two hours when she started in on the topic of Nathan. She had no clue where to start, and so she felt as if she were feeling her way through a dark room as she started in on the biggest event to hit her life since her mom died.

At least this is better than that.

"I have something to tell you guys," said Elizabeth as evenly as she could.

"You already told us how much food you cooked and what you did almost every day you were there. What else could there be?" asked Mitch.

"Well," Elizabeth started, looking around at her three brothers, who were listening so intently to her stories. She thought of how much they loved her, and how wonderful they had always been to her. She thought of how the biggest problem she had with her brothers were attitude problems once in a while, and how lucky she was to have them since everyone else close to her had either died or left. Elizabeth thought of past dates they had approved of and the ones they hadn't. She thought of the trouble Danny had whenever she had a date; the only guy he ever liked was a friend from college, but after he left for the military, Danny seemed to go back to rejecting anyone Elizabeth brought home, however rarely that was, even girl friends. She knew they could eventually accept Nathan, but when would that be, if ever? Much of how her heart would feel after this conversation depended on her brothers' reactions.

More like reaction, since they tend to have the same one, she thought to herself.

Elizabeth continued, "Well, I wasn't alone while I was doing most of those things on vacation. I met somebody."

"That's good—that you met a friend. I was wondering how you had so much fun if you were by yourself the whole time," said Danny.

"What do you mean, you met somebody?" asked Bryce.

Elizabeth immediately sensed that he and Mitch knew what was coming. They were nineteen and fifteen, not stupid, and far from naïve.

She stared at them. They stared right back.

"Well, I met somebody. I met a guy. A guy I really like. A guy I'd like you guys to meet someday soon."

The boys weren't talking before Elizabeth's revelation, but they all felt the sudden silence as they stared at her. The summer noises singing in their small backyard were louder than ever.

"I'm prepared for the worst, so," she paused, "you can just throw it out there."

The boys sat in a kind of stunned silence until Danny spoke. He said, "I don't really know what to say."

"Yeah, me either," Mitch chimed in. "It's not like you haven't met a guy before."

"True," Elizabeth said and smiled. "But Nathan is different. He's so much higher on the list than any other guy I've dated."

More silence.

"Do you want me to tell you about him?" she asked.

Elizabeth looked at Bryce. He had leaned back in his chair and was fiddling with the glass in his hand. He didn't look excited; he didn't look angry. He looked confused and worried.

Bryce cleared his throat and said, "Sure."

Elizabeth wondered what was going through his head. Her nerves were apparent as she quickly gave a description of Nathan.

"Well, his name is Nathan, like I said. He moved to the East Coast just a little while ago. He has a yellow lab named Jax," she said, pausing to look at Danny, hoping this would make a world of difference. It didn't seem to, but she kept going. "He's a high school English teacher, but he wants to work at a big church. He loves to exercise, running in particular. He likes country music, and he drives a Jeep. I met him when he spilled my smoothie all over me, and he bought me a new one. Shirt, I mean. Not smoothie. He loves ice cream and movies, and looking at the stars."

She hadn't paused while describing Nathan, but certainly her elevated tone indicated she was worried about her brothers' reactions. The brothers were looking at each other, which scared Elizabeth because they seemed to have their own code that she had never been able to decipher. She wasn't sure if it was because she wasn't their biological mother and therefore didn't have whatever mothers had to make them know everything, or if it was because she was female and they were each one hundred percent boy. Either way, she waited for their response. Something, anything that would let her know what they were thinking.

"This has to be pretty serious if you told us your first night back?" asked Bryce.

Finally. "Yes, it is. Well, I think so." Elizabeth answered candidly. "We're going to start e-mailing and talking on the phone about once a week. But I didn't want to hide it from you. He took very good care of me when we were in North Carolina."

"You don't need to be taken care of, Elizabeth," said Danny. "You take care of yourself, us, and you used to take care of Mom sometimes. You don't need anyone to take care of you."

Elizabeth didn't like his alarmed tone. Her parents had caused each of them too much heartache and anxiety; Elizabeth had vowed never to be the reason for this kind of tone in one of her brothers' voices. She quickly tried to stymie it.

"Well, Danny, everyone needs someone to take care of them sometimes. Like, remember when I was sick with pneumonia last year, and you, Mitch, and Bryce pitched in and took care of me and the house while I couldn't?"

"Then why can't we keep taking care of you like we did that week? Why do you need someone else?" asked Danny. His demeanor was becoming progressively and aggressively defensive.

"It's not that you don't take care of me," said Elizabeth, starting to plead, until she pulled back to calmly continue the conversation. "You boys are so good to me. But sometimes life gets bigger and stronger, sometimes a person's heart needs another heart it can care for and be cared for in a certain way."

Silence.

"Where does he live?" Danny asked suddenly.

"North Carolina," she said plainly, not giving any time or merit to the way-too-premature thoughts she knew would be running through at least Danny's head and possibly Mitch and Bryce's too.

"When do you want us to meet him?" asked Bryce.

"When we're ready," answered Elizabeth honestly.

"Does he go to church?" Mitch asked the question this time.

"Yes," she said matter-of-factly, not at all surprised that this was one of the first questions asked. She knew her brothers would be instantly drawn to this one tidbit of information.

"You haven't been to church with us in years, and pretty much since Mom died, you've isolated yourself from anything related to it," said Bryce with accusatory undertones.

"Well, maybe that's one thing you can already thank Nathan for. He said some things about his own faith that got me thinking," she said.

"Like what?" asked Mitch. He sounded disbelieving of what Elizabeth was sharing. Not that he didn't trust Elizabeth or believed she wasn't being honest with them, but she knew Mitch had a hard time believing Elizabeth had thought in any depth about anything having to do with faith. Because of that, Elizabeth hesitated. She wanted to clear the idea of Nathan before moving to another topic. Her brothers would be happy with the faith component of Nathan's person, but she refused to use it as bait. So she said, "Maybe we could talk about that another time. Right now, what do you think about me meeting someone?"

They looked at each other again.

"If I don't like him, he's out," said Danny.

"It's not just up to you, little bro," said Bryce. "We all have to like him."

"Don't call me little," responded Danny.

And we're back, thought Elizabeth.

Elizabeth was sure to clarify, "And by all, that includes me."

She had their attention again.

"When is he supposed to come for a visit?" asked Bryce.

"We have no plans for that right now. Just e-mails and phone calls for a while." She knew part of acclimating the boys to Nathan would be an unusual amount of reassurance. She could handle that; love and encouragement were something she naturally gave her brothers throughout the years. Elizabeth tried so hard—sometimes, maybe too hard—to make up for what her parents left lacking.

Elizabeth looked around at her brothers' faces again. She could tell they were uncomfortable with the word *we*. For most of their lives, *we* always meant the four of them: we're going for pizza to-night; we're going to Danny's baseball game; we're working this out before going to school—things like that. Never had it involved an outsider.

She cautiously asked, "Well, what do you say? Will you give this a try with me?"

The boys looked at each other, each in their own state of fear of what might happen should their Elizabeth be too distracted to be all theirs all the time. She supposed their minds were taking the situation to the extreme, but she was a proud sister when Bryce, Mitch, and Danny agreed to this curve ball.

That night, Elizabeth curled up under her light covers. While the bed in her beach house was cozy, nothing could touch the comfort of her room and her bed at her own home. She had always treated her room as an oasis, a place where her dreams could still live while she was growing up, no matter how dramatic or difficult things were on the other side of her bedroom door. She lay awake, thinking of her vacation and everything that had happened, missing the sound of the ocean waves and wondering if her relationship with Nathan would really develop into what her heart was secretly hoping it would. Her mind was running through so many things, but she was too tired to stay awake for longer than just a couple minutes after she snuggled in. Elizabeth's final thought before drifting off was wondering if she was making the wrong choice by bringing Nathan into her family's life. She supposed she'd find out eventually.

Chapter 7

*"Every tomorrow has two handles. We can either take hold of it
with the handle of anxiety or the handle of faith."*
~Henry Ward Beecher

ELIZABETH HIT THE GROUND running Monday morning, getting back into the swing of her regular life before Nathan came
into the picture. School was out for the summer, but she still had
plenty of projects to complete. She did, however, manage to find
some time to do a little daydreaming at work since she didn't have
her brothers around to distract her. An image of her grandma came
to mind; the woman told Elizabeth a long time ago that it's a good
thing Elizabeth was so transparent, because sharing one's heart was
a good thing. "It keeps your heart from growing bitter," is what her
grandmother used to say. Elizabeth never found a way to tell her
grandma that she wasn't that way with everyone. It got worse after
her grandparents and mom died; why would she share a life that was
upsetting and oftentimes embarrassing? Nobody she knew would
understand her situation or all the moving pieces of it. They knew
the situation on the surface, and that was that. Elizabeth had quietly
formed the habit of sticking to herself when it came to the big stuff,
sewing her heart up one tear at a time. It had long ago closed, but
Nathan's presence had her wondering if it might be able to open
again. Could she handle the emotions that would inevitably follow?
She had been tight-lipped, tight-hearted for so long.

As a child, Elizabeth used to dream of princes carrying her to lands of chocolate kisses, and Hawaiian flowers growing abundantly around her Cinderella-castle-size house. As she went through her teen years, Elizabeth's dreams morphed into more down-to-earth but still lofty ones: living in Europe, studying literature and cooking, dating cultured European men. She couldn't put her finger on when she stopped dreaming, but whenever it was must have been many years ago because not doing so had clearly taken its toll on Elizabeth's heart. Yet, she was starting to realize that in the two weeks away from her regular life, she had allowed herself to believe some of those dreams again. Not the Cinderella ones or even the European ones, but the dreams about having a safe heart, a love to call her own, and having her own life away from being a mom to her brothers, love them as she might. Some of her co-workers expected her to feel as mothers feel when their children get older, a sense of loss and sadness that they might be leaving the house in the next few years. But Elizabeth hadn't felt that way. She didn't realize until vacation how desperately she needed to be reminded that there were other, more non-maternal sides to her.

The next two weeks felt like a whirlwind, as if she would never quite catch up from being away from home for fifteen days. At home, her brothers took up much of her time as Elizabeth went back to cooking, cleaning, listening, helping with summer homework, and anything else they needed from her. Mitch and Danny were conditioning because Danny wanted to try out for the football team the following spring. They were getting a long head start, they told her. It wouldn't sound like something a mom has to help with, but there are injuries in football practice, not just in games. She made sure to stock extra healthy food in the house for when they came in from the ninety-plus-degree heat. There was new equipment to buy, listening to them talk about and work on memorizing plays. Bryce didn't need her as much anymore, but she liked to be there for him still. Mostly when he got home from work—as long as it wasn't the middle of the night—she liked to make sure she was awake and alert enough to talk to him about his day. He ran his own errands and helped Elizabeth grocery shop, but he couldn't take away the mom-tired (it's different from other kinds of tired) and the way she thought about the boys at all times.

She did manage to get them all together a few times to go miniature golfing, once to a drive-in movie, one night of a family movie night at home, and a game night at home. The activities the Tenners engaged in together didn't matter as much as the time spent. On family nights, it was a rule not to fight—verbally or otherwise—a rule instituted by Grandma and Grandpa when the boys were young and preferred physical fighting over using their words. Elizabeth and the boys carried on this rule, and for it, she was truly grateful. They may fight at home, but not on family nights.

Another thing Elizabeth loved about these family nights since she got back from vacation were how easy going they were. Where Elizabeth expected anxiety, frustration, and a withdrawal from her brothers because of her new relationship, she found the boys to be perfectly normal, completely themselves. Perhaps the strongest indication of this was the four of them walking down the boardwalk that led to a pier extending over a regional lake. They had just gotten ice cream after miniature golfing, and Elizabeth had come in last place. There wasn't one stone left unturned in regard to their teasing her, simply because of the promises she'd made earlier that she would win this time around. Elizabeth almost always lost at miniature golf, but just to mess with her brothers, she did a little more trash talking than usual leading up to the game. It did her no good; her score was the worst it had ever been. The boys took turns razzing her about not just her score but the way she held her club, how maybe she should get one of the kids playing with another family to come help her, and how un-athletic and uncoordinated she was. All comments were made in good humor, and Elizabeth was able to dish it right back because that's what brothers and sisters do. But she didn't let it go unnoticed that the boys were in exceptional spirits compared to what she had expected. Still careful not to let her guard down, she relished the moment in case it didn't last long.

Elizabeth's times of peace and quiet lay in her morning jogs and in her Tuesday night phone calls with Nathan. Their first couple of phone conversations were everything the beginning of a relationship should be: fun and flirty. They shared a lot on the beach, but talking on the phone—with Jax's barking chorus in the background—was a whole new dynamic, and they realized their relationship was still in its infancy. Yet, that fact in no way hindered Nathan's asking Elizabeth in the second week's phone call if she had thought about God since she'd been home.

"I'm still uncomfortable talking about that stuff, Nathan," she said.

"Why is that?"

"I don't know. I'm just more private in some areas than others," she responded. She was wriggling in her chair even though he couldn't see her. Everything up to this point had made for a wonderful conversation: details about each other's day, more stories of Nathan's family, and sharing laughs over a crazy woman in the news who was suing a local grocer for not stocking something she wanted. *Why couldn't it stay that way?* Nathan accepted her answer, though grudgingly. She all but heard his scowl over the phone. They still talked for a long time each week, and by the fifth phone call, they talked for more than five hours. At 12:45 a.m., Elizabeth had to call it quits.

"C'mon. Just fifteen more minutes?" pleaded Nathan.

Elizabeth could hear the smile in his voice. She could see his laugh lines and his eyes dancing as he teased her through the phone. He didn't want to give her up just yet, and how could she turn him down? The sun had long ago set, and her yawns were getting to be every couple of minutes, but Elizabeth was becoming addicted to Nathan's voice.

"Just fifteen more minutes. I'm always so tired on Wednesdays, and I have a presentation tomorrow."

"Which just three hours ago, you told me you were more than prepared for," said Nathan.

"Yes, but that doesn't mean I want to look hideous when I'm giving it," said Elizabeth.

"Yeah, good point. You should go get some rest," said Nathan, teasing Elizabeth.

"Hey! You better watch your mouth," said Elizabeth, fully playing along.

"Okay, okay," he playfully backed off while they both laughed.

Again, she could hear his smile. She wished she could see it in person. It had been five weeks since Elizabeth had seen Nathan's face as he watched her get in her rental car. Five weeks since she saw the flash of a smile that caused a physical reaction within her. As if he read her mind, Nathan asked her about that very idea: seeing each other again. She had successfully avoided the topic, but she knew it couldn't be staved off for much longer.

"Oh, boy," was all Elizabeth could think to say. She had thought about it at least a hundred times in the past five weeks, but she didn't feel ready. Whether that was for fear or true lack of readiness, she wasn't sure. Nathan interrupted her thoughts when he asked, "What's the 'oh boy' for?"

"I don't know, Nathan. Am I ready for that?"

"For what? It's not as if you've never seen me before. No surprises. I look the same. Maybe I've lost five pounds because I'm not eating all that chocolate with you, but, you know." His voice held teasing, anticipation, hope.

"You know what I mean. I have a delicate life here and besides, what would you do with Jax? He'll miss you." Elizabeth trailed off, knowing the last half of her statement was a sorry excuse meant to dodge the topic.

"Nice try. I have friends who would be more than happy to watch my dog for a few days. And, you don't know if you're ready for me to mess with that life, I get it. But I think we should give it a shot."

She questioned him again, and of course, his answer was unchanged. And to be honest, it was hard for Elizabeth to resist his request. Nathan had followed through on everything he said he was going to do so far—send her a surprise in the mail (candy), call at a certain time each week, e-mail every day, and answer any questions she had about church, faith, and his life. She had no reason to believe that he was anything or anyone but who he said he was, and that should make inviting him to her home that much easier. But when she thought about her brothers and how they might feel, she hesitated. And when she thought about her day-to-day life and the inner workings of why the Tenners do what the Tenners do, she thought of having to explain more about their fragility to Nathan, and Elizabeth wasn't sure she wanted to handle that, wasn't sure she *could* handle that. This relationship was deeper than any previous relationship, dating or otherwise. It also seemed to hold more at stake beyond her brothers' acceptance, but she wasn't sure why that was. Trying to pinpoint it to one certain thing made Elizabeth's head spin.

Elizabeth had spent a good deal of time thinking about when she would be able to see Nathan again, wondering if that would ever even happen with all the psyching herself out she was capable of doing. And now he was asking, and she found herself answering in a manner of sincerity, against her flight-risk instincts, and as though this train was going 100 mph and she had no power to stop it.

"Well, of course I've been thinking about it. A lot. I think—" she took a deep breath – "I think you should come visit soon."

After a brief pause, Nathan said, "Really?"

Elizabeth could hear the suppressed excitement—not wanting to make a big deal lest he scare her away, but not wanting to apologize for being thrilled at his next chance to spend time with her.

"Yes. I think … that … will … be … good." Her words were slow, deliberate, cautious.

They decided it would be good for him to come in three weeks. That was forty-two e-mails, three phone calls, one bouquet of flowers, and three brothers to convince that this is a good idea, that all stood between Elizabeth and Nathan and their next meeting. She decided to broach the subject with Bryce, Mitch, and Danny over dinner on a Thursday night. Not so early in the week that she could ruin the rest of it for them, but not the weekend when it could completely ruin their Saturday and Sunday. The boys were still five weeks away from starting school, but they had enough on their plates: Bryce was working full time in between semesters, and Mitch and Danny were training for football. She reasoned that even if that didn't seem a lot to deal with for a normal family, it was a lot for them. It was a lot for a family that had gone through the kind of trauma that tore her family to pieces. Elizabeth was always careful about what to add to the boys' loads, even if a casual observer would say they could handle much more. They were strong boys, but having Nathan around might be overwhelming for them, so she wanted to ease the blow as best she could.

Deciding on a taco night, she then planned out several ways to tell them—while they were getting their ingredients to make a taco, or three in Danny's case, after they sat down but before they started eating, after they starting eating, or when the food was gone. It ended up so that she found time during dinner; she decided she liked the full mouths—more time for them to think of their answers before automatically saying "no."

Bryce picked up the other boys from school, so they all came home together. Dinner was laid out on the table, and each made a beeline for the table when they saw the line of ingredients set up on the counter that would together make their favorite meal.

"Hey, what's the big occasion? Usually taco night is Friday. It's only Thursday." Danny was the first to pick up on the unusual selection for dinner, though that didn't stop him from assembling three over-stuffed tacos. She wasn't fazed in the slightest because she had grown accustomed to the way her three brothers ate: a lot and all the time. She encouraged them to sit down so dinner could start, but before they could dig in, Danny asked if they could pray.

"Of course," said Elizabeth, caught off guard. "That's a good idea." She was so anxious to get this over with she forgot something they did just about every night. Praying before dinner was not entirely against her will, but still one of the boys always asked her permission out of respect for her anti-faith attitude. And sometimes she actually said no, if she was feeling particularly tired or just didn't want to hear about God that night. When she talked to Bryce about it one night, he said the boys knew how she felt about it, "but our youth leader suggested we ask you instead of being brats and insisting on praying every single night." Bryce said they always prayed on their own whether or not they prayed aloud together as a family.

Elizabeth was learning so much about her brothers since she got home from North Carolina. Aside from them talking about church more, they had many more quiet and contemplative moments, which made them all seem to be growing up faster than she remembered them doing before she left.

Their contemplative moments worried her, if only because their behavior was reminiscent of years past when their family situation was going from bad to worse. When Elizabeth's grandparents died, eight-year-old Bryce ate dinner in his room for three straight weeks; when Mitch was eight years old, Elizabeth dated a guy from work for only two months, but Mitch's behavior at school turned from model-student to in-the-principal's-office-every-other-day; Danny passed through his eighth year without a big behavioral change, but at ten years old, just months after their mom died, he went all but mute for almost six weeks. Elizabeth watched their current actions closely because she had working knowledge of her brothers' hearts and behavior patterns, and she'd sooner commit a crime than be the reason for their heartbreak. Still, her own heart's attachment to Nathan begged for attention.

At any rate, this dinner was happening now, so she jumped back to the moment and started in on a combination of speeches she had practiced before the boys got home. Her words were carefully chosen, deliberate. She wanted them to know this was not a decision she was taking lightly, nor was it a topic she broached without regard to their feelings and how they might react.

"Okay, you know I've been talking to Nathan every week for more than a month now. And we've been e-mailing every day. Well, this past Tuesday, he asked if he could come for a visit. And, I said yes."

Silence. Not necessarily the uncomfortable silence that she expected, but the boys were looking at each other again as they did the night she came home from her vacation. They seemed to be speaking to each other with only eye contact until Bryce used spoken words to include Elizabeth in the conversation.

"When?" he asked.

"In three weeks," said Elizabeth with finality. She wasn't giving them a choice in the matter, because she thought if given a chance to say no, they would.

"Well, we figured it was coming sooner or later. We think we're ready, don't we, guys?" said Bryce, in an equally authoritative, no-choice tone that startled Elizabeth.

"Yeah, Elizabeth. I want to see what this guy's all about," said Danny.

"Really?" Elizabeth was hesitantly hopeful. She had come up with a litany of reasons why it'd be okay that he came to visit because she expected a defensive response and a lot of resistance. Maybe her expectations of frustration made the go-ahead that much more surprising.

"Okay." She took a deep breath. "Well, that was a lot easier than I expected. Thank you, guys," she said sincerely. "You'll like him. I promise."

"We'll see about that; don't get ahead of yourself," Mitch piped in, speaking seriously.

There it is.

"Is there anything I can do to make this easier? Are you sure you're ready?" It was difficult for Elizabeth to accept the ready-set-go attitude around the table. There had to be a catch of some kind.

Mitch spoke again, but he didn't answer her question. Instead, he seemed to bring a question from the depths of his heart, one he seemed to have been yearning to ask for weeks.

"Elizabeth, why do you like this guy so much if he's a Christian?"

Confused, she replied, "What's that got to do with anything? I love you, and you're Christians."

Danny chimed in, as though her brothers had rehearsed this very conversation. "Yeah, but he's going to want you to go to church. You never go when we ask you. Are you gonna go when he asks you?"

She tried not to read too much into their words, but it sounded like they were comparing her commitment to Nathan with her commitment to them. She was honest and said she wouldn't be going to church with him, either. Yet, she again reiterated her question of "Why does it matter?"

This time Danny shrugged, but Mitch piped back in. "We care, Liz, that's all. You should go if Nathan asks you to go to church. Then it won't be just us nagging you."

Elizabeth could only find it in her to shrug her own shoulders and encourage the continuation of the out-of-the-norm taco night. It turned into one of the best nights the four of them spent together since Elizabeth returned from North Carolina. They laughed and talked about their grandparents, about how Grandpa always fell asleep in his chair and then talked in his sleep. They recounted embarrassing stories about each other and giggled their way through dinner. Perhaps Elizabeth's favorite memory of the night came from Mitch's story: their grandparents had taken them to a drive-in movie theater when they were twelve, seven, and three. Danny was just born and was staying at home with their mother. The day consisted of miniature golfing, two movies watched on a sprawling lawn in front of the outside screens, and loads of junk food, which was a total treat since Elizabeth's grandparents always had mostly healthy food in the house. The night had been filled with fun and new things to laugh about, specifically the moment when Bryce got so excited during one of the movies that he flipped completely backwards in his lawn chair. Everyone was stunned until he raised his arms victoriously from under the chair and shouted, "I'm okay! I am okay." Elizabeth, Mitch, and their grandparents, when they were still alive, never let Bryce live that down, but it brought tears of laughter just about every time it was recounted.

For dessert after their taco dinner, Mitch requested a trip to the local bakery. On Thursdays, the owner made a special tiramisu that Elizabeth's family loved. They walked outside from the bakery and sat on a bench to enjoy both their dessert and the live band that was playing on a lower level of the shopping center. Elizabeth loved this beginning of fall, when summer was still holding on, for this very reason. It always seemed a romantic time of year. What she liked even more was that this year, she actually had someone to dream about. But equally tying up her thoughts were her brothers. Their response to Nathan coming to visit seemed too easy. They barely put up a fight; their fight came in the wariness of their words rather than in the words themselves.

At the end of the night, she pulled Bryce out onto their deck and asked him one question that nagged her even amid her and her brothers' great night. Simply put, "Are you sure you and your brothers are ready for this?"

He evaded her question by responding with his own. "What do you mean? I told you we are." His words vaguely matched his fidgeting hands and throat clearing.

Elizabeth nodded thoughtfully and said, "I know, and we had a great night, which would indicate that you three really are accepting of this. But you all seem to be a little quieter than I remember."

"As compared to …?" Bryce asked.

"Before I went to North Carolina. Before I brought Nathan into the mix."

Bryce looked away, distracted by a firefly that Elizabeth turned quickly to catch. Then he said, "Liz, we're fine. It's a little weird, hard to get used to the idea because you sound so serious about this guy, but you know … we'll try to get used to this." He seemed steeled as he spoke his words, as if he was willing himself to say them so that he might believe them.

"You think?" She wanted an honest answer, and she wasn't convinced that's what she was getting. But Bryce's annoyed insistence that they were fine kept her from pushing the issue.

She determined that she could keep everything moving in a positive direction by continuing to shower love on her brothers as she always had. Because in her mind, whether she liked it or not, that's what it always came down to: giving all that she had to three boys who lost everything else at too young an age. But recently, as she began giving little pieces of herself to Nathan, Elizabeth got to wondering if giving to her brothers wasn't default mode that started as survival mode so many years ago. Did she dare challenge that? Did she dare move her heart from its complacent yet comfortable state, onto what she could only imagine would be a roller coaster—and not necessarily one she would enjoy? Could she put up with making life difficult for awhile as they transitioned into a new condition?

She wasn't sure. For now, she was mostly thankful for her brothers' response to Nathan's pending visit, and all that was left was getting herself ready for Nathan's arrival. On paper, that would seem like an easy task as she bought extra food, readied the couch for him to sleep, and planned weekend activities. Yet, in her mind and in her heart, it might as well have been the most challenging event ever to cross her social calendar. Because for the next two weeks, Elizabeth woke up and went to sleep thinking about Nathan's arrival: *Will he still like me? Am I different here at home? What if my brothers hate him? What if he hates my brothers? Am I being irresponsible?*

Elizabeth went over countless questions like these until finally, one week before Nathan's visit, Bryce stopped her and said something that completely changed her outlook. It was before he left for school one morning, and Bryce could tell his big sister was preoccupied.

He said, "Look, Elizabeth. I know you really like this guy. But, speaking from a guy's perspective, you've got to calm down. He knows our situation; he clearly cares enough to come. If he cares enough to visit, he cares enough to try. It's coming, ready or not. Seriously, you've got to calm the heck down. You're pacing all over the place, you're biting your nails, and you're forgetting lunch money for Mitch and Danny. You're driving us crazy."

Bryce's words were like a soft splash of water in her face. From that point on, Elizabeth barely thought of Nathan's visit until the night before he was to arrive. Nathan would be here Thursday midday, which would give them some alone time before the boys got home from school. Her mind trailed off a dozen times that morning, thinking how they would spend those few hours; none of it involved talking.

To prep her brothers for Nathan's visit, they talked about things the family would do when Nathan was visiting. She reminded them that she'd like for the whole family and Nathan to spend quality time together.

"Don't you want to be alone?" asked Mitch.

"Yeah, to do, you know, boyfriend and girlfriend stuff?" added Danny, clearly uncomfortable thinking about his big sister acting in anything other than her usual role.

"We are a family, and that is what is important," she said.

None of the boys responded, but she hoped they appreciated hearing her words. Elizabeth knew she had to make it clear to her brothers that she was not putting Nathan or her own feelings ahead of the family.

"Okay," said Danny. "Well, as long as he can throw a football and will play, it's a start."

"I'm pretty sure he'll want to," Elizabeth said with a little chuckle. They were being protective, and Elizabeth loved it. In all the drama that surrounded her life since almost the day she was born, Elizabeth managed to hang onto a sense of self-worth that many women in her situation might not have had. With her parents not wanting her—her father wanted to abort her, for goodness' sake—and never really having had any close friendships, it would have been easy for Elizabeth to hole herself away as unlovable. But her grandparents and her brothers sought to make sure Elizabeth knew that was not the case. She was sure her brothers did this subconsciously, but nonetheless, it mattered the world to her. Still, with knowing herself and knowing what she deserved out of a mate, it was a unique kind of safety to have young men guard her and her heart. Today, she felt like a pretty lucky lady.

Chapter 8

"Sometimes the most important thing in a whole day is the rest
we take between two deep breaths."
~Etty Hillesum

ELIZABETH HAPPENED TO BE looking out at the driveway
when Nathan arrived. Leaves crunched under his feet as he
walked to the cream-colored door of the Tenner house. There was
an inviting basket hanging on the knocker; it was a rustic tan with
bright blue and yellow flowers bursting from the top of it. She
wondered if he would think that was corny, but at that thought,
Elizabeth decided she was far too nervous if she was worried about
the door decoration.

It was the middle of the afternoon, just as planned. Nathan's
flight was even early. She had offered to pick him up at the airport,
but he insisted on driving. When pressed for a reason, Nathan said
he always preferred to have his own car when he traveled. Elizabeth
didn't believe him, but she let it go. She was about to spend a weekend with a man she adored, and she didn't want any negativity
clouding that.

"Hey there, stranger," she said with a huge smile upon opening
the door. She noticed he seemed a little nervous, evidenced by the
deep breath he took while tapping his leg with his fingers; it made
her feel better.

"Hi," he said, handing her the bag of chocolate he had for her.

She melted into a kiss that came slowly, as he gently put his hand on the small of her back and pulled her close. She slid her arms around him and pulled him closer, begging for more. He obliged. After what felt like ample time getting reacquainted with each other's kisses, Nathan stepped inside for a tour of the house. Elizabeth walked him around, showing him each room and pointing out certain things, like an art piece on the wall, giving a few reasons why she liked certain items more than others.

"This might be more than you bargained for," she said. "I'm kind of nervous, so stop me when you get bored," said Elizabeth.

Nathan seemed to laugh out some of his nerves too. "I'm not bored—don't worry." He smiled at Elizabeth and took her hand, kissing it quickly and simply. "So when do your brothers get home?""Well, Bryce won't be home until late, maybe even after we go to bed. Mitch and Danny will be home fairly soon. Mitch has a soccer thing, and Danny went to a friend's house; he'll walk home."

"You let him do that? Isn't he only, like, thirteen?"

"Yeah, he's thirteen, not three. Remember what we did at thirteen years old? I remember walking down a busy road to the corner gas station before I was even twelve. Besides, we live in a safe place, and it's right down the street, like, ten houses down. I trust him and the people in this neighborhood."

Nathan was quiet.

Elizabeth closed her eyes and tipped her head back. She said, "Eh. That was pretty defensive. Sorry." She paused. "Yes, he can do that. Now, let's start dinner."

Elizabeth and Nathan enjoyed making dinner in Elizabeth's kitchen, just as they had in North Carolina. They talked about families and marriage, relationship generalities that allowed Elizabeth's heart to open up a little more at a time, only slightly withdrawing at various points throughout their conversation, mainly when words like *commitment* or *always* came into play.

Nathan noticed and made it clear he wasn't going to let her slide. He said, "Elizabeth, please don't shy away from this. We're just talking."

"I know, but I come from a land of broken relationships. Broken relationships between people who are supposed to be implicitly bound together, like mothers and daughters, fathers and sons."

"What about your grandparents?" Nathan challenged.

"I see them as the exception rather than the rule. Plus," she said, waving her fork at him, "you tend to move conversations like these toward God, and I am not in the mood for that tonight."

"Come on, Elizabeth. Jesus loves you," he said lightly.

If Nathan hadn't said that with the incredible amount of child-like sarcasm that he did, Elizabeth would have found an excuse to get upset with him. Instead, she laughed spontaneously, and it felt freeing.

Nathan continued, "Plus, I wasn't turning this into a God thing. We're just talking, you know?"

Elizabeth knew this weekend would either push her and Nathan deeper, or they would decide to cut off the relationship before it went any further, and there were many factors that would influence the decision. All the while during their conversation, Elizabeth's mind was reeling with envy that Nathan was so open, wondering what her grandparents would say if they were in the room. She thought of how she was glad her brothers would be home soon; she wanted to get this show on the road. To her, it was sink or swim time.

"So, are your brothers looking forward to meeting me? I know you must have told them *all* sorts of great things about me," teased Nathan.

"Well, after I briefed them about the murder conviction, they got excited," she said.

Nathan cocked his head with a crooked smile that said, "Ha ha, very funny."

Elizabeth said seriously, "They have their reservations, but they know how much I care about you. They're great guys; you'll love them."

Nathan smiled and kissed her temple. "I'm sure I will," he said. "My concern is them being okay with me."

Danny and Mitch walked through the door just past 6:30. Elizabeth heard them coming in, so she put aside her butterflies, went into mom mode, and greeted them like every other day: with a smile and a hug.

"Hey, guys, how did you end up home at the same time?" she asked.

"Mitch saw me walking when he was getting a ride from Joe," said Danny.

"I see. Well, welcome home. Happy weekend!" Her voice was high pitched, and her smile was tight.

It was uncomfortably silent for a few moments before Danny said, "What's up, sis? You seem nervous."

"Yeah. Well. It's an important weekend." *What the heck?*

"Why?" he asked seriously.

"Danny," she said.

"Elizabeth," replied Danny, still serious.

It was quiet; it was still uncomfortable. Nathan was standing off to the side, not sure what to do. Elizabeth, too, seemed to have no idea what to do or say, either, to her little brother who seemed clueless about the fourth body standing in the kitchen besides Elizabeth, Mitch, and himself.

"Danny," she said it a little slower this time, in a singsong question that had a last-nerve feel to it.

"Elizabeth," Danny reciprocated the slow speech. Then, a slow smile spread across his face, and he said, "Relax. Have you lost your sense of humor in the last twenty-four hours?" He turned to Nathan. "Hey, man. I'm Danny."

Tension broke, and the evening began.

Bryce didn't get home in time for dinner or dessert, but it seemed to be going well with the other two boys, not more than two awkward silences. After dinner, Elizabeth pulled out the ice cream cake she made the day before and had stashed in the back of the freezer (after all, she lived with three boys) and started serving it around the table as everyone chatted. Elizabeth appreciated Nathan's patience with the boys' questions and sometimes rude demeanor, particularly when the boys acted less than impressed with Nathan's job as an English teacher.

The only hitch she saw so far was that despite Danny's teasing when he first got home, he was quiet the rest of the night. He ate, nodded at the appropriate times, even chuckled once or twice, but Elizabeth could tell it was forced. Maybe that's how it had to be at first, she thought.

Elizabeth nudged Nathan, suggesting that he tell Mitch what his ultimate career goal was; she knew it would intrigue her little brother.

"What I really want to do is work in a church," said Nathan.

Mitch's face lit up again.

"Doing what?" he asked.

"Not sure yet. Youth or marriage ministry, maybe," answered Nathan.

"Don't you have to be married for the marriage ministry?" asked Danny, confusion pouring from his voice in the first words uttered in several minutes.

"Yes, yes, you do," said Nathan, eyeing Elizabeth. Her eyebrows were raised as though unsure of the conversation, so Nathan continued slowly, "But someday I will be. Until then, we'll see where there's a need that I can fill."

Elizabeth could see Danny's mind was jumping to an uncomfortable conclusion—it was written all over his face—but she wanted to keep moving through the evening, so she didn't dwell on it. For now.

After dinner, Mitch helped Elizabeth clean up the dishes because it was his turn, and Danny asked to be excused to finish his summer reading. This was the first time Danny had ever made such a request, but Elizabeth wanted to give him a chance to sort out what she was sure were his many feelings, some of which might be confusing and overwhelming. A flashback brought to mind Danny's mute weeks following the death of their mother. She wanted nothing more than to shield him from further heartaches, but she wasn't convinced her relationship with Nathan would cause just that.

Elizabeth had deliberately said an extra-long goodnight to Danny, listening to anything he wanted to say. Although her sweet little brother told her about a good grade on his math test, Carole Ann in his Spanish class, and a joke about the cafeteria food,

nothing on the subject of Nathan was brought into the conversation. Elizabeth took her cues from Danny, believing he was sorting
before speaking out his feelings. Plus, she needed to be an adult, not
a mom, just a woman falling for a man as other twenty-six-year-old
women do who have no teenage boys to think about.

"I had a great time at dinner tonight with you and your brothers," said Nathan as Elizabeth entered the kitchen, where he had
waited.

"I did too. I wish Bryce had gotten home earlier, though. He
must have had to work late. Sometimes he works until after mid-
night on Thursdays."

"I'll meet him tomorrow, though, won't I?" Nathan leaned
against the kitchen counter, holding a cup of the coffee he had
started when Elizabeth was saying goodnight to her brothers.

"Yeah. He was so sweet; he said to me yesterday, 'Elizabeth,
don't freak out, but I took off this weekend so I could meet Nathan.'
He told his boss he had an important family matter and needed the
time off." She helped herself to a cup of coffee.

"That is sweet," said Nathan. "Those boys really love you. And
respect you."

"Thanks. I just wish they had a real mom to look up to. I know
I leave some holes, but they know I do the best I can," she said
casually.

It had been so few times over the years that Elizabeth could
remember talking about parenting with anyone. When her grandparents and then parents died, some people tried to talk to her about
the responsibility of taking care of three boys—as if they had to
remind her how difficult it was, or how much energy it took, or
how being a mom or, in her case, a sister acting like a mom, was
a twenty-four/seven, no-time-for-anything-else, emotional roller
coaster of a thing. She was mature enough to know her birth parents weren't parents at all, just two big kids who never reached
farther than the conceiving part of "parenting." Elizabeth remembered thanking a few people for their advice but assuring them she
would manage just fine. Specifically, she remembered some men
and women from her brothers' church coming to her during the

funeral. We can help, they told her. Your brothers have told us what you all go through, and we'd love to be there for you, they told her. In a kind, detached, diplomatic way, Elizabeth told them she appreciated the offer, but to please stick to helping at church and not her home. Bryce had gotten upset with her because, as he put it, people from church were only trying to help, they were showing the love of Jesus, he had said. It had been all Elizabeth could do not to laugh, but since their mom had just died, she cut her brother some slack by telling him they could show that love at church but not at their house. Then, from what Elizabeth felt was out of nowhere, Bryce said—in a voice fuller and more mature than she thought could be mustered in the short span of his life up to that point—"Elizabeth, we show that kind of love in this house every day. I hope someday you can see that."

She had been too stunned to speak, and she and Bryce never talked about that conversation again. They talked about church and Jesus, though; Bryce, Mitch, and Danny made sure of that. And, it seemed, so would Nathan.

Elizabeth was looking directly into Nathan's eyes. He listened to her so intently; she savored every second of it and took advantage of the attention.

Nathan said, "Seeing the way you interacted with your brothers was interesting. I saw a whole different side to you tonight. The mom side."

"Yeah? Well I'm not a mom. I'm a sister," said Elizabeth pointedly.

"But you take care of those boys without an ounce of evidence of how it tires you out. It comes so naturally; I don't know how you do that. They treat you like a sister and a mother."

"I'm really quite something, aren't I?" teased Elizabeth. Her sarcasm was an attempt to hide the fact that she felt a serious conversation coming.

Nathan smiled at her sarcasm, but confirmed her suspicion. "I wonder if you realize how much God has helped you along."

And there it was. "What do you mean?"

"Think about it. I know the youth leaders at your brothers'

church have helped; I think He put them in your path for a reason, and He's held you up all these years."

"How? You just told me how impressed you were with how my brothers treat me," said Elizabeth as honestly as she's ever said anything to Nathan.

"I am impressed. But I think God has built you up all these years," he said.

Elizabeth took an agitated deep breath. Then she said, "I'm not sure about that. I certainly didn't feel Him building me up when my mom was MIA, or when my grandparents died. Or when the state said they'd take away my brothers if I didn't volunteer to take care of them. At twenty-two, I didn't feel Him helping me all those nights in college when I was a student, employee, mom, and sister, constantly switching from one role to the next. Sometimes in the same breath."

"I'm not trying to invalidate what you've gone through. I am just saying ..." Nathan trailed off as he looked at Elizabeth. She looked hurt, frustrated, and confused.

"Yes?" She was pressing for an explanation, because the one he'd just given her felt insulting. And if she had taught Nathan anything, it was that she was a fighter; letting things lie wasn't her strong suit.

"I am just saying," Nathan continued slowly, "that I hope you can come to see God's grace. It's a gift, and He's really good about extending it to all different people, especially those who think they don't need it."

"Whatever you say, Nathan."

They were quiet for a few minutes, so Elizabeth got up to put on some music. Halfway through the first song, she finally voiced what she was thinking.

"You know, I might be thinking more about God, but I definitely am not where you're at. I don't have a heart like yours, so sometimes I'm going to say things that you might not like or want to hear, things about what I think about my life and God's role in it, or lack thereof."

"I know that," said Nathan. He wasn't smiling, but he didn't seem upset, either. He was biting his lip, looking painfully close to saying something.

Elizabeth looked at Nathan. He was again looking deep into her eyes. Right now, Elizabeth knew he saw a woman who was doing her best to search for some good answers because she couldn't ignore such a strong tug at her heart for something more than what her life was. But Elizabeth was also a woman who had been battered a little more than Nathan by life circumstances. He had his share of heartache. Still, Elizabeth certainly could have been worse off, but the emotional damage left by her family dynamics was no minor etch in her story.

"How about we let this go for now?" said Elizabeth with a sigh and a slightly mischievous tone. Her desire to distract Nathan from this topic quickly became her number one priority.

"What do you want to do?" Nathan seemed to know exactly what was coming from Elizabeth.

They kissed for what seemed like only a few minutes. Their kissing went from soft and sweet to strong and passionate, and back and forth again and again until they were both tired enough to stop. Elizabeth reveled in every moment of this. Not only the physical attraction, but the feeling of intimacy and the act of not thinking—or caring—about anything but that single moment. She was wrapped up, carried away, for all intents and purposes, in a whole other world.

Searching for words to bring them back to Earth after they silently but mutually decided to stop, Nathan said, "That was fun."

They both laughed at the obvious but simple statement because neither could think of anything else to say or do.

"It was," said Elizabeth. "I love kissing you."

"And I, you," responded Nathan.

Nathan and Elizabeth ended the evening in her bedroom with a box of chocolate chip cookies and a bottle of wine, still enjoying the sound of each other's voice in person rather than on the phone as they talked into the wee hours. Eventually, it was time to call it a night. After getting ready for bed and saying quick goodnights, Elizabeth and Nathan spent the night in separate rooms.

They weren't sleeping together, and Elizabeth didn't want to give the boys the impression that they were. Elizabeth's decision not to sleep around was still very important to her. For one, women who slept with her dad were part of the reason that her family was in shambles for the first part of Elizabeth's life. And two, there was only one other guy with whom she had felt comfortable enough to consider sleeping with, but he had been her best friend in college, not her boyfriend. And look where that went. Nowhere.

Elizabeth's thoughts before she drifted off to sleep were of two things: Nathan's kisses and wondering what Bryce's reaction would be to his big sister's new boyfriend when the two of them finally met in the morning.

By the time Nathan woke up Friday morning, Elizabeth had already showered, eaten, and was sitting on the front porch talking to Bryce.

"Good morning," said Nathan. He kissed Elizabeth on the cheek and turned to Bryce with a firm handshake. "It's nice to finally meet you. I'm sorry you had to work so late last night."

"Eh, Elizabeth probably told you it's pretty normal," said Bryce with a shrug. "Sometimes people don't really see the 'closed' sign until the bus boys are sweeping under their feet."

"I thought you worked at a hotel?" asked Nathan.

"It's attached to a restaurant, which is where I worked last night," he said.

"I see," said Nathan, nodding. "Well it's nice to meet you, man."

"It's nice to meet you too," said Bryce. "We've heard a lot about you."

"All good stuff, I hope," said Nathan, winking at Elizabeth.

"If you know Elizabeth, you know what she told me," he said with a smirk.

"Did she tell you how we met?"

"Yeah, how you were so graceful with the smoothie."

"Thanks for that, Elizabeth, yes," said Nathan, sounding

embarrassed but not enough to blush even in the slightest. "Did she tell you about the second time we ran into each other?"

Bryce took a sip of coffee and answered, "Yes, the movie theater."

"Movie theater?" Nathan was confused.

"I think it's time to make you," Elizabeth pointed at Nathan, "some breakfast. Come on, I'll make you—"

"Elizabeth, sit down," said Nathan with a mock-serious expression on his face.

"Not a movie theater?" asked Bryce, confused and intrigued.

"No," said Nathan. "That is not how we ran into each other the second time." His words were pointed as he looked at Elizabeth with an expression that said, "I can't believe you."

"And here I thought you would stick to only embarrassing yourself this weekend," Elizabeth said to Nathan, rubbing his arm somewhat forcefully.

"No," said Nathan, smiling a truly mischievous smile.

Nathan recounted for Bryce their second encounter, fully embarrassing Elizabeth. Bryce got a good laugh out of the story.

"Thank you, Nathan, my brothers always need more ammunition for picking on me," said Elizabeth.

"Too much is never enough, Elizabeth," said Bryce with a wink.

Mitch and Danny came down for breakfast, and both of them seemed unusually awake for a Saturday morning.

"Good morning," said Elizabeth with the same smile she gave them when they got home last night. All morning, Elizabeth worked herself up to keep herself as steady as possible. She resolved to rein it in and keep her voice inflection and her actions as close to natural as possible. It was a high-stakes weekend, so a normal heartbeat, steady hands, and an even tone were near impossible. But she would try.

"Morning," the two said almost in unison. "Hey, Bryce," said Danny. "How was work last night?"

"It was fine. Super busy. Hey, listen to this story about Elizabeth," he said with amusement.

And ignoring Elizabeth's stink-eye, Nathan retold the grocery bag fiasco for Mitch and Danny. They laughed even harder than Bryce, fully enjoying the images Nathan drew up, images Elizabeth thought to be embellished descriptions of her not-so-graceful walk from the store.

After everyone settled down, Bryce continued his conversation with Danny. He asked, "Did you have a good day yesterday?"

"Yeah, it was fine," said Danny.

"Fine. Every thirteen-year-old boy's day is 'fine,'" Bryce teased. Then he switched gears, asking Elizabeth and Nathan, "So, what are we doing today?"

Nathan answered, "Your sister said we could hang around here; play some football in the backyard, some other games inside, maybe miniature golfing later, then dinner and ice cream?"

Everyone seemed to agree to the plans, so after breakfast, they moved on with their day. While changing her clothes for their touch football game, Elizabeth's head crammed itself with nagging thoughts and questions.

I wonder how today will go.

Well, I hope.

Just be yourself and let the boys be themselves. Don't make a big deal of things. Just relax.

Stop thinking so much; just go.

Unfortunately, some of Elizabeth's fears came true; the day was not everything she hoped it would be. Danny and Mitch were bickering over the smallest things, and when Danny was tagged on a third down, he slammed the ball into the ground as though he were trying to bury it. Elizabeth tried taking deep breaths and letting the boys work through their frustrations, but nothing was changing. Their behavior wasn't escalating, but it wasn't improving, either. Especially Danny's. This was not her sweet, little Danny. This was a brother who she had seen with new eyes since coming back from North Carolina. He was in between boyhood and manhood, trying his best to deal with everything that comes with this stage in life. Elizabeth had thrown him a big curve ball, and being the most sensitive of the Tenner boys, she should have expected Danny to need the most amount of adjustment time. Slamming the football, re-maining quiet at dinner last night, keeping to himself right now—these were telltale signs of trying to cope with transition, something her family had always fumbled through because their transitions usually involved a great life change that came without warning.

In those split-second moments when a mother would have the exclusive right to tell her sons what to do, the sister in Elizabeth wished the choice to guide her brothers' behavior wasn't hers to make. So right now, in an effort to avoid an argument, she let her two youngest brothers battle it out, and she tried to enjoy the time with Bryce and Nathan. At least the two of them seemed to have a lot to talk about. That was a good sign, right? She listened in on their conversation, even later after football as she pretended to nap while they were watching television. Mitch and Danny chose sepa-rate activities when a few neighborhood boys came looking for two more to fill their street hockey team.

"What church do you guys go to?" Nathan asked Bryce.

"Liz didn't tell you?" asked Bryce.

"Nope," Nathan said, casually shaking his head.

"Oh. Well, we go to RockPointe Christian Church. It's a huge church, but we really like it," said Bryce.

"How'd you get started going there?" Nathan wanted to know.

"Believe it or not, Liz got us started. After our grandparents died, one of Liz's friends from school asked us to go to church. Her friend knew what we were dealing with at home and told Liz church might be able to help. She was, admittedly, excessively skeptical, but she told us that if she was going, we were all going, as a family. Liz always wanted nothing more than to be a whole and functioning family. I'm sure she's told you that our parents … well, they sucked as parents. We went to church, and Danny, Mitch, and I loved it, but Liz … I don't know. We started going every week, practically begging her to take us. She came for a few years, but after Mom died, she took it upon herself to take care of us and decided that we had made a home for ourselves at the church without her, so we didn't need her to go with us anymore. The youth pastors there really took us under their wing, which seemed to give Liz a much-needed break."

"Liz never told me all that." Nathan seemed concerned but happy that Bryce shared so much. He said, "She knew your youth pastors had really helped you boys, but she doesn't like to talk much about church."

"Don't I know it. Anything else we talk about, she hangs on to every word. Mention church and it's 'mmhmm' and 'good.' She always supported us going, but I think she was just glad we asked to go to church instead of a lot of other places doing a lot of other things."

"Yeah, we're working on that," said Nathan with some disappointment in his voice.

"Good luck, man," said Bryce.

Nathan laughed, "Yeah."

Bryce seemed so sincere, Elizabeth noticed. Nathan seemed discouraged. Is that really how they saw her? That anything surrounding their life with the church was a topic she didn't want to hear about? Bryce was right on one point: she was glad they chose church activities over who-knows-what-else. But the other thing—her not caring about that part of their lives—that wasn't true. Or was it? She had only met the boys' youth group leaders a handful of times, she never escorted them to birthday parties, and on only two occasions had she gone to church with the boys on Christmas Eve. A wave of guilt washed over Elizabeth without warning. How had she ignored such a huge part of who her brothers were as young men? But almost as quickly as the wave came, she cast it away. This weekend was a Nathan weekend. Thinking about her brothers would bring her into mom mode, and she was putting forth a concentrated effort against that this weekend.

Elizabeth hoped Nathan and Bryce would linger on the topic for a little while longer so she could hear more of their thoughts, but they didn't. Instead, they turned their discussion to things she was not interested in—science magazines and cars.

When she "woke up," she wanted to play miniature golf. Mitch and Danny had just gotten home, so everyone piled in Bryce's car, and for the next two hours, the Tenners and Nathan had an intense miniature golf competition. And these two hours took Elizabeth by surprise as they turned into what she had wanted out of the weekend: everyone laughing, smiling, and having fun. Together.

Friday night, Elizabeth, Nathan, and the boys lounged in the living room. They watched two movies, one picked by Nathan and the other picked by Mitch. Before they started the double feature, Nathan noticed a coffee can with what looked like pictures of DVD covers on the front of it. It sat on the fireplace mantle with two clothes pins clipped to the edge of it.

"What's this?" asked Nathan.

Everyone looked at him, but it was Danny who volunteered an answer.

"Oh, that's how we decide who gets to pick the movie we watch. All our names are in there on a clothes pin, and whosever name gets picked out gets to choose the movie."

"Hmm," said Nathan. "That's different. Fair, but different."

"It helps us to choose faster. It used to take *soooo* long to pick a movie we could all agree on. This way, we all get a turn," said Elizabeth.

"It wouldn't take so long if you were up for watching better movies, Liz," teased Mitch.

"Hey, I pick good movies," she said.

The boys laughed almost in unison. "Yeah, right!" Mitch said. "Remember that awful movie you chose last time? What was it? *You've Got Mail*?"

"That is not a bad movie! Nathan, tell them!" she said, mockingly defensive.

"Sorry, guys. That's a great movie," said Nathan.

"Thank you!" Elizabeth was playing indignant.

"What else has she picked?" asked Nathan.

"Nathan!" Elizabeth couldn't believe he was encouraging her brothers. He was egging them on. Again she played indignant and defensive, but she loved the back and forth; a bond was building between the five of them.

Bryce and Mitch each came up with a short list, and Nathan ended up agreeing with them.

Elizabeth stared at her brothers and Nathan. *"Anyway,* what are we watching tonight, Mitch?" His clip had been pulled out of the coffee can.

Mitch answered, "I picked *Double Jeopardy.* Nathan picked ... I don't know. Nathan, what did you pick?"

Guests always got to pick at least one movie. Elizabeth, Bryce, Mitch, and Danny all looked at Nathan and a found a smirk on Nathan's face.

"What's that look for? What'd you pick?" Elizabeth was curious.

"I picked ..." Nathan held it behind his back for a moment before busting out with it for everyone to see. *"Miracle!"*

Elizabeth smiled, and her brothers just looked over at her. "What? I didn't tell him to pick it."

"What's wrong with *Miracle*?" asked Nathan, clearly thinking he had made a good choice. "Hockey. Tension. Perseverance. Good stuff."

"It's one of my favorites, actually, so they've seen it a hundred times. But, oh well! Guest picks, right boys?" Elizabeth was all smiles.

"Yeah," the boys all answered in staggered responses. Elizabeth was happy to see that the not-again looks coming from her brothers were the exact ones they would give her when they didn't want to do something but knew they were going to have to do it anyway. They were being themselves, and Elizabeth felt desperate for that. If the boys could be themselves with her while Nathan was around, there was hope for furthering Nathan's presence in the Tenner family.

Then, Elizabeth caught her thoughts. She couldn't push herself past this weekend. Not yet. Eventually, maybe, but not yet. For now, she continued to watch the boys interact with Nathan. They talked a little bit through both movies but for the most part remained quiet. The Tenners did not like talking during movies.

Elizabeth found herself not only thinking how much she loved seeing the boys and Nathan spend time together, but also how attractive she found Nathan in a big brother-ish role. She made sure to tell him so after her brothers had gone to bed when he came outside after being on the phone. She was leaning against her deck railing, looking out past their backyard.

"Hey, pretty lady," he said as he wrapped his arms around her middle.

Elizabeth turned around to return the greeting. "Hi there. How is Jax?" Nathan had called a friend from church to check on him.

"He's fine. Moping around for me, as usual, though."

She smiled in response as she leaned her body into his, kissing him for what felt like only a second.

"Well, hello there." Nathan was surprised by her impulsive kisses but wasn't about to slow her down. "What was that for?"

"You really want to know?" she asked.

"I think so, yeah. Because whatever it was for, I'll be sure to keep doing it," said Nathan with a small laugh.

Elizabeth giggled. "Well, it was for two things. One, it was for how much I loved watching you interact with my brothers. You're a natural with them, Nathan."

She showered him with little kisses on his mouth. Nathan clearly loved every second of it, but he pulled back and asked, "As a high school teacher, I hope I'm good at it. And two?"

"And two, being with you makes me forget I have a mom hat. It makes me want to be a teenager who sneaks around to make out with her boyfriend," she said coyly.

Nathan smiled, and the couple shared a few more sneaky teenager moments. Back inside, they plopped down on the oversized chair in Elizabeth's bedroom to watch another movie. After a little while, Elizabeth became distracted, and Elizabeth could see Nathan watching her out of the corner of her eye.

Probably because you're fidgeting like a crazy person, she said to herself. The roller coaster of emotions Elizabeth had been experiencing since Nathan came into her life was still something Elizabeth could not get used to. Though her family life had been dramatic, Elizabeth always knew how to take control of a situation and control her emotions. Both were always out of protective instincts for her brothers and a strong contempt for her parents. But with Nathan and everything he ushered into her life, Elizabeth felt most of the time as though she was fumbling her way through. And tonight, when she knew how to be a sister and a mom to her brothers and a girlfriend to Nathan, figuring out how to mesh the two started to stress her out as the night settled in.

Finally, about halfway through the movie, Nathan pressed pause and asked Elizabeth to open up.

"What's on your mind? You seem distracted," said Nathan.

"It was a long day. I'm just tired," she said.

"It was a long day, but you didn't seem too tired downstairs. Now you're squirming and not really watching the movie. So what's up?"

Elizabeth studied him, then said, "You know, sometimes the things you say sound so unrealistic. Like you're a character in a movie, and someone has already written your lines for you."

"What do you mean?" he asked.

"What you just said. How are you so perceptive?"

"Because I pay attention, Elizabeth," said Nathan. "I'm not really sure what you're looking for here." He sounded confused, maybe even a little bit frustrated.

Can you blame him? You're lovey-dovey, then defensive. Pick a gear and stay in it awhile.

When Elizabeth didn't say anything, Nathan continued talking.

"How about this," Nathan suggested. "You give me a chance to help you sort through something."

"You're going to use a godly perspective," said Elizabeth matter-of-factly.

"Will that bother you?" asked Nathan.

Elizabeth hesitated, and then said hurriedly, "Maybe."

Nathan smiled. He said, "Let's give it a shot."

Elizabeth sighed. "Well, it's hard going from mom to teenager, like before, I mean. I don't know how to stay in teenager— Let's not call it that. I don't know how to stay in non-mom mode. Put God in *there*; I dare you."

"Well, first of all, to separate what you're going through from God's presence is something I can't do. And second, I know this is an adjustment, but I need to know you're going to at least try, or else we've got some waiting to do before this goes any further."

"What do you mean?" she asked, somewhat defensively.

"Elizabeth, I have watched you watch me since I got here Thursday. You're watching me with the boys, like this is a test run for the future. You can't be thinking seriously about a long-term future together without considering the fact that you can't yet open your heart to something deeper."

This took Elizabeth back a bit. She thought they had a great day. He was right about the test-run part. So what was the problem?

"Look," Nathan started slowly, but sped up as he spoke. "We have been talking every week for almost two months. We've written to each other every single day. I just … I guess I expected to feel a little deeper of a connection from you this weekend."

Elizabeth blew a puff of air, blowing her side bangs off her temple. She said, "I knew this was going to happen. I knew I shouldn't have even started this fantasy. I knew that when you came here, you would see my real life and decide you didn't want to be a part of it. I knew—"

"Elizabeth, stop." His stern tone stopped her from continuing. "That's not what I meant. What I meant was, I expected to talk about things, like the way Danny's been acting. Or about how you and Bryce seem to tag-team it sometimes when nobody's watching. Or about how you're resisting this relationship so subtly, but you have no good reason to do so. Everything you're thinking about is an excuse."

Elizabeth was extremely uncomfortable with Nathan's insight. So much so that she responded in anger. Tears sprang to her eyes, and she said, "Well, then leave. If you've got me figured out, and you're so sure I won't be able to give what you want any time soon, then leave."

"No."

"Nathan, why are you pursuing this? You would make this so much easier if you just realized what a dramatic mess you stepped into, and walk away."

Nathan looked at Elizabeth with half pity, half adoration. Then he smiled and said, "I don't suppose 'God told me to' would be an acceptable answer for you?"

She, of course, shook her head.

He answered her skepticism: "Elizabeth, I have not been shy about telling you that I am a praying man. It's how I make my decisions, especially the big ones. Even when this doesn't make sense to me, or to you—which is something you're not shy about admitting—my gut tells me to keep going. My gut is telling me, 'Stay.' So, here I stay. I really care about you. And you know what else? I'm not going to let you get away with wasting time."

"Wasting time?" she asked, confused.

He clarified, "Wasting time not moving forward. There's no movement in your life; you're just surviving."

"Please don't judge my life," she said in an icy voice.

"Elizabeth—"

"You're darn right I'm surviving. It's a technique I perfected when every person who was supposed to take care of me either didn't love me, died, or left." The tears didn't fall, so she talked through them. "Don't talk to me about living versus surviving. I'm doing the best I can, and your God-stuff isn't helping. It may have helped my brothers, but they're still being taken care of."

Nathan didn't respond, so Elizabeth stared at him for a while without saying a word.

"What are you thinking?" Nathan finally asked.

"Honestly?" asked Elizabeth, tears still in her eyes.

"Of course, honestly," said Nathan.

"That you make me really uncomfortable and I don't know if I'm ready for this," she said. "You're making me feel all these things, and it's not all good."

Nathan let out a deep breath before he answered her.

He said, "Maybe it's time, Elizabeth, that someone takes the reins from you for a bit. And can I be hopeful and wonder if, after thinking 'I'm not ready for this,' you've also thought 'but maybe I can go ahead with this anyway'?"

This time Elizabeth let out a loud, frustrated sigh. She said, "Ugh! Again with the charm."

"Elizabeth, I don't know what to tell you. I'm just being honest. I want you to stop being afraid."

Elizabeth thought for a moment before she responded to Nathan. Finally, she said, "Look, I don't know either. I like you. I like you very much. But this is where I'm at right now. I *am* afraid, because I don't have just me to look out for. This is my life. Take it or leave it."

Nathan wasn't satisfied. He said, "Well, I'll say one thing for your guarded heart. It certainly makes you stand up firmly for who you believe you are." His words were filled to the brim with frustration. He and Elizabeth both struggled to keep their voices down because the boys were sleeping. But Elizabeth matched his frustration.

"Who I *believe* I am? What the heck does that mean, Nathan?"

"It means you think you can't handle this, but I think you can." He took a deep breath before finishing. "Because I have faith that God and I can melt your heart like chocolate in the sun."

Still uncomfortable with Nathan's perception of her and her life, Elizabeth couldn't help but laugh at his last comment. Nathan and Elizabeth's second night together wasn't as free as the first, but Elizabeth noticed it was a kind of tension she had never felt before. It seemed to be a necessary tension, one that she thought might eventually iron out.

Strange, she thought to herself.

Saturday was spent at the county fair. The morning started off easy, with everyone in an agreeable mood. The boys were still a bit on the quiet side, but Elizabeth hoped they were tired from watching movies the night before. Nathan and Elizabeth had mostly settled their late-night disagreement. Nathan's disappointment lay in the fact that he did not feel their relationship was moving any deeper. Elizabeth was frustrated that Nathan thought God could fix everything. She didn't need to be fixed. They had agreed to move on—for now—but Elizabeth could feel a slight distance from Nathan on Saturday. From the boys too, which made for another roller coaster of a day.

Her hopes that the boys were quiet from being tired diminished as the day went on. Danny was the quietest, withdrawn even. Mitch was on and off with making conversation, and Bryce seemed at a loss for words. In the middle of the day, during a potbelly pig race, Elizabeth realized something: they probably had a lot of questions going through their minds, such as if she fell for Nathan, where would Elizabeth live? Would she move away? Then where would that leave the boys? Elizabeth figured Danny was most anxious out of her three brothers; he was always the most worrisome. That, she surmised, was a survival tactic from when their mom had started checking out as a parent long before her death.

Elizabeth had no clue how to make this better for them other than having a serious heart-to-heart with each brother, but that was going to have to wait until after Nathan left.

Saturday night, the boys were exhausted when they got home, so they went to bed earlier than usual. Elizabeth and Nathan had the living room all to themselves, and they did what they did best: talk for a long period of time about serious and not-so-serious things.

"Elizabeth, I don't mean to déja vú here, but what's up? You seemed extra quiet and distracted all the way home."

"What do you mean? Everyone was quiet. Another long day." Elizabeth finished putting away the fudge and cookie mixes she had purchased; Nathan helped.

"Yeah, but I could tell you had some pretty heavy stuff on your mind," he said.

"Again with the insight," she said, almost under her breath.

"Elizabeth, stop. C'mon, talk to me." Nathan sounded like he was getting irritated with Elizabeth's commenting on his words rather than responding to them.

"I'd rather do this," said Elizabeth slyly, right before she pursued giving him an unapologetically passionate kiss. Elizabeth wondered if this would be enough of a distraction for Nathan to stop trying to help her sort out her feelings.

"And another déja vú," said Nathan. "You're good at distracting me."

They shared another kiss, but this one was less intense. After it was over, Nathan teased, "So I'm just some random guy you've chosen to 'hook up' with?"

Elizabeth didn't respond well to the teasing. "What was the air quote for around 'hook up'?"

"Liz, I was just joking. We're not hooking up; we're just kissing."

"Is that okay with you?" she asked. If she was honest with herself, she believed Nathan would be expecting certain things as the relationship progressed. Elizabeth didn't date often, but she got the hint from the few she did have about what men expect at a certain point and after a certain number of dates. Actually, she was surprised the topic hadn't come up sooner. She was equally surprised when Nathan told her that it was absolutely fine, that just kissing was completely okay with him; in fact, he said it with no pretense in his tone of voice.

"*Why* is it fine with you?" asked Elizabeth. She had her eyes squinted, curiously, testing him on what his answer would be.

"First of all, you're getting defensive again. And second of all, because I don't want … I'm not … I'm not having sex until I get married," said Nathan. "Even though I will want, with every fiber of my being—trust me on that one—to do so beforehand." He sounded, not embarrassed, but expecting to be made fun of for what he just revealed.

"Like the celibacy and purity clubs the high schoolers do?" Elizabeth's voice held a bit of disbelief.

"Are you making fun of my decision to wait until marriage?" asked Nathan with mock indignation.

"Hmm," Elizabeth paused for a moment. She changed her tone when she said, "I guess not. No. It's a great choice." When she pressed him for why, Elizabeth was not at all surprised to learn that Nathan's celibacy choice was part faith, part practicality. He didn't want to be anyone's "baby daddy"—said with a mix of humor and disgust—unless he was married to the baby's mom. She conceded.

"Great. I'll wait for you. You're okay with that. Let's move on," Nathan stated matter-of-factly. He started walking toward the counter to plug in his cell phone.

Elizabeth's carefree smile was halted at his last words.

"Wait for me? What do you mean 'for me'?" Elizabeth's defensive tone was back.

Nathan hung his head and gave a deep, audible sigh. Then he said, "Mmmm. I didn't mean to say that." He pursed his lips together.

"But you said it, so what did it mean?" asked Elizabeth, ready—again—to hold her ground until she got an answer. His words were so distinct. Wait for her? First of all, that was very dramatic sounding. Second, she could barely handle the *now*, and he brings up a future tense?

You're picking a fight. Let it go.

Nathan looked at Elizabeth, who was looking at him, obviously expecting a clear, straight answer. Her eyes were wide, her forehead creased, and her hands firmly on her hips; it was the standard woman pose for "Tell me right now."

"Liz, I don't know how you're going to feel if I tell you my true answer. You've been pretty up and down this weekend and—"

"Try me," she said, cutting him off again. His voice had dropped significantly, as though he was truly uneasy about sharing his thoughts. But she had to know. For her sanity, for her boys, for her future—she had to know.

"Okay." Nathan took a breath. "Liz, I would love it if we got to spend the rest of our lives together. I would really, really love it. That said, I will wait for you. I will wait for you to accept Jesus' love and grace. I will wait for you … physically. You don't need me to save you, and that's not what I'm here to do. But I will wait for you to come around. I know you want to. And I know how you feel about me, and I think we're headed in a good direction for achieving all of what I just said. So. I will wait."

Nathan didn't say anything while Elizabeth seemed to be processing what his words meant. "I, um, I'm not sure what to say," she said, because she really didn't. *He is so honest.* This started as a slip up, but still. The rest of their lives? Her brothers hid out in their rooms for half the weekend, for goodness sake. She was barely hanging on as a sister, mom, and girlfriend, and now she had the pressure of Nathan wanting to spend the rest of his life with her. Elizabeth knew that the kind of life she had—with the exception of her grandparents and her fierce devotion to her brothers—had taught her to run when it came to something like this. And even with the exceptions, she saw her grandparents as an extremely rare example and her brothers as common-sense responsibility. She didn't know how to be okay with someone wanting to stick around, because her own parents had seemed allergic to it. Still, she knew enough to know that having Nathan around was nothing if not wonderfully comforting. So at this moment, all she could think of was, "You're right, I don't need saving. I am not the kind of person who will say 'I need you,' and not because I don't want to let down my guard, but because it presupposes that I need you to live, which I don't. But, it's nice having you around, and I guess we'll see if this stuff you're talking about comes true."

The three sentences of her response were said slowly and with small cringes on her face as she said the words. She was nervous, never having been here before.

"I'd really, really like that," Nathan said in a husky whisper through a big smile and wet eyes that slowly made their way up after facing the floor during her short speech. And when they made their way to Elizabeth's face, he saw tears in her eyes too.

Chapter 9

"In the grip of grace, you're free to be honest."
~Max Lucado

Elizabeth was surprised Sunday morning when Nathan wanted to go to church with the boys. Surprised, because she figured he would want more alone time with her. She knew Nathan wanted her at church, just like her brothers wished. But she was still separating Nathan from God, so Nathan's request to go to church felt like a blind side. Elizabeth weighed it over and over, tossing it back and forth like a ping-pong ball—her favorite mind game. Going would satisfy all the men in her life, that she knew. But not going sat a lot easier with her. At the last minute, she decided not to go, a decision that plainly hurt both Nathan and her brothers.

"Why won't you come?" Nathan asked her while holding her hand and trying to understand. He was kind of whiny, and his eyes were pleading. But nothing could stop Elizabeth from being defensive, her natural tone for anything that might soften her heart, but especially church.

"I haven't gone in years. And I don't want to jump at changing my lifestyle just because someone new is in my life. I—"

Nathan cut her off. "So, even if you might want to go, you won't go because you think it's just my presence making you want to go? Even if it's something positive and you have a great deal to gain from the experience?"

"Why do you take things to the extreme?" asked Elizabeth,

certainly not backing down, but rather defending herself and her stance. She recognized her defensiveness, but moved forward with the conversation as though she hadn't.

"I'm not," said Nathan as he let out another frustrated noise. "I'm just making sure I've got it right. You might want to go, but you think you only want to go because I'm here."

An exasperated sigh slipped from Elizabeth's lips. "Yes."

Nathan responded by putting his head back to the wall and returning her exasperation. The lines on his face said he was upset, and his words did nothing to contradict his expression. "Fine. But I want to go. Will this bother you? Will we have an argument over it later?"

"I don't want you going without me," answered Elizabeth, hoping he would stay with her. *Now who's whining?*

"Why not?" asked Nathan.

"Because, then it's just going to be everyone at church saying to one more guy in my life, 'We gotta get her here on Sundays.'" Elizabeth's mocking voice was reminiscent of a child mimicking an adult. "If you really want to start *this* discussion, we can, but I don't like people talking about me like that, and I really don't want them knowing there's one more man in my life who wishes I was at church. It's none of their business."

"Well," Nathan started. He stopped when Elizabeth gave him a stern look as though to say t*read lightly.* "Well, it kind of *is* their business."

"How do you figure?"

Nathan recounted the conversation he had with Bryce while she was "asleep," which Elizabeth fully remembered but had kept to herself. He concluded that people care so much about the boys that it's natural they would care about her too. Elizabeth's aloof posture, both physically and emotionally, didn't budge during Nathan's speech. Not until the boys came down from breakfast did Elizabeth take a small step back on her stubborn no-church decision. Danny looked upset; his eyes were red, and he was wearing a hat, which was an extremely rare occurrence.

Danny grabbed a banana so quickly she barely had time to say

"Hi" or "Bye" before he was out the door. Mitch was only slightly slower, so she caught Bryce's arm before he could slip away too. It was a light grip, but enough to make him turn around for her.

"What's up with you and your brothers this morning?"

Bryce looked—very maturely, Elizabeth noticed—over at Nathan before meeting her eyes and answering quietly. "Danny overheard you and Nathan talking last night and again this morning."

"So?" Elizabeth asked, still confused.

"Liz, I don't know. Don't worry about it." He rubbed his forehead as he spoke, again looking wise beyond his nineteen years. "I gotta go."

Elizabeth gazed at the door as it shut behind Bryce, unsure of how to finish her conversation with Nathan after the encounter with her brothers. After several awkward moments, she chose to continue wiping the table from breakfast. She cleared her throat and, aware that Nathan was watching her, stubbornly continued the conversation.

"Where was I? Oh yeah. In the grocery store, there are these two older women who I always see and who say to me, 'I saw your brothers in church on Sunday. I wish you'd come. I tell them every week to bring you, but they always tell me how busy you are.'" Elizabeth's mimicking of the older women again made Nathan laugh, but it didn't deter him from trying to convince her to spend the morning at church.

"First of all, do you want to talk about what just happened with your brothers?"

Her response was immediate when she insisted she didn't. She was more than thankful when Nathan accepted her answer. But her demeanor went right back to the cynical side when Nathan went for the church stuff.

"Well, I still want to go," he said. "Your brothers go to a huge church, and those two women are probably the only ones who say that to them."

"Whatever. It's still uncomfortable." In a vain effort to completely throw him off, she added, "Do you realize we are arguing over an institution that rejects people who don't believe what they believe?"

Elizabeth was still wiping the table from breakfast, acting unsatisfied with the job she'd done so far. Nathan shook his head, apparently unwilling to fall into the argument Elizabeth was starting. "I am not getting into a theological discussion with you, because my main message to you about Jesus has always, always been love and grace. I stick to those points, and your brothers do too, because they are infallible truths and the cornerstone of our faith. Theology gets people into arguments," he waved his hand as though covering the whole world. "And by the way, like it or not, I am another man in your life who wishes you were at church."

He finished there, but in such a way that indicated there was more he wanted to say. The couple was in a standoff, Nathan with his near-begging approach to get Elizabeth to walk out her front door and through the sanctuary doors to what he described as her long-awaited saving grace. Elizabeth stood still, knowing there was no one or nothing that could prod her heart enough to make those first steps. Not here, not now. As she looked into his unusually hard brown eyes, she saw a man who wasn't done fighting for what he wanted. He was on the brink of saying something, she could tell. He proved himself right a minute later when he said, "Fine. I will stay home with you."

"What? Really? Why?" She straightened her posture, completely surprised at his concession. She was sure there would have been another little tangle of back and forth.

Letting go of his set jaw, Nathan said in one long, drawn out breath, "It'll give us some alone time while the boys aren't here before I have to go back to North Carolina."

"Mmmm, I like that idea." Despite his still-distant vibe, she moved closer to Nathan so she could kiss him. He put his hand on her back to draw her closer. Their kisses became deeper. She seemed to have moved Nathan past irritated and back into being so enveloped with Elizabeth that nothing else mattered. After a particularly passionate moment that had Elizabeth against the wall, Nathan backed off. Holding her at arms' length with his hands firmly on her shoulders, he asked, "Can we take a walk?"

"What? The boys aren't here, and you want to take a walk? I had something else in mind," she said with a sly smile, trying to lean in again. But Nathan stopped her.

"Liz, please," he pleaded. Nathan looked at her with his head cocked to the side, his eyes pleading with her to understand. "Liz, can we take a walk?"

This must be the physical stuff he was talking about. How inconvenient.

"Whatever," she said as she rolled her eyes. She may have sounded less than thrilled but ultimately was happy to comply since he had stayed home from church. Thinking about his confession the night before about not sleeping with anyone until he was married, Elizabeth figured this was his attempt to keep his eye on that prize. It wasn't easy to break off moments like these. And this was nothing she had ever thought deeply about. Her decision not to sleep around was grounded in not wanting to get pregnant without a stable foundation of a life backing her up.

On their walk, Nathan roped Elizabeth into a lively evaluation of the weekend so far. He tried to talk about church again too. This time she gave in because she could tell he didn't want an argument; he just wanted to talk. Plus, Elizabeth figured he was just redirecting his passion from before.

"You know your brothers better than me. How do you think it's going?" he asked her.

"I can't completely tell," she said while shaking her head. "I've never been in this situation before." She had a smile on her face, but inside she had a cage of butterflies fluttering like mad. "They've all been kind of quiet, but Danny especially. His behavior has been out of the ordinary, but I haven't known what to say to him. I'm not really worried about Bryce. I can't figure out Mitch. He seems to go back and forth. Maybe I'm thinking about it too much."

"I can tell you I haven't felt too awkward; I expected them to be a little gun-shy. I'm having a great weekend with you and your brothers. Your life here is nothing like I thought it was going to be." His hands were hidden in his pockets; Elizabeth couldn't help but notice how serious he looked.

"How so?" she asked.

"It's smoother, for one. I thought you were kind of roman-ticizing it when you told me about it on vacation. And it's just ... different. You're so grown up," he said with a chuckle. "It's weird seeing you as a mom. You were so woman-ly in North Carolina. And in your e-mails," he added.

"As opposed to now, when I'm ... not ... very ... womanly?"

They laughed together.

Nathan responded, "No, no, that's not what I meant." He paused. "You're a beautiful person, Liz. I'm even luckier than I thought I was." His sincerity rang of a five-year-old's who knows no other way to be.

When was the last time she was in a situation that had the potential to be so life-changing? *Could be? I think we're too far for* could. When was the last time someone tilted her foundation like this? In such an honest, endearing, thrilling way, Nathan's presence in her life was a catalyst for her life taking on a new look, a new meaning, even. The last time her foundation was tilted like this was when her grandparents died. Not even her mom dying shook her world to the extent the previous event did; her mom's passing was more relief. Thankfully, so far this experience with Nathan hadn't brought the kind of devastation the other big events had. The only negative elements were her brothers and Nathan's fixation on church. But on a scale mea-suring how much it would affect her life, her relationship with Nathan was about as high on the meter as it could possibly be.

"Nathan ..." Elizabeth trailed off because she was unsure of what to say next. So much was at stake. So much had already been put out there. So much could go wrong, but so much could go her way.

"Hmm?" asked Nathan.

"Nathan ... you ... I don't ... Hmmm."

Nathan laughed lightly at her indecision of whether or not to speak.

She sighed and finally said, "I like you," as though no other words would have satisfied the moment.

Nathan laughed and said, "I like you too, pretty lady."

———————————

Nathan was scheduled to leave Monday morning. The boys all had plans and so said their short-and-sweet goodbyes early. It was just Elizabeth and Nathan when Nathan loaded his car. True to the rest of the weekend, Elizabeth seemed to go up and down with her emotions in just a short amount of time.

"Why are your arms folded like that?" asked Nathan as he put his bag in the backseat.

"Why do you have to know everything?" asked Elizabeth, sounding annoyed at Nathan's acute perceptions.

"Why do you sound so angry?" he asked, sounding exasperated and not at all accepting of her attitude.

"I'm not angry," she said.

Nathan looked at her as though he didn't believe her.

"I'm not," Elizabeth assured him. "I'm not. I'm uncomfortable. I'm confused. I'm still kind of hungry," she said, trying to make light of the moment.

"What are you confused about?" Nathan's voice went up noticeably at the end of his question.

"It's been pretty up and down this weekend."

"So?"

"It's a lot to deal with. And I've been rude to you," she said, keeping her words short in an attempt to hide the intense emotion she was feeling. Elizabeth was unsure of herself and of their relationship, but she didn't know how to protect herself from how far her emotions had already taken her. Her arms were still folded, the frown on her face seemed to have gotten deeper, and Elizabeth's whole body seemed to be drawing inward.

"You weren't rude. You were honest," said Nathan with compassion, rubbing her arm.

"If my brothers talked to me the way that I've talked to you a couple times this weekend, I would tell them they were being rude," she said.

"Well, we are in a relationship. You were upset. You can be yourself, and I'll still like you the next day. One thing I learned from my pastor back in California is that if you expect to have a healthy relationship, you should be able to trust that you can have a fight and still like each other after the fact."

Elizabeth sighed and said, "Sometimes I don't believe you exist."

"Even when I'm standing right here? In front of your face? About to give you a big hug?"

Nathan's strong arms wrapped around Elizabeth and swayed her gently. He kissed the top of her head, and then he pulled back just enough to slouch down and be eye level with her.

"Listen to me, Elizabeth. I'm strong enough to hang in there. I promise. Even when I'm annoyed or I don't understand. Now, I want you to enjoy the rest of your day, find out what the boys really thought of me, and I'll talk to you tomorrow."

"Are you sure? Because, you know, now is your time to really cut ties and be free," she said, testing him one last time.

He gave her a kind of scolding look and said, "You know what makes me feel free?"

"I suppose you're going to tell me," she said, looking at the ground and kicking small rocks lying at the wheels of Nathan's rental car.

He put his fingers under her chin and drew up her face so their eyes met. "I feel free when I'm in church, singing a favorite song. I feel free when I'm swimming in the ocean or on a long jog. And I notice I feel free when I'm with you. Being with you makes me feel free, just like being in church, swimming in the ocean, or running."

"If you say so," said Elizabeth, betraying her facetious tone with a widening smile.

"I do say so, but you know, you also make me feel like I have to turn the charm down a little bit so you'll think of me as a believable man with whom you could fall in love."

Elizabeth laughed, "Don't let my wit fool you. I'm taking

you in, one cheesy line at a time."

When Elizabeth returned from grocery shopping and an hour-long jog after Nathan left, all three of her brothers were home. Danny was upstairs in the office doing pre-work for school, and Mitch and Bryce were engrossed in a television program. She went around the house watching all three of them, and then she called them together to the kitchen. When they didn't come right away, she mentioned she had cheesecake; suddenly, all three were before her.

"So?" she said, hoping they'd start in on their feelings of the weekend as they did when they were younger and she offered them chocolate chip cookies and milk. Elizabeth was ready for anything they were about to say. She had practically raised three boys; that makes a woman tough. She could handle this. She knew they could be harsh, but they could be sensitive too.

"So, what?" said Mitch. "The cheesecake looks good. C'mon, dish it out." His face was expressionless save for the impatience for the dessert.

"Mitchell!" She yelled, in a half-annoyed, half-joking manner. Elizabeth's brothers all looked at her with serious faces. It was not every day she used his or Danny's full name. Suddenly, they understood that she meant business.

"What did you think?" she asked again.

Silence. Elizabeth was afraid of this silence, more so than any harsh comment they might toss out. To Elizabeth, silence meant fear, confusion, and anger that they were afraid to express. She forgot to breathe until Danny spoke up.

"Well, you want us to be honest, right?" he finally asked as he cut a rather large piece of cheesecake.

"Of course. Whatever it is. Be honest. Just remember I'm a girl. Not just your sister. I have feelings." She gripped the back of the kitchen chair in anticipation of what they'd say. The boys exchanged glances, wondering who would go first. Apparently, their eye contact said Danny would.

"Well, I liked him. He seems like a decent guy. I liked how he played along with our movie thing and never once acted like he was going to take you away from us."

He looked like he wanted to say more, so she prodded him to go on.

"I just … it's just that … I'm not … It's weird. It's different," he said.

There it is. "Okay. Good different or bad different?" asked Elizabeth cautiously.

"I don't know," he said, his face twisting uncomfortably.

Okay, thought Elizabeth, *uncomfortable doesn't mean impossible. At least he was being honest.*

The two other boys said they felt the same way. They liked him, but it was uncomfortable. Their response was more than she had hoped for, so she should be grateful. *Should* be. But as her brothers continued eating and talking, she was brought back to when she was eighteen years old; Mitch was seven, Bryce, eleven, and Danny was only five. She had been doing her homework upstairs when she heard her mother downstairs yelling at Mitch.

"Give them back, you little brat!"

Mitch screamed, "No! I want Lizzie!"

Elizabeth hurried downstairs to see what was going on. Mitch ran to her as soon as she rounded the corner into the kitchen.

"He took your car keys, Liz," her mom said with a combination of astounding immaturity and contempt.

"What do you care? They're mine," said Elizabeth to her mother, with no warmth.

"My car won't start, and I need to go out," she said.

Elizabeth turned to her little brother and gently asked him to go up to her room, where she promised they'd play cards in a few minutes. He obliged, but their mom yelled after him, "That's right, go upstairs!"

His face contorted in a quiet fit of rage that Elizabeth had never before or since seen from Mitch. He turned to his mother and coldly said, "I hate you! I wish you'd died, not Grandma and Grandpa."

Their mom started toward Mitch, but Elizabeth stopped her. Once Elizabeth thought he was safely upstairs, she said to her mom, stoically, as she had gone into survival mode for her brother, "He is seven. What is the matter with you?"

"He stole the keys!"

"*My* keys. Grandma and Grandpa left me that car. And since you do nothing around here, I need it to bring the boys to school and to go to the store to, you know, buy groceries." Stoicism turned to bitter sarcasm.

"Oh, shut up! You don't care about those boys," her mother said.

"More than you ever have," said Elizabeth.

"Whatever, Elizabeth, just give me the keys."

"Why? So you can be gone for a week while we're stuck here? Have one of your stupid boyfriends pick you up." She could have spit at or slapped her mom, she was so angry.

"You'll leave one day, you'll see."

All of a sudden, Mitch rumbled back down the stairs and was again in front of Elizabeth. He screamed, "No she won't! Elizabeth will never leave us!"

"Mitch! Go upstairs!" Elizabeth instructed Mitch out of concern for him. But he didn't go; instead, he kept yelling at their mom. "You leave! You always leave!"

"It's because I have better things to do!" their mom yelled back.

All of a sudden, Bryce was at the door to join the argument. He yelled, "So? We don't care! We like Lizzie better, anyway!"

"You're a brat just like your brothers and your sister," she said, directing her words at Bryce this time. "This is none of your business."

The rest of the argument was a back and forth of biting words to her brothers and resentful glares to Elizabeth from their mother. But Elizabeth never forgot Mitch's words: "She'll never leave." These experiences and others left Elizabeth with an initial fear that bringing Nathan around would immediately trigger the boys' memories of all the adults from whom they had requested and expected love but who had either left or died. Though Elizabeth had no plans to leave, who knew what the boys were tossing around in their minds? For now, all she had to go on were the few awkward silences during the weekend and the subdued mood that filled the house for a lot of the time since she returned from North Carolina. And now, the "I don't know" conclusion to Nathan's visit.

In general, Elizabeth was still spending quality time with her family as she'd always done, but the boys' discomfort didn't seem to go away. Usually 100 percent of Elizabeth's time and energy would be devoted to her family and their needs and wants, but now she was on the phone all night on Tuesdays and talked about Nathan from time to time. There were little and big signs that the boys weren't okay with this change in their age-old routine, such as less conversation at the dinner table, averted eyes when she talked about Nathan, and them not letting her help with their homework. Another thing Elizabeth noticed was Mitch and Danny taking phone calls in their rooms. She didn't worry too much because they still met all their curfews, nobody had called her into school, and they still went to church every week. If something fishy were going on, she was confident she would know. Elizabeth spent the better half of the next week wondering how and when this would all eventually settle, if ever. She hoped it would get better with time, that none of the boys would act out or get progressively angry. She would find out in time, she supposed.

The Saturday night following Nathan's visit was the kind Elizabeth loved. The sky had turned to just a deep enough blue that the tall trees were a black shadow. The warm wind let her know a storm was making its way in. She didn't care; she loved storms. Loved the before, during, and after. They seemed to stir within her every bit of hope she held in her heart. She supposed the feeling came from relating the pouring rain to some serious and much-needed soul cleansing.

Lying outside on the roof of her car, Elizabeth finally thought about God. If Nathan were here, he would say that he loves the storms *God* creates. If her brothers were out here, they might say something similar. She considered this new man in her life and the person Nathan seemed to be asking her to be. There were so many thoughts and emotions tied to just saying or thinking Nathan's or God's name, she didn't even know where to begin.

First, she thought about Nathan: the feelings she had for him, the desire not to rattle her family, and the pull to have a life that would be considered normal for women her age. She'd never been in this situation before because she had managed never to become this involved with a man, but Elizabeth knew she was falling in love with Nathan. She knew it by the way her smile grew as she thought about him, from the way she watched him try with her brothers, and she knew from the sinking feeling in her stomach every time she thought about not having Nathan in her life anymore. Her brothers were always first in her life, because who else did they have? She wasn't about to jeopardize that and give them one more person not to trust. But that fact put her nowhere closer to deciding what she was going to do with Nathan—in her life and in her heart. And if she really wanted to believe what Nathan said, that God was in charge—then shouldn't she agree that He brought Nathan for a good reason? What if Elizabeth didn't like the reason? What if the reason was to start separating her from her brothers? Could she handle that? Yes, she wanted her own life, but Danny was still so young, Mitch still needed a strong parent figure, and she wouldn't leave Bryce to go it alone.

But I'm not a parent, she thought. *I'm a twenty-six-year-old woman who is very attracted to a man my age.*

But you did agree to care for these boys at least until each turned eighteen.

That means I'm not allowed to be in a romantic relationship?

But what if this relationship takes you away from them?

It can't if I don't let it; this relationship doesn't have to control me.

There it is! That's it.

Her last thought—*this relationship doesn't have to control me*—brought Elizabeth back to Earth. All this time, Elizabeth was feeling like she was out of control, that she would play everything by ear and see where her feelings for Nathan led, see what it brought to her family. But in that one moment, she realized: that doesn't have to be the case. What was that verse Nathan told her about? About choosing freedom? There were a few; she thought of the ones Nathan had recited from memory. It talked about Jesus relieving one's burden, something about Jesus' burden being easy[1]. Elizabeth remembered another one: that for the sake of freedom, Christ made us free[2]. But what was that one about us choosing to live a free life? With a strange sense of clarity, she remembered the phrase: "Everything is permissible for me, but I will not be mastered by anything[3]." Just as she had controlled whom to let into her life over the years, she could decide if this relationship was something she wanted to pursue. Nathan couldn't tell her what to do, Bryce couldn't tell her what to do, nobody could, and her feelings didn't have to be the ultimate say-so.

"I can decide for myself," Elizabeth said aloud. But that didn't feel right either.

She started thinking about God again. Yet another verse came to her mind that Nathan told her about in an e-mail: "Something about leaning on God's understanding instead of your own[4]," Elizabeth said aloud. Elizabeth thought about the way Nathan seemed to feel so peaceful when he made decisions. Like when he told her about his decision to move from California to North Carolina. Nathan had said that on paper the decision looked crazy: leave a successful career, his family, friends, and hometown, for a town he had seen once, with no promise of a job, and being acquainted with only one person. But in the throes of his decision-making, Nathan felt little turmoil; in fact, he was insistent that the peace he felt in his heart when imagining himself living in North Carolina far outweighed the anxiety or sadness of leaving home. Plus, there was the way he described his decision to pursue their relationship, that his gut instinct, after much prayer, had told him to stick it out.

She wondered about her brothers and how they made decisions. In trying to figure it out, Elizabeth realized Bryce was somewhat right: she did shut out their attempts at bringing church or God into conversations. Elizabeth could remember—though vaguely—hearing her brothers say "Pray about it" to each other when a big decision came up. For example, Danny's decision to try out for the football team, Mitch's decision to go on a missions trip to New Orleans, and Bryce's decision to break up with a girlfriend. Elizabeth supposed the only reason she remembered these instances was because she distinctly recalled thinking to herself, *That's ridiculous. Prayer won't help.* Because people made decisions all the time without God's help. *Didn't they?* So why was this one—this decision to love Nathan, make room for him in her life—seemingly impossible for Elizabeth to make without wondering what God would say? She had no idea why the notion wouldn't go away, but it was undeniable and categorically unavoidable.

So, in an almost painful effort to move up and out of her cyclical habit of thinking about God just far enough that she didn't let Him move anything in her heart, Elizabeth offered up a prayer that read more as a one-sided conversation. But if she was honest with herself, she had no idea what she was doing, so she couldn't really worry about the aesthetics of it all.

"God, I want to believe you're listening. But I still don't know what to say. I can't make a decision about Nathan. I'm asking you to guide me in the right direction, so that the least number of people get hurt and everything works out the way it's supposed to." Her eyes weren't closed and her head wasn't bowed, but presenting herself "as-is" was as far as Elizabeth was willing to go.

She waited, knowing she was naively hoping for an immediate revelation. Yet, another unavoidable element came along: a strong sense of peace seemed to wash over her entire body. So much so that she relaxed her shoulders wholly and completely for the first time in recent memory.

"Well, that's new," she said aloud to the chilling night air.

She rested in that peace for another twenty minutes before she allowed herself to be sprinkled on by a few droplets; the torrential downpour came just moments after Elizabeth stepped inside the house. And though the storm was big enough to cause fright, it was her phone going off that made Elizabeth jump. The boys were at an overnight youth group event at their church. She was relieved when she saw it was Nathan. Relieved because it wasn't someone from church calling to say something was wrong with her brothers, and a little confused because it was Saturday night. It wasn't Tuesday. She answered the phone cautiously, hoping nothing was wrong. But he answered back and started up the conversation as normal as any other time they had talked.

"How was your night? Anything great happen today?" he asked. Elizabeth loved that Nathan asked how her day was, because he asked it with interest. Yet, she couldn't help but be alarmed at the impromptu call.

"Not really. I just spent a few hours lying outside on my car, watching the stars. It's not Tuesday." She wasn't going to waste time looking for an answer to this late-night weekend surprise.

"No, it's not. It's Saturday. You're smart—one of the many things I like about you." Nothing in his tone suggested that there was a specific reason he called.

"Is anything wrong?" she asked skeptically.

"What do you mean?"

"Nathan. What's up? You've never surprised me with a random phone call." She wasn't giving in, and judging by his audible sigh— which she could only imagine was accompanied by an eye-roll— her resistance and fear was getting to him. A little at a time, but still some.

"No, I suppose I haven't. But I was sitting here, thinking about you, and I decided we've moved past the follow-*all*-the-rules point in our relationship. I figured it was time to have this conversation."

"What conversation?" She was confused.

"The moving-forward conversation."

 Silence.

"Elizabeth?"

"Yes?"

"What do you think?"

"That we already had this conversation last week."

Nathan answered casually, "Kind of. But I want to move forward in the sense that we don't have to schedule our phone calls anymore, things like that."

"Like what things?"

"Like random phone calls, maybe text messages, just … a little more spontaneity."

"I don't know," said Elizabeth, unsure of Nathan's proposal to step up their relationship.

"Is this really a surprise to you?" asked Nathan.

She thought for a moment. "Well, I guess the topic isn't a surprise. Just the Saturday night phone call. I'm … glad you called." She sounded almost defeated. Contradictory to her earlier resolution, this relationship seemed to be on a freight train headed for her. And moments like this—when Nathan pursued her and was clear about his feelings for her—made it hard for Elizabeth to believe she could do anything to stop her beating heart from wanting to be more and more involved with this man and in this relationship. Every step he took toward her—literal or otherwise—was met with one of two things: acceptance or resistance. There seemed to be no schedule as to which would rear its head on any given day, but at least she was aware of the dynamic duo fighting for first place. She gauged which feeling won by the words that slipped out of her mouth without a moment's notice.

"You're glad I called?" Nathan sounded incredibly hopeful on the other end. Elizabeth closed her eyes and took in a deep breath, thinking, *Am I really this lucky?* and *Am I really ready for this?* at the same time.

She continued, covering her doubts, "Yes, of course I am, Nathan. Hearing your voice a little more often wouldn't be the worst thing." Elizabeth could hear the ends of Nathan's mouth curl up into a smile that she found irresistible.

"This is a very good thing, Elizabeth."

"Don't get ahead of yourself, Nathan. It's just one phone call," she said, afraid he would take this admission and new permission to a place for which she wasn't yet ready.

"I know, I know. Relax, we'll go slow."

"Hmm," was all Elizabeth said. But the next moment, she jumped into a nagging thought of hers from the past few days. "I've been thinking of a lot of 'what if's' this week."

Nathan asked, "Like what?"

She said, "What if my brothers don't adapt to the idea of my making a life with someone who doesn't live here? Someone who might take too much of my attention? Someone who would take me away from them?"

Nathan knew some of her concerns, and so she could be truthful about them. He had hit her heart, and she wanted to share it with him. Because of this, she was unsurprised at his candid reaction.

"Elizabeth, I understand some of that. But," he said, hesitating on a deep breath that seemed to take forever to let out. "But, please help me understand. How do you expect to start figuring out *that* stuff, when just one extra phone call throws you off?"

Now it was Elizabeth's turn for an extended deep breath before she said, "I don't know." Nathan was waiting for Elizabeth to keep talking; she knew he could sense that her gears were still turning. "I just … don't know." She recounted her memory from when Mitch told their mom that Elizabeth would never leave. Both were quiet for a few moments afterward. It was Nathan who broke the silence.

"All I'm saying is, one step at a time. Don't get so caught up in the long term, when you can barely handle a random phone call."

And in that one instant, Elizabeth's emotions and frustrations came to a head. Her words might as well have formed icicles on her phone as she repeated, "*Barely handle?*"

For the next thirty minutes, Elizabeth and Nathan chased each other around in a conversational circle that would have exhausted professional orators. Elizabeth insisted she needed to combine short and long-term thinking in order to make the right decisions for her family. In turn, Nathan would tell her she was going about it all wrong, that one step at a time would be better, especially since she was having trouble with the small ones. Each succeeded in exaggerating their emotions, getting more than a little defensive, and making accusations. Finally, after a particularly defensive comment from Elizabeth that if responded to may have started a dangerous tangent, Nathan's cooler head prevailed.

"Look," he said. "I'm coming up again in a little more than a month. Can we put this conversation on hold until we're together?

I was hoping to come on Thursday again, giving us another long weekend."

His tone was not friendly, patient, or compassionate, but rather was exhausted and acutely desperate. She knew he truly cared for her but that their differing opinions made him want to climb the walls. Besides, Elizabeth knew the conversation would be easier in person because she could see his whole reaction as they talked; she just wasn't sure she could put it out of her mind for that many days.

Nathan kept talking. "Listen, I'm not telling you to just not think about it until then. I'm just asking that you don't rush to any conclusions without me and without hearing what else I have to say. We need to cool it for now. Maybe if the weekend goes well enough, we can have a family discussion. You know, one with me, you, and your brothers."

Elizabeth said flat-out, "That scares me."

"Well, regardless. I just want to talk about it when we're together, okay?"

She conceded. Normal talk about their days, the news, and other surface topics continued until they got off the phone two hours later. Even though the beginning of their conversation weighed heavily on her mind, the sound of Nathan's voice stayed with her when she got into bed and snuggled under the covers. For the next five weeks until Nathan's visit, Elizabeth basked in the comfort Nathan sent her way, no matter how many hundreds of miles he was from her and how different life seemed to be getting with the boys. She couldn't remember their household being this strained in years, but still, every day she hoped for a new start.

When this whole situation began, Elizabeth had seen small signs of the boys withdrawing from her. They still talked to her about the same things—sports, friends, sometimes even girls. "You are one, after all!" Mitch had told her once. She still went to Mitch and Danny's church league soccer games, to Bryce's performances when he was playing his guitar and singing. But even so, the boys seemed to have an underlying tone of sadness. Elizabeth also noticed they kept bringing up church far more often than she ever remembered. Just a couple of days ago, Mitch asked her, "Are you gonna come to church with us this week, Lizzie?" The question had come out of left field to Elizabeth, since she hadn't gone in years and the boys hadn't requested her company in the pews since Nathan's visit.

"No, Mitch. Why do you ask?" He had just shrugged his answer. She pressed for more.

"What's up, kid?"

"I just thought that since, you know, Nathan goes to church and you're really into him and all, that you'd finally give it a shot."

Elizabeth noticed he didn't say Nathan's name very naturally or altogether kindly. It was a touch of sarcasm mixed with bitterness. Maybe a little envy too. She asked him, "Why would I go just because Nathan goes?"

Her little brother was old enough for mature conversations like this, but still he just shrugged his shoulders for his answer. Finally, he said, "I don't know. I guess I just thought you would. People do crazy things when they're in love."

Again with the left field: "in love." But she stayed on topic.

"You were *thinking* I would or *hoping* I would?" Mitch's casual conversation and aloofness couldn't fool her. She knew where his mind and heart were at. He seemed glad of that too, evidenced by his half smile before he responded, "Both, I guess."

Elizabeth thought maybe she could test the waters with him a little bit, to see if he'd be honest and also because she couldn't help but wonder what went through his mind when it came to Elizabeth and church.

"Why do you want me to come to church so badly?"

Mitch looked at her out of the corner of his eye. He was fiddling with a rubber band as he spoke. She couldn't remember the last time—if ever—Mitch spoke to her with this level of emotion; he seemed ready to explode. She made sure to pay extra close attention, since apparently she usually didn't when the boys talked about church. He cleared his throat and began speaking:

"Elizabeth, you don't have it easy. You never have. Our church—our faith—has helped Bryce, Danny, and I get through some of the most difficult situations in our lives."

She was thankful Mitch noticed a twinge of hurt, as he quickly added, "You've helped too, of course. But ..." he looked down before meeting her eyes. "Jesus is so much bigger than our situation. He's a safe place. And I guess, I just really want you to have a safe place."

Touched and stunned by his words, she didn't know which to acknowledge first. Still betting on Mitch's maturity, she said, "You guys are a safe place. Nathan is turning into a safe place."

"It's not the same, Liz. It's just not the same. If you gave it a real shot, you'd see that."

"See what?"

Mitch sighed, the heaviness of the conversation weighing on him. "You'd just see it. How much of a difference a relationship with God makes."

Still, Elizabeth questioned how he could be so sure. And still Mitch stood strong without missing a beat. "It's hard to miss, Liz."

He was being so open, so honest. She couldn't quite read his eyes, partly because they were darting to and fro, and partly because this was a look that Mitch had once in a great while. But Elizabeth, much to her dismay, had not paid attention to any kind of pattern of when the expression showed itself. Elizabeth didn't want to push her luck, so she wrapped up the small but weighty discussion by giving Mitch a long, motherly hug and saying, with a thick voice, "Thank you for caring so much."

Mitch returned her hug, and then quickly ran out the door to go for his thrice-weekly jog. Elizabeth watched after him, thankful that her brothers were kind, big-hearted young men. Given the alternate possibilities, especially considering their situation, Elizabeth felt exceedingly, undeservedly lucky. And, as was natural these days, thinking about being lucky led to thoughts of Nathan. Just a few more weeks and he'd be visiting again, holding her hand and kissing her lips. He'd be there to interact with her brothers and would more than likely request her presence at church. Nathan was nothing if not consistent.

Bringing up Nathan's impending visit with the boys wasn't altogether easy, but she was fairly pleased with herself when she managed to sneak it into casual conversation. Yet, what bothered

Elizabeth wasn't the lackadaisical reactions or even the non-reactions. No, what bothered Elizabeth was the inconsistency of their reactions. They seemed less accepting than last time, but agreed nonetheless. She could find no pattern, no rhyme or reason for their behavior these days. Never before, in all her years of taking care of Bryce, Mitch, and Danny, was Elizabeth so unable to read them. She had always prided herself in being able to figure out what they were thinking to help them problem solve.

Still, Elizabeth kept moving in the same direction: toward the idea of making room for Nathan in her family's life. She would continue to gauge responses and general attitudes, hoping that all the pieces would fall into place at some point.

Chapter 10

"Most of the shadows of this life are created by standing in one's own sunshine."
~Ralph Waldo Emerson

FINALLY, THE LATE SEPTEMBER day of Nathan's second visit arrived. If her nerves were fluttering before, they were in full-force freak-out mode now. She had driven her brothers crazy again with nervous movements, forgetting lunch money and other mom things she did on a regular basis. Once again, they told her to relax, that it's not as if Elizabeth had never seen him before. But how could Elizabeth explain all the reasons she was nervous? Did they really want to hear about how much she cared for him? How scared she was for what the future held, because she feared that both losing him and keeping him would cost her dearly. Could she really talk to them about how she had never felt this way before, and she wasn't sure she was doing it right? She didn't know how to fall in love, how to have a relationship. For all Elizabeth knew, she was lucky to have made it this far without failing miserably as a girlfriend. But she must be doing something right, she thought, as Nathan showed up with a colorful bouquet of flowers and an even brighter smile, ready to spend another long weekend with Elizabeth and her family. He pulled in just after ten on Thursday night. His hair was a little tousled, which was absolutely adorable to Elizabeth, and on his walk up to the front door, a crooked smile covered his face and matched the bounce in his step. Elizabeth watched him from inside and was grateful he couldn't see her. She had an even bigger smile than he, and she couldn't stop blushing. Nor could she stop her heart from the erratic beat it had started up.

I've waited a long time for this. I wonder how long it'll be mine before I can't have it anymore. Just as quickly, she considered, *What if it stays mine?*

Nathan had stopped at a twenty-four-hour market and bought fresh strawberries, a container of cool whip, and a bottle of Elizabeth's favorite wine. Upstairs, they spread out a blanket in the middle of her room and had a sweet indoor picnic. They laughed, giggled, kissed—long ones and short ones—and altogether enjoyed each other's company like teenagers in love for the first time. Once the strawberries were gone, Nathan got a serious, deep look in his eyes that she hadn't seen since they'd met during the summer.

"What is it?" asked Elizabeth, hoping it was nothing bad.

"What do you mean?"

"You have a look in your eyes. I've only seen it once, when you were talking about your grandparents. It looks …"

"It looks, what?" Nathan was now amused; his eyes sparkled, and the corners of his mouth were turned up slightly. He clearly enjoyed the idea that Elizabeth knew him well enough to know a nuance like a specific expression.

"It looks like you have something you want to say. Something very important, but you're not sure of the words you want to use."

"I'd say you nailed it," said Nathan. "I do have something to tell you. But first …"

And with that, he moved to her side of the blanket, wrapped his arms around her, and gave her a long kiss. Afterwards, she was breathless. She leaned in for more, and he happily obliged.

After a few long moments, Elizabeth laid her head on Nathan's chest on the blanket, listening to his heartbeat; they were smiling and breathing in sync with each other. She asked him what it was that he going to tell her before they started kissing.

Nathan moved to lie on his side so he could face Elizabeth. He brushed a few hairs off her face and lightly touched her cheek.

Nathan's smile said volumes, but he went on anyway.

"Elizabeth, I haven't … We haven't known each other very long. But we've shared a lot. You know I want you in my life on a permanent basis. And I know we said we'd talk about that this weekend. But what I need to tell you, and what I need you to take in and let soak in before we have that discussion, is that I love you."

Elizabeth's expression read like a shell-shocked soldier who had just been told of an immediate deployment. Her raised eyebrows and wide eyes must have scared Nathan some too, because Nathan took it as his cue to continue talking in a rambling, nervous kind of way.

"Anyway, there it is. And I mean it. Completely, with my whole heart. And I want you to know it through more than just my words. I will show you, Liz, that I love you."

Her head shook imperceptibly as Elizabeth tried to figure out how to respond. She wasn't angry; she knew that. She was a little alarmed at how they had known each other for such a short period of time and yet, he said those three words that, to her, should not be said until much later than three months. Nathan was talking about wanting to stay in each other's lives on a permanent, romantic, life-partner level. And if Elizabeth took the time to go to the heart of the matter, she wanted that too. How she made such a quick decision like that for something that was deep, deep down, she wasn't sure. She could barely decide what she wanted for breakfast in the morning, let alone something that affected the rest of her and her brothers' lives. But with Nathan, her heart strings seemed intricately linked to his from the early moments of their relationship. He gave her butterflies and made her feel safe. He was thoughtful, considerate, and mature. Certainly, her feelings for him were very strong. She hadn't voiced any of this yet, because that was an entirely different matter than just thinking it, and she lived in constant fear of what her brothers would think. But knowing those feelings were inside her gave Elizabeth a sense of peace and comfort; it stilled something within her that until recently had been persistently restless.

To convey her strong-like-but-not-yet-love to Nathan, she leaned up toward him and kissed him softly. Knowing she had to say something rather than nothing, Elizabeth finally responded, "I love everything you just said. Can we leave it at that and talk more about it tomorrow?"

Nathan smiled as he pushed her hair back again; he seemed to understand that her mind and heart were swirling. She had an entire life here that would need figuring out if they decided their futures were going to be tied together permanently. But for now, she simply wanted to spend time with the man who had captured her heart, pretend there was nobody or nothing else to think about, and enjoy the fairy tale she felt she had fallen into.

What Elizabeth expected to find the next morning was that same peace, an inexplicable joy bottled up inside her that she'd have no choice but to spread around. Had she not just last night thought about how still Nathan's presence made her feel? Instead, what she found was an irritability that wouldn't go away. Here she and Nathan had the entire day to themselves, but she couldn't un-irritate herself—not until early afternoon when Nathan asked her what was wrong, and she finally articulated what was bothering her did she start to feel better.

"Why are you so anxious?" he asked. All morning her quick, nervous responses and glances had been bothering him.

She breathed a deep breath and said, "I think the reality of the situation is finally hitting me."

"What do you mean?"

She spread her arms out helplessly. "I can't just walk out on my family."

"I'm not asking you to walk out on your family." Nathan's voice was full with concern, compassion, and some confusion as his brow furrowed.

Yet, it was clear to Elizabeth: falling in love meant choices to make, changes to move into. "But you can't just walk away from your job," she pointed out.

"You're right; right now, I can't. We just started the year." He shook his head, almost laughing at the conversation Elizabeth seemed to be jumping around in.

"So," she said. Elizabeth was now a mix of frustration, anger, anxiety, and sadness. Each emotion played out separately, then together, and Nathan was watching it unfold on her face. Elizabeth's crossed arms and creased forehead let him know not to say anything right away. She knew it wouldn't last long, though. And she was right. Deciding to cross what had suddenly become a stone wall, Nathan stepped nearer to Elizabeth as he asked, "Liz, what's this all about?"

She went on to explain, almost in one breath, how she realized that falling in love with Nathan—and telling him so when she was ready—meant either Nathan had to move to New York or she had to move to North Carolina, and that as it was, she was lucky enough to make it to work every day with matching shoes on her feet, let alone have to make such a monumental decision. In a whine that would have made a fussy child proud, Elizabeth explained that she felt unable to make the decision. She wasn't quite sure what she expected from Nathan after explaining her revelation, but what she got was a fight. Nathan exclaimed that saying "I love you" didn't mean he was moving in the next day and that nothing would ever get better if she kept such a whiny and helpless attitude. "Your brothers wouldn't be the young men they are if you adopted that kind of immaturity. So, seriously, Liz, cut it out."

Elizabeth's head snapped back in surprise. Words flew from Elizabeth to Nathan and back, about making decisions, not understanding the other's point of view, one not trying and the other trying too hard, and of course, what it always came down to—the boys. After several minutes of pounding, defensive voices, Nathan and Elizabeth hit the bottom of the well of their fighting words. Speechless, the room only sounded with their heavy sighs. They both were highly successful in making the other angry, and since it was their first significant argument, the interaction turned awkward when it was drawing to a close. Elizabeth walked to the fridge to get a glass of water, and Nathan used the distraction to restart the conversation as he followed her to and from the refrigerator back to the couch.

"Look, Elizabeth. I *know* that right now, all we can offer each other is long distance. I'm fine with that, *for now*. What I need to know is that you are too. And that eventually, someday, we can discuss a solution for this. Are you willing to do that?"

Elizabeth could do nothing but stare at this man who verbalized every thought that came into his mind, no matter how uncomfortable his ideas made her. When she let her own thoughts settle through the rest of the day, Elizabeth realized that before anything else, she needed to sort out two very important pieces of this puzzle: once and for all, how she felt about God and how she felt about Nathan and his presence in her life. Because God was such a huge part of Nathan's life, she knew that topic wouldn't be ignored. And if something could be reconciled in that department, Elizabeth needed to figure it out. Then she could decide if she could wholly commit to Nathan. She thought about the night she spent lying on the roof of her car, dipping her toes in these thoughts but never thinking them through any deeper. She supposed it was finally time to do so.

Elizabeth told Nathan her revelation Friday night over dinner. The two of them had Chinese takeout since the boys wouldn't be home until it was time for dessert. Elizabeth started the conversation; Nathan had just filled his mouth with noodles when she began talking.

"I realized something today," she said.

Nathan nodded for her to go on.

"When you were talking about having me in your life permanently, and I was all frustrated, I remembered something that I realized a couple weeks ago on that Saturday night you called me out of the blue." Her rambling words and sweaty palms revealed her nerves, but she didn't care. This was too important to shut down about. "I realized that I have two things to figure out: how I feel about you and how I feel about God."

Nathan raised his eyebrows.

"Does this shock you?" asked Elizabeth with a slight smile on her face, feigning offense.

"I'm proud of you," said Nathan. "I want to hear more."

Elizabeth took a deep breath. This was a lot of sharing for her, and it just kept getting deeper. "I don't know what more to say. Just that I need to figure out those two things before ... well, before I can give you a full commitment?" She ended on a question, hoping he would understand. It made Nathan grin as Elizabeth added, "Does that make sense?"

"Of course it does, Liz. Of course," Nathan assured her. He gave her a quick kiss.

"So that's it for now?" asked Elizabeth.

Nathan smiled and said, "For now."

Okay, I can live with that, she thought. *Now I'm ready to try the weekend.*

She wondered how the second round of quality family-plus-Nathan time would go. The first one left everyone afraid of the come-what-may approach Elizabeth and Nathan were taking. But heart-to-hearts with the boys and some thinking on her own propelled Elizabeth into an ownership role of her and Nathan's relationship: not only could she steer her decisions, she could also see that there wasn't just one right way for this situation to go. She had choices, and they didn't have to be black and white, one (brothers) or the other (Nathan). Now all she had to do was successfully communicate that to her brothers; after that, she thought the figuring-it-out part might come a little easier.

All three boys got home around 8:30, and the ice cream cake Elizabeth had made was ready for the taking.

"Hi, guys!" Elizabeth and Nathan said at the same time. In response, Bryce, Mitch, and Danny said hello but with small smiles.

"How was your day, Mitch?" asked Elizabeth.

"Fine." It was the typical tone of a fifteen-year-old boy, but with Elizabeth's heightened emotions, it worried her. She moved on to Danny.

"And yours, Danny?" asked Elizabeth.

"Same. Fine. What's for dessert?" he asked.

"I made ice cream cake," answered Elizabeth casually in an attempt to set the tone for the night. Their words were short and nondescriptive, but that could have been because they were hungry; she had told them a special dessert would be waiting when they got home. And one of the things she loved about her brothers was that no matter how old they got, her special surprises hadn't gotten old. The boys let out various praises for the cake, and just like that, her brothers seemed to jump six steps ahead in their ease with Nathan being around for the weekend.

"So, Mitch, how is your sophomore year coming along?" Nathan asked, starting up the interaction between him and Elizabeth's brothers.

"It's okay. More work," answered Mitch. Still short and sweet, but anything was better than "fine."

"Are you in any sports?" asked Nathan.

"Yeah. I thought Liz would've told you."

"She did, but I thought you could tell me about it," said Nathan.

"You could've just asked, 'How's soccer going?'" said Mitch. His eyes rolled just enough for Elizabeth to reprimand him. Her mom hat hadn't lost its strength.

"It's okay, Liz," said Nathan. "Mitch, how is soccer going?" He didn't miss a beat. Probably because dealing with snarky teenagers was in his job description.

"Fine, I guess," answered Mitch.

"More than fine," bragged Elizabeth. "Mitch is one of the best on the team. He starts every game."

"That's great, man," said Nathan.

Mitch only nodded in agreement.

"What about you, Danny? Are you looking at any sports once you get to high school?" Nathan asked the youngest brother.

"Football" was Danny's only response.

"When do you try out? Next spring or summer?" asked Nathan.

"Spring, I think. But I don't know if I'll make it," said Danny.

"Why not?" Elizabeth and Nathan asked at the same time.

"I just don't know," he shrugged his shoulders. "I'm kind of small. I need to up my endurance. The coach is pretty tough. And … I've never done it before, so I just don't know," he said. Danny sounded annoyed that he had to explain his answer.

Everyone was quiet for a minute because of Danny's defensiveness.

Nathan seemed unsure of what to say as he looked from side to side, and Elizabeth wanted to wait until her emotions calmed down before speaking.

It was Mitch who broke the silence. "I think you'll make it, Danny. I'll make sure we train you leading up to tryouts like we did all summer."

Danny kept his head slightly downcast, but he sent a look of appreciation to Mitch.

Conversation continued this way—forced, stalling, awkward—for another thirty minutes. After they curtly covered Bryce's day and other random information, the boys asked to be excused from the table sooner than Elizabeth would have liked. She kindly reminded them that the group was leaving at 9:30 the next morning for the annual Tenner Family Fall Day.

Already confused and upset by the boys' subdued demeanors, she became more discouraged when Mitch and Bryce mumbled an "okay" and Danny quickly and quietly muttered, "K, goodnight." She watched her brothers walk away, staring after them, not knowing what to feel. Finally, she said, "Well, that didn't go as I'd hoped."

Nathan put his hand on her back and agreed, "No. No, it didn't." The awkwardness was almost too much to bear at times. Elizabeth had silently cringed as Nathan kept forcing conversation. She wanted to rewind the night and start over, or at the very least stand up and just scream from the discomfort of it all. Eyes barely met, voices were solemn for the most part; it was painful. When the boys walked toward their room and Nathan held his hand on her back, Elizabeth toyed with the idea of asking Nathan to leave, for the mere fact that the boys seemed intensely uneasy. She felt sorry for them. But talking herself down from that anxiety was easy when she registered Nathan's presence behind her: no way could she let him go.

I could talk about the night with him. Maybe he can give it a good perspective.

And what, relive and analyze every silent and awkward moment? No, thanks.

Instead, they lay on the couch for a time, wearing their sneaky teenager hats again. Just before one a.m., they said goodnight with a final kiss, although she wasn't ready to part. Not physically, anyway. But Elizabeth's night alone in her bed didn't seem so bad, not when there was a man downstairs who made her feel safe. Scared sometimes from the intensity of her feelings, but for the most part safe. And that feeling—safety—was a new one, as her life hadn't allowed for a resting place in a very long time. In her ever-cynical way, Elizabeth fell asleep while safety and fear battled for the foregrounds of her heart and mind.

———————————

Elizabeth had arranged for her, Bryce, Mitch, Danny, and Nathan to spend the late September day first at their favorite farm, then out to dinner, and finally with some chill time at home. A visit to Sam's Pumpkin Patch had been an annual event in Elizabeth's family for many years, at least since Danny was little. Elizabeth and the boys picked apples and pumpkins, bought fudge, took a horseback ride, and Elizabeth always watched the boys do two things in the main lodge: attempt to lasso a mechanical bull and play one of the arcade games. Elizabeth was anxious to see what the day would be like with Nathan along for the tradition. When she originally suggested that they go the weekend Nathan was visiting, the boys had mixed feelings; they weren't totally sure they were at ease with the idea.

At least they're being honest with me.

They eventually came around to the idea, if for no other reason than they felt they had no choice in the matter. But when Bryce, Mitch, and Danny walked down for breakfast, they seemed to be making an extra effort to be comfortable. More than the night before, anyway. Elizabeth appreciated the effort but hated that they had to go to such lengths in the first place.

Nathan's initial visit was better than Elizabeth thought it would be. This time, it seemed to be the opposite: the boys seemed to be so up and down; she knew they wouldn't be able to fake it for too long if inside they hated what was going on. She knew that in between visits, they had gotten mad almost every time she was on the phone, and Elizabeth could tell they saw how distracted she sometimes was. Still, she had gone ahead with having Nathan come visit, thinking things would even out. She certainly didn't expect this bumpy of a weekend.

"Good morning," said Danny.

Elizabeth turned from the stove where she was cooking eggs. "Good morning," she said, adding a smile.

"Morning, guys," said Nathan.

Why does he sound so casual when things are so unsettled? Elizabeth wondered to herself.

"Good morning, Nathan," said Mitch.

"Did you guys sleep all right?" asked Elizabeth.

"I guess," said Mitch. "I'm looking forward to today." He was rubbing his hands together and yawning, still in his plaid pajama pants and plain white t-shirt.

When the group arrived at Sam's Pumpkin Patch, the first thing the brothers wanted to do was choose a pumpkin. It was still early, and Mitch had a reputation of being particular with his pumpkins. If they chose early, he'd get his pick of some of the best pumpkins the patch had to offer, or so Elizabeth said.

Because of the boys' detached attitudes the night before, Elizabeth watched their demeanors and actions very carefully. She tried to do this discreetly but was sure everyone noticed she was slightly anxious. She noticed that Nathan, Bryce, and Mitch looked completely relaxed, while Danny appeared somewhat discontented. Nathan wasn't to be deterred, though; he willingly left Elizabeth's side to look at pumpkins with Danny, about which Danny seemed to have mixed feelings. He awkwardly accepted Nathan's help.

Mitch was acting naturally as well. Sometimes he was near everyone else; other times, he was far away—all in search of the perfect pumpkin.

Bryce seemed to be acting himself too. He stuck pretty close to Elizabeth, helping her find a big pumpkin as he did every year. But he was intently eyeing her while they scoured through the fresh patch.

"Are you having a good time, Liz?" asked Bryce.

"Yep. You?"

"Yeah," he responded, though unconvincingly.

Elizabeth's eyes were squinted in Bryce's direction.

"What?" he asked.

Elizabeth decided against voicing her thoughts and concerns in favor of continued observation. She'd rather not initiate an intense conversation at a time when they should be having fun.

"Relax, will you?" He sounded frustrated.

She rolled her eyes and responded under her breath, "Sure, no problem." *With you three going up and down like a see-saw? Easy as pie.*

When the pumpkins were picked and in the car, the group went through every other Sam's Pumpkin Patch tradition. Again, Elizabeth watched everyone carefully and on the way home decided it was an up-and-down day. They were fine during pumpkin picking, but Bryce, Mitch, and Danny walked off by themselves during apple picking; Danny and Mitch were all but mute during lunch and dinner, yet during dessert Mitch explained in minute detail to Nathan why he's so picky about his pumpkin. Bryce was fairly even all day. What should she make of their behavior? Elizabeth had the advantage of knowing her brothers intimately, given the fact that she'd been their primary caregiver for eleven years. She was well aware that while her brothers were trying, they were unsettled. When Danny and Mitch were quiet during dinner, Elizabeth hated it; the situation caused a physical reaction within her that resembled the recoiling of a boa constrictor: her insides seemed to bunch up and tighten so that she could hardly breathe.

She was thankful for Bryce's mostly normal state, but the one thing that bothered her—and it was big—was when she saw after dinner, from a distance, that Bryce seemed to be comforting Mitch. She couldn't tell at first, but Bryce's arm around Mitch's shoulders confirmed it. Elizabeth felt her heart and the rest of her insides constrict again.

Her physical reactions alone were enough to exhaust her, given that she went from good to bad to worse and back all day. Deep sighs filled the ride home, and Danny, Mitch, and Bryce went downstairs almost immediately after stepping in the front door. Nathan and Elizabeth headed upstairs to hang out alone, but when Elizabeth walked into her bedroom, she wasn't sure whether to throw a screaming fit, throw a crying fit, or just throw things. Caught in the middle of all her emotions, Elizabeth simply lay on her bed, looking at the ceiling.

"Do you want to tell me what you're thinking?" asked Nathan, sounding cautious and defeated. All day he acted like nothing was wrong, until the car ride home when his demeanor became as heavy as the rest. It wasn't like Nathan to keep his feelings inside, that Elizabeth knew. So she could only imagine his disappointment might go even deeper than it already had in this complicated situation. Whatever he was feeling, he was feeling it intensely, she decided. Maybe he was ready to go; maybe this was too much to handle. He got the ball rolling on the conversation, so she'd find out eventually.

"I'm thinking many things," she said.

"Give it to me," said Nathan quickly. "Go."

"I need some wine," she said.

"And some chocolate," added Nathan.

"Today was hard," said Elizabeth.

"Yes," he said, nodding.

"We're not ready," said Elizabeth flatly.

Nathan asked, "By *we*, you mean ...?"

"My brothers and me. We're not ready for you, for this change. I thought we were fine because of last time, but this ... this was too much up and down."

"I disagree," said Nathan. He seemed—compared to his usual disposition—to be all but out of words. She was about to say something that she was sure would bring Nathan back to his regular verbal energy level.

"I think you should go home," she said.

"Liz—"

She sat up. "Nathan, I told you. I warned you fair and square."

"Liz, did you think this would be easy? Are you really going to make me go home because you're unwilling to push through the discomfort?"

"I don't live in a fantasy world, Nathan. I have three other lives to worry about," she said defensively. "I'm not willing to push through the discomfort? Do you know what this is like for me? It's exhausting, that's what it's like. And I can't try as hard as you want and need me to in order to make this work with you. I have no energy left after trying to gauge how my brothers are doing and engaging everyone in conversation and …" she trailed off, but finished a moment later, "it's a lot."

Nathan agreed with Elizabeth by nodding his head. But he wasn't letting her off easily, either. He responded, "Yes, it is a lot. And it's hard. It'll probably be difficult like this for a while. But, Elizabeth, I really, really believe that if you give it more time, talk to God about it, and trust your brothers, we'll come out on the other side more than okay—all of us."

Elizabeth's eyes began to water as soon as he said the word "yes" because she knew that even with as much of a fight as he put up, Nathan saw it. He saw how tiring this was for her; he saw the amount of pressure she felt. His words and actions revealed that he understood. He was leaning toward the brash side, but of all Nathan's shortcomings—the few Elizabeth had so far seen—she could deal with brash. Elizabeth learned long ago to have stamina for fighting, so not only did it not intimidate her, but she welcomed it sometimes. She liked to know she still had it in her to fight for what she knew was right. Plus, Nathan's brazen attitude and the fight he was putting up was *for her*, which was in direct opposition to the fights her sorry excuse for parents would put up.

Her thoughts, which had a distinct habit of carouseling even during important conversations, came back to the way Nathan stuck God into his short but heartfelt speech. As usual, she called him out on it. She had the same frustrated expression she had had on her face since the conversation began.

"I sandwiched Him in there, yes," said Nathan, with a sly grin and raised eyebrows.

"Sneaky." Elizabeth was almost smiling now.

"Sneaky?" asked Nathan, feigning indignation. "Clever. And right."

Elizabeth rolled her eyes and explained that she was not faithful like Nathan. She had a real-world fight going on that she still wasn't sure God was involved in. Nathan counteracted her—as always—with insisting that God is involved in "real world" stuff because He created it and He cares. Their voices were lower than just a moment ago, but Elizabeth felt no less anxious about what went on with her brothers earlier in the day. Plus, she knew they were once again at a moot point. Nathan unwaveringly told her he was not going home, and Elizabeth returned the adamancy by not letting the God talk go any further.

Nathan let a minute go by while Elizabeth stared out the window; she seemed to be considering all she and Nathan had just aired out. Usually when God was brought into the conversation, Elizabeth halted it. *I wonder if he did that on purpose so I would stop talking and think about what he said.* Maybe, because Nathan seemed to decide that the discussion would be on hold for now as he said, "How about I get that wine and chocolate, we put in a movie, and you fall asleep on my shoulder?"

She looked over at Nathan, who was standing with his heart in his hand. He loved her, this she knew. He could tolerate more than she gave him credit for too, but could she and her brothers tolerate all of it, that was the question. Choosing the side of her heart that was melting like chocolate in the sun, as he once stated it would, she said to him, "Now that is a suggestion I completely agree with."

─────────────

Sunday morning came and went similar to Nathan's previous visit. Bryce, Mitch, and Danny went to church, while Elizabeth and Nathan went for a long walk. The last time they went for a walk, she tried to steer clear of God talk. This time, she had a feeling it would be inescapable. Nathan had fished around earlier in the morning to see if they could go to church with her brothers. Elizabeth weaseled out of it, but she knew that habit couldn't last very long. If she wouldn't *go* to church, she had a feeling she was going to be forced to at least *talk* about it. Not five minutes down the road, her suspicions were confirmed.

"Are you any closer to going to church with your brothers?" Nathan asked. To her, this was a loaded question. But she knew that, to him, it was just a way of seeing if her heart had moved at all closer to the God he believed in. Little by little, Elizabeth was understanding that it was nearing time to decide: she either believed or she didn't. Knowing she didn't have to decide this moment helped ease the anxiety. But she had to start at least thinking about it, talking some about it with Nathan and maybe her brothers. It was a mix of curiosity about what they all shared and a strong desire to shut them up on the topic.

Oh well. Now or never.

"I just don't know. I'm still hesitant. I want to make sure I'm going on my own terms."

"May I add—once again—that if I am making you want to go to church, that's a good thing. The Bible even says so," said Nathan.

Elizabeth laughed. "Oh really?"

"Yes, really. Iron sharpens iron. I'm sharpening you by encouraging you in your faith."

"I don't have a faith," said Elizabeth, almost so quickly she couldn't stop the words if she wanted to. Nathan's body seemed to deflate just enough for her to notice.

"Can I ask, again, what is your main reason for not wanting to go to church?" asked Nathan.

"Sure, you can ask," she answered, but she stopped there.

"Well?" asked Nathan.

"Well, what?" she answered mysteriously with a wink.

Nathan looked at her, un-amused. "What's your main reason for not going?" he asked flatly.

"Oh! You were actually asking," Elizabeth winked at Nathan again but realized he didn't seem to be in a joking mood. "I don't know, Nathan; it seems to be a strong combination of things."

"Let's hear 'em," said Nathan.

"Why are you so open to hearing all my negativity toward the church?" she asked boldly.

"I'm awesome. C'mon, no distractions. Talk to me," said Nathan.

"Ugh. Okay. One. I still don't like the institution of the church as a whole. Two," Elizabeth was holding up her fingers as she counted her reasons, "I don't want the attention of going to a church my brothers have gone to for ten years. And three, it seems like an easy out."

"An easy out to and from what?" asked Nathan.

Elizabeth answered honestly, "It just seems so ... soft. Too easy. Jesus loves me, just like that?" She snapped her fingers. "Seems too easy."

"It's a great thing, Liz," said Nathan honestly.

"Clearly you didn't hear what I just said," she said.

"Elizabeth, loving and accepting love from Jesus is anything but an easy out. It takes commitment. It takes courage. It takes gumption."

"Gumption?" asked Elizabeth suspiciously. Nathan was too animated for a topic that made her squirm. Her anxiety grew.

"It's one of my favorite words. To stand up and say things like, 'I have a Savior who loves me,' and 'I will stand for what's right,' and 'I forgive you,' and really mean it? Those things absolutely take gumption," Nathan told her.

"Yeah, those are some big things you just said." Elizabeth was shocked by Nathan's explanations but not entirely surprised that his English teacher self overflowed into the God talk.

"They are," agreed Nathan. "But it's the life I choose to lead."

"It's—it seems like—" Elizabeth couldn't seem to finish her thought. Finally she choked out, "It seems like a lot of pressure."

He nodded slowly, as though carefully considering what he wanted to say in response. His answer did nothing to ease her nervousness. If anything, her body involuntarily squirmed even more. "You know what I've found? The more I focus on the love and grace, the easier the truth comes along."

For a minute, neither Elizabeth nor Nathan said anything; they simply walked hand in hand, breathing in the deep, crisp fall air. She was letting Nathan's words sink in, trying—silently and with increased effort—not to throw out everything he said.

"Okay," Elizabeth finally said. "Let's let that simmer for a while."

"Okay," said Nathan. His tone held finality, but once he started his next sentence, Elizabeth realized his finality was only related to her second issue with the church; he quickly moved on to another one of her concerns.

Nathan asked, "Well, what about the institution part?"

"I keep looking for positive things the church is doing, but so much of what I keep seeing is corruption and hypocrisy."

"For example?" he asked.

"Like those churches you see in the news. Protesting soldiers' funerals and abortion clinics; pastors who abuse their families; how much they hate gay pride parades? That's not love. I've heard the argument that that's only a handful of them, but that handful really matters. How can I even want to become part of a group who thinks that some people are any less human than you or I?"

Nathan seemed to be again thoughtfully considering her words and how he would respond. When he did speak, Elizabeth could tell it was important. She listened more closely than she had to his previous statements.

He said, "When I was ten years old, my aunt and uncle split up; we had all gone to the same church. You know how my church responded? They kicked us out. All of us, our entire family."

"Seriously?" Nathan's admission angered Elizabeth. "How did you deal with that?"

"I became determined to get involved with a church that would stand for—once again—the love and grace of Jesus, instead of focusing on the punishment," said Nathan.

"Different churches behave differently?" Elizabeth sounded surprised.

"Absolutely," said Nathan.

"Hmm," she said.

"Hmm, you'll keep thinking about this? Or hmm, you're tired of talking about it?"

Elizabeth laughed softly and answered, "Both."

"What would you like to talk about?" Nathan asked her. By now, they were back at Elizabeth's house, and Elizabeth was happy for Nathan's release from the conversation. She had gone easy on him when it came to the institution aspect of her decision not to go to church. Elizabeth had strong opinions on how others should be treated, and she knew those opinions contradicted much of the behavior she saw from people who called themselves Christians, both on the news and in her hometown. Nathan's admission that his church excommunicated his family didn't help her feelings on the matter either. But the softer side—and, if she was honest, the more reasonable side—told her that if Nathan and her brothers went to church every week and were the men and young men they were, then it couldn't be all bad. She'd think about that later. What she wanted to think about now was the fact that her brothers weren't home yet, and she was filled with passion for this man. Nathan asked her what she wanted to talk about, but a better question would be what did she want to do. Elizabeth answered her own question by bringing Nathan into a strong kiss, but it only lasted a moment until the boys came in the door from church.

Elizabeth and Bryce made brunch while Nathan, Mitch, and Danny watched a football game in the living room. She kept checking in, but each time she did, nobody was talking, laughing, or even smiling; they were just staring at the television. Again, Elizabeth didn't want to start a big conversation with Bryce about how her brothers were acting, so they just talked about how church was that morning, his classes this semester, and her upcoming projects at work.

When they all sat down to eat, Nathan offered to pray. "Heavenly Father, thank you for this day. We ask that you bless this meal to the health of our bodies. I also thank you for the welcoming hearts of Bryce, Mitch, and Danny. Please continue to bless and guide them as they work their way through the school year. We love you, Lord. Amen."

Elizabeth looked up just before Nathan had finished so she could watch the boys. When her brothers opened their eyes, they looked at each other with curious and unsure expressions. The reason for this was answered later that night, long after Nathan had left.

Chapter 11

*"There would be no passion in this world if we never had to
fight for what we love."*
~Susie Switzer

ALL RIGHT GUYS, WHAT'S up?" she asked.
Elizabeth looked around the table for an answer. Nathan
had left a few hours earlier, and dinner was underway. The boys
used their full mouths as an excuse not to respond. She looked
at Bryce first since he was the oldest. He played with his food,
staring at the chicken and rice as though doing anything else
would carry grave consequences. Mitch looked to Bryce, and
when Bryce didn't look up, Mitch looked quick to Danny and
then to Elizabeth, but only for a quick second before he looked
out the window. When Elizabeth looked at Danny, he wasn't
even touching his food. He was propping his head up with his
left arm, with a pouty look on his face. He, too, was looking at
his food, but his sad eyes and downturned mouth indicated tears
were about to wet his cheeks.

"Seriously, guys," Elizabeth said again. "What's going on?"

This time, they all looked at her, probably because of her
no-nonsense mom tone that rarely, if ever, took "no" or silence
for an answer.

"Danny," said Bryce in a fatherly tone that startled Elizabeth.
She looked over to Danny; a tear fell slowly down his right cheek.

"Danny, what is it?" asked Elizabeth. She let him take a deep breath before he spoke. When he did, she couldn't believe what she was hearing.

"I got in trouble Friday at school," he said.

"You did?" She tried her best to sound more sisterly than motherly. This was one of the rare times she was confused as to which hat to keep on. "What kind of trouble?"

"The teacher made me leave the classroom," he said.

"Why?" she asked, altogether confused and afraid of what she might hear.

Danny didn't answer. Starting to lose her patience, Elizabeth repeated, "Why? Why did you have to leave the classroom?"

He took another deep breath before he said, "I started a fight."

"Danny!" Out of the corner of her eye, she saw Bryce give her the "calm down" signal. She tried her best.

"Elizabeth, we have been keeping something from you," said Bryce.

She was too stunned and scared to say anything, wondering how bad this was about to get.

"Danny has been getting in trouble since school started. Friday was the worst, but he promised," Bryce paused and gave Danny a hard look, "that it would be the very last time. Right?"

"Yes, sir."

Getting in trouble? Why hadn't she known—or even suspected—that something was that wrong? And why hadn't they told her? And how did they keep it from her? And, 'Yes *sir*'? When and where did that start? She was anxious, confused, and hurt. She dealt with the confusion first. "Danny, what's going on? You've always been able to talk to me."

The tears he had kept under control for the past few minutes now let loose. Through them, he said, "Not anymore."

"What ever, ever gave you that idea?" She quickly moved to his side, stroking his head and trying her best to balance mom and sister.

"Because you spend all your time with Nathan! When he comes here we do stuff together for some of the time—"

"About half the time," Mitch cut in.

"Fine, about half the time," Danny continued, still tearful. "But the rest of the time, it's like you want to be alone. You never needed adult time before. I'm not saying I don't like him. He … picked a great pumpkin," he said slowly, obviously reaching for something positive to say. "But he's taking you away. I miss you when Nathan's here. And when you're on the phone, you can't help me with my homework. Bryce is cool, but he's not you, Lizzie. You can't leave us. We're like the four musketeers, remember? But if you're not here, there's not four—there's only three, and we're not a family without you."

Elizabeth was holding Danny's head as he cried, thinking that the fallout she'd half expected since the first time the boys met Nathan was finally upon her. She knew they were having a hard time letting her go, even just the sliver of her heart that she was asking for. Mitch and Bryce weren't consoling Danny like they usually did, so she understood that they knew all of this and had decided not to share it with her. She'd talk to Bryce about that later; right now, she had a crying thirteen-year-old on her hands.

"Sweetie," she tried to hold Danny's head up, but he hadn't quite stopped crying. "Sweetie," she tried again. "Listen to me, okay, Danny? Listen. First of all, I haven't gone anywhere yet—" Danny's eyes grew wide at "yet" so she quickly amended her words. "I mean to visit, I haven't gone away to visit. Second of all, Danny, if you are hurting or upset, I want to know. Sooner than this." She looked at Bryce. "Okay?"

"What if I'm upset and you're on the phone? Or you go to visit Nathan and I'm upset then?"

He was pushing and testing the boundaries as any teenager does. But Elizabeth wouldn't give in; she had already decided Nathan was someone, some*thing* worth fighting for. Besides, the Tenner siblings matured too early for sugar coating and niceties; she'd tell them the truth, no matter what. In this case, it meant letting Danny know she would still want to hear his troubles, but he would have to wait until either she was off the phone or when she got back home.

"WHEN you get back home? When are you going away?"

She just about rolled her eyes, struggling with her feelings for Nathan and wanting to protect her brothers. Her loyalty to Nathan was winning, though she couldn't figure out why. In the past, any display of heartache from her brothers would cause Elizabeth to immediately change her course of action. Her loyalty to her brothers wasn't changing, but the way she handled her own heart seemed to be shifting. She finally answered him. "No immediate plans, Danny. In the future is what I meant. But what I want you to take away from this is that you will *always* have me, and I always want to know when you are upset. Okay, bud?"

Danny didn't answer; he just sniffed.

"Danny, okay?" she asked again.

"Okay." His silence was short-lived; she could tell he wanted to say more, so she waited.

"Elizabeth?" he asked.

"Hmm?"

"I'm sad," said Danny with such honesty that Elizabeth could barely hold her own tears.

"Because I've been spending more time with Nathan?" she asked.

Danny only nodded his head. Elizabeth's words were simple, but her tone was that of speaking to a young adult. She was direct, not willing to risk Danny's trust, and not wanting to embellish the reality of the situation.

"Danny, did you know this day would come eventually? I mean, I had to meet someone sometime. I love Nathan. And he loves me too."

"Well that's good for *you*." He looked up with his big, brown, still-teary eyes. The poor boy had never seen two adults truly love each other, so he had to no idea what that looked like. And he had no idea that it could be good for an entire family if handled and displayed properly.

"That is a good thing for *all of us*. He really likes all you guys. He wants to keep coming around and getting to know you and help you with your homework like he's done a couple times, stuff like that."

"I don't know," said Danny.

Elizabeth had always credited Danny as being more mature than other boys his age. She believed this to be a result of his being raised by his sister and brothers rather than his mom. Danny had always known he came from a different kind of home; Elizabeth knew that Danny knew they were all doing the best they could. But at the end of the day, he was still a thirteen-year-old boy acutely sensitive to anything that could possibly shake his foundation, one that had trouble being laid in the first place.

"Well," said Elizabeth. She chose her words carefully. She wanted to continue being honest with her brothers, even if it wasn't exactly what they wanted to hear. "We're going to keep trying."

Danny made a frustrated noise. Her persistence contradicted the lack of resolve she showed Nathan, but in this moment, she was fighting for her side.

"Danny, can we talk about this tomorrow night? We'll go on a date night, just you and me. That way, I can think about everything you've told me, and you can think about everything I've told you. How does that sound?"

A sniffle and a quiet "okay" came out at the same time. Dinner was finished quickly, but mostly in silence and heavy sighs. It reminded her of the families she sometimes saw at restaurants where an onlooker could clearly see that nobody wanted to be at the table; everyone would rather be doing their own thing. Every time she saw that scene, whether in real life or in a movie, she was grateful that wasn't her situation. Her family could thoroughly enjoy each other's company. But tonight, heavy hearts and weighted minds kept spirits low and conversation to a minimum.

The phone happened to ring for Mitch just as they all asked to be excused. Before he disappeared up to his bedroom to take the call, Elizabeth asked who was on the phone; it was the third time that week someone had called for either Mitch or Danny. But all either of them ever said, including this time, was that it was a friend from church.

Later, after Elizabeth knew that at least Danny was asleep and Mitch was in his room, she took Bryce outside to talk. The first thing Elizabeth did when they got there was to slap Bryce on the shoulder.

"How could you not tell me he was feeling this way? And that he's been getting in trouble?" Elizabeth's arms were animatedly moving to her sides. "We have never kept anything from each other when it comes to this family!"

Elizabeth knew this was about to be a full-blown argument, but she didn't care. Elizabeth and Bryce had it out once in a great while, the tensions of pseudo-parenthood sometimes too heavy to bear. Neither was scared to fight with the other, which made their arguments all the more brutal. Yet they were complete, air-it-all-out fights since everything was always put on the table; this also meant all ill-will was usually over and done with by the end of the conversation. Nothing lingered, which Elizabeth and Bryce both appreciated. They had enough on their plates without carrying one more unresolved issue.

"I promised him, Liz. He made me swear. And besides, we both know that part of what he said is true." Bryce's tone was bordering on biting.

"Actually, almost all of what he said was true. When Nathan is here, I don't spend as much time with you guys as I used to, and sometimes I will be going away to visit him. How can you not understand this? You've been in love before, you know how it feels. What am I supposed to do? Just forget about it?"

Bryce stared at her. It was chilly outside, so his short, angry breaths were coming out in big puffs of air. He tried to keep a controlled voice but was failing as he went on.

"Elizabeth, I do understand. I'm the second oldest in the family, and we take care of the boys together. You took care of me until I got old enough to take care of myself. Then I started helping you. But you know what? Danny's not even close to that age. He doesn't even understand yet how much you really do for him. He knows what you do, but he doesn't think about it on a regular basis. He doesn't think about how you handle all the bills. He doesn't think about the fact that you read cookbooks or that you should be starting your own family. He loves, respects, and admires you, but he doesn't truly appreciate you yet. And that means he will not understand for a long time what it means for you to leave now and then to visit Nathan. He's a bright kid, but he's used to the people who take care of him leaving, and that is how he will see this. He will see this the way he still thinks about what Mom used to do. It isn't right, but that's the way our life is. Those two weeks you were gone on vacation, when you *met* Nathan, he was a mess the whole first week. The second week, he was only okay because he was counting down the days until you'd be home. I don't understand how you thought he'd be okay with this."

"I thought there would be some fighting at home, some bad attitudes until we got used to it, but I didn't expect acting out in school. And I didn't expect you to lie to me," she said angrily. Elizabeth, too, was getting more and more frustrated.

"I didn't lie to you," said Bryce, defending himself. "I just didn't tell you. I was hoping it would stop before we had to tell you."

"That is a lie, Bryce," said Elizabeth strongly. They were quiet for a few moments until Elizabeth spoke again, "So you're telling me I shouldn't be with Nathan?"

"First of all, are you really in love with him?"

She didn't pause when she said, "Yes."

"Elizabeth." Bryce let out a big puff of air while tipping his head back, his tone accusatory.

"Why? Why 'Elizabeth' in that tone of voice?"

"Because you should have stopped this before it got this far. Man, you knew you couldn't afford this. I mean, do you even have the energy? Do you even have the energy to be in a relationship right now? Danny and Mitch still need you. *I* still need you." At this point, Bryce almost sounded like he was pleading.

"So I'm supposed to give up just like that—" she snapped her fingers, "just drop it like it never happened? I'm *not going anywhere*, Bryce. I'm still here for you guys, and I will continue to be." She slapped one hand into the other for emphasis on her point.

"You always said family was the most important thing to you." His voice was getting louder still; so was hers.

"It is! Don't you dare accuse me of putting anything else before my family; I'm trying as hard as I can here."

"Well these past few months it has definitely felt otherwise."

"Something else entered my life, Bryce!" she said impatiently. "Again, what was I supposed to do? Just throw in the towel because it's kind of difficult in the beginning? Because I didn't have the answer to the next fifty years right in front of me?"

Immediately Elizabeth caught herself: *I sound like Nathan.*

"No, but our faces could have flashed in front of you for a second! Just for a second so you could have remembered what you'd have to give up if you went through with this! How long were you going to let it go? How long are you going to let this be difficult?"

"Why does it have to be one or the other? You guys or Nathan." She moved her hands as though weighing her options. "That is *ridiculous*. Why can't I have both?"

Bryce didn't have an answer for his older sister. Elizabeth drew in a deep breath and went back to the first part of their conversation, because she was barely ready to accept the idea that they had been talking about her behind her back. If anything, this stung the most.

She said, "So you've all just been talking about me, about how horrible I've been these past three-and-a-half months?"

Bryce rolled his eyes. He said, "That's extreme. But we've talked, yes."

"Way to stab me in the back. I thought we worked together on stuff like this. Why haven't you come to me?" she asked, frustrated.

"We were hoping it would settle down a little more. I guess we didn't know how serious you two are about each other," said Bryce.

"Well, now that I know you've been talking so much behind my back, I feel betrayed, manipulated, and angry. Which are three things I have worked hard at keeping out of *your* life by helping take care of you boys and shield you from Mom and Dad's stupidity. And now it's going to be more complicated than it had to be in the first place. Because heaven knows, no matter what we decided, the situation would be anything but simple."

Bryce looked at her, and she suddenly knew exactly what he was thinking.

"You think I just brought this on all by myself, huh? You think I was irresponsible in North Carolina and just forgot about you boys and went with my own feelings? Let me tell you something Bryce: It's insulting that thought would even go through your head. If you seriously think that I would give up my life with you boys for some fling, you don't know me at all. If you think I would even *consider* giving up my life with you guys for *anything*, you haven't paid attention the last eleven years! You don't think this has been on my mind every single day since almost the moment I met Nathan? You don't think I've been holding my breath, waiting for this exact thing to happen? You really suck for letting me get to this point without as much as a hint that something was up. I thought we had made some progress since Nathan's first visit, but I guess not. Thanks for nothing."

With that, Elizabeth stormed inside and slammed the door. She knew it could have woken up Danny, but at this point, she did not care. They'd all seen each other at their worst, and this was certainly one of those times. She thought it could eventually be okay, but how to get there—and when it would happen—was Elizabeth's biggest worry. She thought of when she pretended to be asleep and listened to Bryce and Nathan talking. The scene had given her a lot of hope for what was to come. She remembered wondering if the boys were talking to anyone at church about their situation. If they were, she reasoned church, too, would probably see her as being in the wrong. What was she supposed to think about everything that went on over the last three days? Nathan telling her he loves her, her own increased level of sharing more of her past and present deep-down feelings, admitting to Bryce that she loves Nathan, up and down emotions from everyone, and finally, a nice, big blowout with Bryce.

As usual, she let everything fight for the number one position at the forefront of her thoughts. Every time she tried to fall asleep, images of her and Bryce fighting, then Danny crying, then Mitch not saying a word, then Nathan kissing her, all came flying at her. The only thing that finally calmed her mind was settling on "we'll deal with this later" and fantasizing about the moments surrounding when she and Nathan met. Because up until recently, her reality had been better than her dreams. Now, the reverse was true. And close to three a.m., there was one sudden thought that kept Elizabeth from sleeping. She realized she had told her brother—and finally herself—that she was in love with Nathan, but she hadn't yet told the subject of that love.

"What time is it?" said Elizabeth aloud. She looked at the clock. "Two-fifty in the morning. Oh well."

She dialed Nathan's number; he answered groggily. "Hello?" Even his groggy, sleepy voice made Elizabeth smile.

"Hey, Nathan," she said casually.

"Elizabeth? What time is it?" he asked, confused.

"Ten till three," she said.

Nathan seemed to wake up quickly. "What's wrong?" he asked.

"Nothing," Elizabeth giggled. "I just have something I need to tell you." She took a deep breath and said it. "I love you."

"What?" Nathan sounded like he didn't believe what he just heard. She could picture him rubbing his eyes, confused and wondering if this was a dream or if it was reality. But Elizabeth wanted him to get back to sleep.

"You heard me. Now go back to sleep; we'll talk tomorrow."

Elizabeth hung up before Nathan said another word. She waited a full five minutes for Nathan to call back. When he didn't, she assumed it was due to his being completely baffled; she imagined he thought it was a dream, and if he wondered whether or not it was real, he wouldn't want to call Elizabeth back because it was late at night. With that task finally checked off her heart's to-do list, she quickly drifted off to sleep, ready for sweet dreams. There was more to figure out, that she knew, but she was in love. And that was nothing to feel less than elated about.

Elizabeth's dream brought her to a dirt road on the side of a mountain. She saw herself in a pick-up truck, wearing a white v-neck shirt and blue cropped sweatpants. She looked to the driver; it was Nathan. He said with a huge smile and child-like giddiness, "Get out, we're here!"

"Where are we?" asked Elizabeth. She was excited too, but she didn't know why. She had no idea where they were or what they were doing. The dirt road was wide enough not to cause her any fright, and the rest of the scene before her was something she had never seen. Large rocks stood guard at random places on both sides of the two-way road. The mountain was reddish, but that might be from the glaring sun that streamed from the perfectly blue sky. A blue, she noticed, she might never have seen before. It was a strong, solid color with the sun its only visitor. Nathan was leading her to the edge of the dirt road, to the edge of the mountain. Her trembling lasted only a second; Nathan was too excited for her to be afraid. She knew he wouldn't lead her into anything dangerous. She trusted him.

"Come see!" he said excitedly.

Out of the truck, Nathan took Elizabeth's hand in his. She felt its strength, how he obviously never wanted to let go. He had her, strong and steady. He started down the dirt road; Elizabeth finally looked ahead after staring into Nathan's eyes, and what she saw took her breath away.

"We're walking into the sunset!" She voiced her observation with awe.

"We are. But first, we have to stop here," said Nathan. Confirming her suspicion, he led her to the edge of the mountain. She still wasn't afraid, especially when she saw what was laid out in front of her. They stopped, and when Elizabeth looked out over the cliff, she could see the entire world spread out before her like a live world map, nations and waterways and world-renowned landmarks at her fingertips. The two were standing above the center of the Atlantic Ocean; she could tell by the geographic locations of everything her eyes were taking in. To the right was Europe, where she could see vineyards in Italy and beautiful castles in Germany and Scotland. She tried to grab a grape from a vineyard, but Nathan told her not to touch; this was only for looking. Farther to the right, she saw Asia and Australia. Elizabeth even thought she saw the North Pole far in front of her; she jokingly asked Nathan where Santa and his elves were hiding. She looked over to the left and saw the whole United States: the Golden Gate bridge, lights in Las Vegas, the Rocky Mountains, the St. Louis Arch; she saw the hole where the Twin Towers had been, and the Statue of Liberty. She saw beaches in Florida, azaleas, and roadside peach stands in the Carolinas and Georgia.

Yet, in a moment, her dream shifted gears, when in one small corner to her top left-center, she noticed her family. Her brothers were sitting at a table, all three of them soaked in tears. All three boys were staring straight ahead while their eyes acted as leaky faucets for their tears. Why were they crying? Why, when she went to ask them, could they not hear her? She shouted louder and louder; still they did not hear her. She told Nathan to help her, but he just stood there, watching. Just like the grapes, he said, this is for looking only. But in her heart of hearts, Elizabeth couldn't watch that kind of heartache play out on her brothers and do nothing about it. No, she had to get to them. But no matter how loudly she yelled, they didn't hear her. No matter how many times she tried to grab them to shake them or hold them, she couldn't get her arms around any of the three boys. And when she started moving toward them, she couldn't get to their table. After running for what felt like an hour, Elizabeth realized she hadn't moved off the mountain. Not one step.

Monday was date night with Danny. Elizabeth spent the day-time being nervous about it, even though Nathan tried to comfort and encourage her. Elizabeth and Nathan talked about how the alone time for her and Danny would be healthy; Nathan even suggested she might gain some insight on how to better help Danny transition. Nathan also made it a point to talk about Elizabeth's impromptu phone call on Sunday night. She assured him that yes, it was real; no, it wasn't a dream; and yes, she was sure that's how she felt. This admission prompted Nathan to a greater confidence about Elizabeth's impending conversation with Danny.

"Let him see that you love me, Liz. He'll come around. So will Mitch," Nathan had said.

She tried taking his words to heart, but it was difficult when both Danny and Mitch seemed much happier the less contact they had with her. Still, she prepared for the date with Danny and had one short but important conversation with Mitch before she and Danny left for dinner. It was a conversation that she wanted to have on a date that included only Mitch and herself, but Mitch said he was too old for a date night with his sister. *Lame* was the word he used.

"Mitch, I need to know exactly how you're feeling about me being with Nathan." She used her firm voice, but it was more sisterly than it was motherly.

Mitch answered, albeit slowly and after he clapped his hands together and took a deep breath. He said, "I … I am still getting used to it."

"That's okay," she assured him. "That's normal. Are you thinking you can eventually get used to it?"

In his short pause, Mitch's face tightened as if it pained him to have to talk about this. "I'm really not sure," he said slowly. "It's not that I don't like him. It's just that you're our older sister, you know? You've never *not* been there for us, and I mean, I still need you. We all do."

Mitch's last words rung in Elizabeth's ears through her date with Danny, where the conversation was similar yet expanded.

"Okay, buddy. I need you tell me how you feel. Remember, you be honest with me, and I promise to be honest with you." She was trying to be firmly delicate.

Danny nodded.

Elizabeth asked, "Have you thought any more about what I said?"

He was fidgeting with his hands but managed to answer her in a regular voice. "Yes, I thought about it. But …"

She waited.

"But … I am not going to like it when you go away," he said.

"Why not?" She knew the answer, but she wanted to hear it from Danny.

He said, "Because Mom always went away, and you're not supposed to."

Evidence of the scars their mother left on her sons was obvious when statements like this came out of her brothers. Danny seemed genuinely pained uttering those words. She wasn't surprised at his honesty; Danny had always been able to articulate his feelings well. Everyone in the Tenner family held that skill. Elizabeth guessed it was because theirs wasn't a household where you weren't allowed to share your feelings. In fact, it was always encouraged. If not encouraged, most certainly provoked, if only because their mother was such an immature fighter; she was fueled by her kids fighting back.

Elizabeth's suspicions—and Bryce's words from their blowout not too long ago—were confirmed. She said to her little brother, "Honey, I will always come back."

"Yeah, but what if one time you don't? What if you like somewhere else better and you stay there?"

"Danny, I could never love anywhere else more than I love where I am with you and your brothers."

"Then why wouldn't you stay here all the time?" he asked.

Her eyes and heart begged him to understand.

"Danny, you know how sometimes you go to your friends' houses and sometimes they come here?"

"Yeah," he said, clearly not thinking this was the same. His look was a mixture of "duh" and "what's that got to do with anything?"

She answered plainly, "Well, it's just like that."

"But you'll be gone longer than when I hang out down the street," he reasoned.

"Yes, Danny, I will be. Because he lives farther away, so I have to travel to see him. But it's not fair for him to always come here, right? So I have to go there sometimes."

Elizabeth was saying everything with a mix of matter-offactness and compassion, sometimes one more than the other. She could see the wheels turning in his head, checking to see if the words she said matched how he felt in his heart.

"I guess that makes sense," he finally said.

"Does that mean you're more okay with it?"

"I don't know."

She smiled and said, "Maybe is good. We can work on maybe." She tousled his hair and pulled him into a hug, because she really loved her brothers, and sometimes she needed their hugs more than they needed hers.

A steady stream of thoughts kept up for the next few days, and every one of them led her no closer to a solution that would satisfy everyone. No matter how she sliced it, no matter who stayed or traveled, someone was left out. Or, worse, someone was left with a broken heart. The only thoughts on which Elizabeth could settle in a resolute manner were these: her brothers were more uncomfortable than she thought they would be; Nathan loved her; she loved Nathan. The last two thoughts were a pleasant surprise for a woman who rarely invested in any relationship regarding anything or anyone past chocolate, wine, or her brothers. Plus, Elizabeth realized that half of one of her puzzles—one being Nathan and the other being God—was figured out. Now, if she could get on board with the God thing, Nathan swore the situation would improve. Regardless, her brothers continued to be uneasy about her relationship with Nathan.

And so, four nights after the fight with Bryce, Elizabeth had enough of not thinking about or talking to her brothers about anything but homework and Nathan. After dinner on Thursday, she called a family meeting. Surprising herself, Elizabeth prayed—well, more begged—silently about the meeting before Bryce came from upstairs, and Mitch and Danny arrived from downstairs. She asked, "God, please help me here. Please put our hearts in the right place. Please help me keep my patience. Please."

Elizabeth took a deep breath and said to her brothers, "All right, guys. Time to talk. I was put in my place the other day about where you guys are with this whole Nathan thing. We've talked about it separately, and now we're going to talk together."

"You first," Danny said to Elizabeth. His arms were crossed and he was staring down at his bare feet. *So up and down. Not five minutes ago, he was laughing to the point of tears with Mitch over a video game.*

Yet before Elizabeth could get started, Bryce interrupted. "Elizabeth, I'm sorry I blew up at you the other night. That wasn't fair." He spoke honestly; she and her brothers gave him time to finish his thoughts. "What I told you was true; that we still need you, and that you should've thought more carefully about getting into this … situation. We like Nathan for you, Elizabeth. He takes care of you, he respects you. But our life is what it is, you know? It's hard to bring others in. But I—we—can't tell you what to do."

This was another reason Elizabeth absolutely loved this family. She knew that Bryce meant what he said, and that he was saying it in front of his brothers on purpose. She had hoped for an apology the day after the argument, but he was doing it now so their brothers could try to follow suit.

Sometimes my boys are such men. Elizabeth was eager to see what would follow. "So, what does this mean?" she asked.

Bryce answered, "It means that for now, we'll keep trying to get used to Nathan."

Now there were tears in Elizabeth's eyes. She was proud of her brothers for putting up with feeling uncomfortable. She had her hands on Danny's shoulders and told them it could get easier, but they had to keep being honest with her. When she got her chance to talk, she assured them that things could change, that she would be honest with them if they gave her the same courtesy, and she promised that big decisions would be family decisions. So for tonight, with their promises made to each other, an ice cream night ensued.

With only one more day left in the week, Elizabeth stayed up later than usual after the boys went to bed. She moved around the house with a mother's ease, cleaning and picking up after those she looked after. She thought about Nathan and what he might be doing. They had talked at least a few minutes every day that week, mostly because of Elizabeth's surprise phone call Sunday night and because of Elizabeth's multiple reassurances to Nathan that her decision wasn't rash. Rather, it had been thought out and realized earlier that night at dinner, and so the couple had settled into a new talking routine. But more than a routine, it was a call-when-you-want, less-rules-than-before kind of thing. Which is why on this night, what at one time might have been a surprise, was a welcomed 11:30 p.m. phone call from Nathan. She answered playfully, and he returned the joy, their easy conversation going for about ten minutes before Nathan grew unusually quiet.

"Is everything okay?" Elizabeth asked, confused by a sudden drop in the temperature of the call. He assured her he was fine, but, confusing her even more, asked her to hold on while he did something "real quick," which turned into four-and-a-half minutes. That's a long time when one is already confused about a situation. When Nathan finally came back on the line with a casual "okay," Elizabeth had about reached her breaking point of confusion. "Okay, what? What is going on?"

"Open your door."

She did just that and found a dozen white roses covering the face of a man whom she loved. Taking them, she discovered a smile so wide she almost didn't want to kiss him so it would stay there.

"What in the world are you doing here?" she asked excitedly.

"Do I need a reason to surprise my girl? I didn't want to wait any longer to see you; last weekend was a tease. I took tomorrow off, and here I am."

Brief were Elizabeth's thoughts about her brothers; she just as quickly remembered that she was an adult with a love life, one she was enjoying as it developed. They flirted and giggled quietly until reaching her bedroom where the two did what came most naturally: mix good conversation with kisses here and there. Their easy talk included a discussion about the family meeting. Nathan was pleased about Elizabeth's pre-meeting prayer.

She told him, "I think it might have made a difference."

"Yeah? Might have?" he asked, bordering on sarcasm.

"Yes. I felt calm and peaceful and almost hopeful—" Elizabeth halted her words when she realized Nathan might as well have had

"I TOLD YOU SO" stamped across his forehead. She pushed back. "You can't *prove* it was the prayer that did that."

Nathan smiled and said, "Whatever you say."

Banter continued back and forth, while the couple teased and laughed and tickled each other. At some point in the early morning, they fell asleep. Elizabeth was on her bed alone but was holding Nathan's hand as he slept next to her bed on the floor. When the alarm went off for the second time Friday morning, Elizabeth barely had her head off her pillow before Bryce walked in to get her out of bed. His head jerked back, and his startled gaze quickly taking in Nathan and Elizabeth. He pointedly told her breakfast was ready and wasn't the least bit shy in closing the door with authority.

Downstairs, Danny peppered Elizabeth with questions. He saw an extra car in the driveway and wanted—in no uncertain terms—to know why it was there. Casually mentioning that Nathan surprised her didn't go over well. Their expressions displayed unbelief, and an additional flash in Bryce's eyes spoke of anger. Few words were spoken aloud, but they might as well have had a full conversation with the fiery looks being tossed among everyone in the kitchen. Had she not just said that these kinds of decisions would be family decisions? But, thankful that they had to go to school, she simply said they'd talk about it that night at dinner. Handing off Mitch and Danny's lunch to each of them, she gave them a kiss on the cheek and sent them to the bus stop.

"Why isn't Bryce taking us today?" asked Mitch.

"I need to talk to him," she said quickly, feeling guilty for being the reason her brothers probably wouldn't enjoy their day. When they had shuffled out the door, Bryce all but tore her arm out of her socket with how hard he whipped her around. It didn't scare her; it would just be another one of their arguments. "Are you out of your mind, Liz? They're going to think you lied to them."

"They are not, Bryce! They know me better than that! He just showed up last night. What was I supposed to do?" she said, indignant.

"Tell him to find a hotel!" His words were loud, dramatic, forceful.

Elizabeth didn't know what to say; anything would have been adding fuel to the fire. All she could force out was, "Bryce, you have to get to school. Later. I love you. Goodbye." She barely had time to think, let alone have a conversation about the war going on inside her, the battle between understanding how her brothers could misconstrue Nathan's surprise and wanting so desperately not to have to defend the situation.

Nathan was waiting for Elizabeth in the living room. From the kitchen, she quickly tried to come up with a decision. She knew deep down what would win out, but she ran through every other possibility before she let herself concede to the inevitable. Allowing herself an inner temper tantrum, Elizabeth let go within her a string of profanities, cursing the difficulty of her situation, the setbacks that shouldn't be setbacks. After collecting herself and her thoughts, and wiping the two tears that escaped during her inner tirade, Elizabeth walked confidently into the living room. She knew Nathan had heard everything, but she still thought it best to tell him the bad news. With a tense expression, she said, "Nathan, I'm sorry, but you need to go home."

"Elizabeth, I—"

"No, Nathan. I need you to go. They need to know they can trust me. They need to know I am not leaving them, physically or otherwise. You showing up unexpected makes it look like I lied to them." Her words were hurried and anxious as she finished getting her things together for work. Her pseudo-confidence was crumbling, but if she kept moving, maybe she could avoid Nathan seeing right through her.

"You think they feel like they can't trust you?"

"I think their foundation has shifted a bit," she said.

"You're still *here*. I'm just here with you," said Nathan, walking closer to Elizabeth. She knew he was trying to stop her from moving so he could hold her while they talked, but she wouldn't have it. Being in Nathan's arms meant risking her resolve, something she often lost with Nathan. She kept God and others at bay, but Nathan had a free pass almost from the beginning. She didn't want to induce that now, but it seemed that in this moment, she had no choice.

"Liz—" he begged.

"Nathan, you need to leave for now. I'm sorry." There was no talking around this; her decision was made.

Nathan looked defeated, but he kept talking. "I wish you'd let me talk. And I wish you weren't asking me to go."

Elizabeth had tears in her eyes when she finally stopped moving around and responded to Nathan. Her eyes were steady and her body tense. "What I keep thinking about is a friend from college. She was dating a marine who was out in California for training. She had a class formal in New York. The boyfriend flew here from California to surprise her. But when he got to her apartment, she already had a date—with a friend of hers, but still a date. She wouldn't take her boyfriend because she felt the right thing to do was to honor her commitment to her date."

"And where are they now?" Nathan asked with a sigh.

"Been married eight years, just had their first child. A beautiful baby girl."

Elizabeth looked at Nathan. Through his eyes, Elizabeth was sure she saw compassion mixed with anger, understanding mixed with disbelief. She was relieved when he accepted.

He asked, still sounding defeated, "Are you still coming in three weeks?"

"I want to." Nathan told her that wasn't an answer; he asked for a yes or a no; she gave him an I-don't-know. Yet, it was all she had, torn between whose feelings to consider first: hers, Nathan's, or her brothers'.

Elizabeth didn't slow down to take a breath until she was a few minutes down the road on her way to work. Stopping to talk to Nathan for the quick few minutes didn't count; her heart had still been pounding well above its normal pace. Once she took the moment to process the string of events that had just taken place, the anger came in waves, along with the assaulting thought that her brothers might never be happy with Nathan in their lives, and the daunting feeling of how unfair that was. Elizabeth had given up so much by raising the boys and never complained about it; so why, this one time when she'd fight hard not to sacrifice what she wanted, were they so resistant to it?

She banged the steering wheel and kicked her feet in a fit of anger, but despite her anxiety and frustration, Elizabeth felt strongly that she should go to North Carolina in three weeks. As she decided this, something suddenly came to her mind: Nathan hadn't said anything about God in their conversation. She determined that he had probably forgotten.

Or maybe he tried when I kept cutting him off, she thought to herself. *I wonder if it would have mattered if God was mentioned. It's not as if He's done anything for us, anyway.*

Elizabeth reasoned with herself that she and her brothers had made a commitment to go forward with Nathan, making a concentrated effort to be comfortable with his and Elizabeth's relationship. Part of that commitment was accepting the fact that Elizabeth would go away sometimes. The boys would be fine for one weekend. Between now and then, Elizabeth could will her brothers into being more comfortable with the situation. Three weeks. Twenty-one days. That was enough time to thaw some hearts. Right now, she had to focus on getting herself together enough to go into work, which seemed a Herculean task this morning. The weight was slowly but surely boring into her rock-solid resolve not to accept Nathan's faith-based help. She recognized that if something as simple and mundane as going into work felt like the last straw, then she most certainly was dissolving at a far faster pace than she realized.

For the rest of the day, Elizabeth pondered on and off over her conversation with Nathan. He was always trying to tell her how much God cared and how He shows grace to people's hearts when they feel anxious or sad; why didn't he do that today?

It dawned on her that maybe Nathan was showing instead of telling today; his actions certainly displayed grace. Elizabeth wished she could feel that, the grace and peace Nathan talked so much about. Even this morning, Nathan had been angry, but he stayed so calm. For what felt like the hundredth time since she met Nathan, Elizabeth wasn't sure what to do with her thoughts and feelings, so she put them aside for the time being. Instead, she thought about some ways to connect with her brothers over the next three weeks. Some restoration was in order for the Tenner family since her last effort was thwarted by Nathan's surprise appearance. She wrote down her ideas and thought of when she could bring them to fruition. Planning was good for her; Elizabeth looked toward the next two weeks with a renewed sense of hope.

Chapter 12

"Cynicism is not realistic and tough. It's unrealistic and kind of cowardly because it means you don't have to try."
~Peggy Norman

H ER PLANS WOULD WORK well—except that for the whole following week Elizabeth felt like she was walking on eggshells again at her house: Bryce kept conversation to a minimum, and Mitch and Danny seemed particularly moody.

Elizabeth had talked to each of the boys privately about Nathan's surprise visit; they seemed to believe her, but by their shifting glances, she knew they were at least a little unsure. She talked to them about the pros of having Nathan around: he goes to church, he likes football and soccer, he's one more to outnumber Elizabeth for movies. All to no avail. No amount of genuine effort to get the boys into the idea of Nathan was working for her. His surprise caused a greater stumble than she anticipated. Her renewed hope was quickly fading into the background of her familiar fear and anxiety. But still, she held her ground and reminded each of them that she would be visiting Nathan in three weekends. A feeling of discouragement flooded her heart when she received verbatim responses from Mitch and Danny in different conversations.

"Do you have to go, Liz?" they asked.

She answered, "Yes, it's my turn to go there. He's been here twice."

"*Three* times," Bryce interjected. Elizabeth didn't dignify his snide remark with a response.

"But we need you here," Mitch and Danny had both said.

"You understand it's only for the weekend, right?" she said.

Mitch and Danny had nodded their understanding but seemed to do so grudgingly.

By Friday night, she couldn't take the icebox that was her house any longer. Elizabeth deferred to her written-down list of ways to improve her family's mood by making the evening all about her and the boys. She got their favorite foods ready for dinner and dessert: a taco line and cheesecake. She pulled games from the closet and took out a few movies she knew they'd love to watch that she would never pick if it was her choice. Elizabeth wanted to believe the boys would respond with big smiles, but she had to be realistic. This never-ending transition made their dispositions anything but predictable these days. Still, when she heard Bryce's car pull into the driveway around seven, Elizabeth was ready to hope for the best. Elizabeth hoped that if she stayed hopeful and positive, they would too. She greeted them in the driveway so she could surprise them with the food as they walked into the house.

"Hey, guys! Happy Friday! Did you have a good day?"

"Fridays are always good, Lizzie," said Danny, upbeat. Elizabeth smiled at the name he called her; "Lizzie" hadn't come from Danny in a happy manner in a long time. The last time he said it, he had been crying because he felt like Elizabeth was about to leave the family.

"I agree," Elizabeth said. "But I thought this Friday we could go for an *extra*-good day." She opened the door wider. When the boys saw everything she had prepared, they seemed genuinely surprised, like they'd never seen their kitchen full like it was.

"Is Nathan here or something?" asked Mitch.

"No," answered Elizabeth, confused and deflating a little bit. "Why would he be here? This is for us! Family night. Tacos, cheesecake, games, movies. Like it's always been." She added, "Like it's always going to be."

The boys looked at each other, probably doubting Elizabeth's last statement, she figured. But Bryce jumped in and volunteered to go first, so the night began. Elizabeth knew Bryce was, again, trying to encourage Mitch and Danny to join in, and it worked. Within twenty minutes, everyone was eating something, laughing every few minutes during one of their favorite movies, and completely comfortable with each other.

After eating three tacos each—except for Danny, who ate five—Elizabeth, Bryce, Mitch, and Danny finished off the entire cheesecake while they watched a second movie. Once Danny ate his last bite, just as the credits were rolling, Danny said, "Now, what are we going to eat while we play Settlers of Catan?"

"Danny you can't be serious," said Bryce, staring in disbelief at his little brother.

"Yet, I am. I say: another round of tacos," he said as he clapped his hands together.

"We ate everything already," said Mitch.

"Oh yeah. How about ..." Danny looked at the ceiling, heavily contemplating what next he wanted to eat. Then he remembered. "Oh! Those chocolate covered pretzels."

"We don't have any of those either," said Elizabeth.

"Let's run and get some, then. Liz, you and Mitch set up the game, Bryce and I will go to the store." Danny's enthusiasm left little room for debate. His siblings laughed, but they indulged Danny. He was in better spirits than he had been in weeks, and they all wanted to keep that going.

Bryce won the game, which was no surprise since he always won. What did amaze all four members of the Tenner family was that the entire bag of chocolate covered pretzels was gone by the end of the game. So much for being full.

Amidst yawns and big bedtime stretches, Mitch asked for a third movie. Elizabeth and the other brothers obliged, just as they had with Danny's run to the store. They obliged, but with full knowledge that they were all tired well beyond being able to watch an entire movie. A strong sense of family, of togetherness, dominated the Tenner siblings that night. They were one unit, the team they hadn't been in weeks, since before Nathan had entered the picture.

Not one sibling wanted this night to end; it was too familiar, in the best sense of the word. Even so, not thirty minutes after Mitch pressed "play," Elizabeth, Bryce, Mitch, and Danny were asleep in various places around the Tenner family living room.

———————

Elizabeth awoke before her brothers Saturday morning. Before her eyelids were open, she considered what a great night she and her brothers just had; it gave her a hope for the future of her relationships with her siblings and Nathan. This steady stream of thoughts about her brothers, Nathan, God, and anything else that related to those three things started up each morning the moment her body registered a sense of being awake. The stream was its own entity; it needed not one cup of coffee, not one bit of warm-up in the mornings. It was on a dimmer switch at night when she was falling asleep—fading, but not completely gone. But in the mornings, there was no dimmer, only "on" or "off," but it was always—always—stuck at "on."

Elizabeth thought about her great night with Bryce, Mitch, and Danny, and about going to North Carolina in two weekends. She tried to figure out a way to bridge those two things; how could she go from being in a great place with her brothers to talking with them about something with which they weren't completely comfortable?

A solution to that problem didn't come on Saturday, as the weekend followed the boys' recent pattern. As Friday was fun and light, Saturday was discouraging. Elizabeth found a bad test grade in Danny's homework folder that Bryce had signed, and Mitch got mad at her for being on the phone with Nathan for two hours while he and Danny watched a movie. It mattered, he said, because he wanted her to watch the movie with them. Reasoning that she watched two movies with them the previous night and played a long game of Settlers of Catan, Elizabeth let herself sit on the porch to talk with Nathan. She even managed to be mostly present for the conversation; only part of her was in the living room, removing the hurt from her middle brother's face and heart.

With such up and down cues and words from her brothers—the three people in this world who not only mattered most to her but for whom she was responsible—it was no wonder that Elizabeth had such a time completely settling herself in this relationship with Nathan. Continued encouragement from Nathan helped some, and despite her brothers' attitudes, she actually thought she was doing a good job of balancing the men in her life.

Elizabeth prepared homemade pasta sauce on Sunday afternoon for dinner, and she used this time to remind her brothers that she would be going to North Carolina soon. She asked if there was anything special they would like for the weekend between now and then.

Mitch was the first to respond. "You know, Liz, you don't have to do special stuff for us just because you feel guilty."

What she wanted to say—no, scream—was, "Well then, what would you like me to do? If I'm doing something for you, I'm accused of doing it out of guilt. If I'm gone, you're upset. Make up your mind!" But, of course, she remained calm in her response, even if his words did bring her down a couple notches. She said, "Mitch, we've *always* done fun stuff together. We hang out because we're a family that likes to hang out with each other."

Nobody said anything.

"Well, we'll think about it this week," said Elizabeth, conceding to the silence.

After dinner, Elizabeth pulled Bryce aside to talk on the porch. She was becoming frustrated with his on-and-off support. He sometimes encouraged Mitch and Danny, but tonight he was quiet during dinner, not offering any suggestions for next weekend, nor did he back her up on not having to feel guilty about visiting Nathan. She wondered if the boys were still talking about the situation among themselves despite the promise they'd made to keep everything out in the open.

"What's up, Elizabeth?" Bryce's tone conveyed that he knew this was going to be an important discussion.

"Why were you so quiet during dinner?" she asked.

"I didn't have anything to say," he said, shrugging.

"Well, I could've used your help," she said.

"What do you mean?" asked Bryce in a flat tone.

"I mean, we've been a team for a long time, and now it feels like you're hanging me out to dry. You're confusing me. You start out by helping me, like Friday at dinner, but it's only once in a while, and it never goes further than your first sentence."

"Welcome to the club," said Bryce with no compassion.

"What is that supposed to mean?" asked Elizabeth.

"Exactly what I said. Welcome to the feeling that your main support has left you out to dry."

"Again, what is that supposed to mean? We already had that conversation. And I've still packed every lunch. I've still helped with homework. I've still been making dinner almost every night. And next weekend is the first time I will be gone since I first went in the summer."

"Liz, I don't know what else to tell you. All I know is Mitch and Danny have talked to their youth leaders at church enough about this to where the youth leaders are talking to me about it. Nathan being here, you being on the phone with him almost every night, and now you're going there … Your mind and heart used to be 1,000 percent here. Now it's split in half, and I hate seeing what it's doing to the boys."

Elizabeth got defensive about her brothers talking to people at church. They already knew too much, in Elizabeth's opinion, about the Tenner family. She didn't need them to think Elizabeth was the same kind of mom her mother had been. Bryce assured her that the youth pastors were actually trying to get Mitch and Danny used to the idea of Nathan, especially since he was a Christian. But Elizabeth had a hard time believing that. She kept trying to argue that point, but Bryce stopped her.

"This is not about church, this is about our family," said Bryce, now becoming more engaged in the conversation. "It has nothing to do with getting along with Nathan. He's a great guy. It's the fact that you are not here, emotionally and soon physically, as much as we're used to. It would have been this way no matter who you brought home."

"Well, I thought you guys were going to keep trying?" she said, still defensive.

"We are, but it's still going to go up and down."

Bryce, like the others, was wise beyond his years. Elizabeth knew this, but moments when this quality shined always stunned her, threw her off a bit. She quickly found her footing, however, and went back to the Jesus stuff, which is what Elizabeth had taken to calling all talk surrounding church or God or Jesus. She said, "Oh, and by the way, I once called Nathan a Christian, and he corrected me. He said he's a follower of Christ rather than 'Christian.'"

Bryce smiled. He was drumming his fingers on the porch railing.

"What? Is it some church talk or joke I don't get because I don't go?" she said, annoyed.

"No, no," Bryce said, smiling. "That's ... that's pretty cool. That man loves Jesus, Liz."

"Right, and if that's what you boys are all about, then why isn't this okay?" Elizabeth felt like she kept asking this question, and had not yet gotten a satisfactory answer.

Bryce took a deep breath and looked at his older sister. She could see he was trying to put his thoughts into words. When he finally did, he slowly said, "Remember when we were little, and Grandma and Grandpa took you and me to the zoo? I was, like, six or seven, so you must have been about thirteen."

"Yeah?" Elizabeth was unsure of where Bryce was going.

"Do you remember what happened when we got home?"

Elizabeth's brow furrowed. "No ..."

"Well, I do. Mitch was only three, and Danny wasn't even one. Mom had begged Grandma and Grandpa to leave them with her. I remember because they fought about it. We got home from the zoo, and Grandpa saw Mitch sitting in the living room watching television, and Danny was in his high chair in the kitchen. Grandpa called for Mom, but no one answered. Next thing I know, Mom is running into the house. I guess she had left for a while, trying to be back before we got home. But she didn't make it. She had left her three- and one-year-old sons home. Alone."

"I don't need you to tell me what a terrible mother we had."

"My point, Liz, is that she left us time and time again. Mitch and Danny were born into a life of being constantly left and let down. More so than you and me, because at least we can remember Grandma and Grandpa more than they can."

The brother and sister were quiet for a few minutes before Elizabeth told Bryce she didn't have an answer.

"I don't know, Liz. Pray about it." With that, Bryce went inside to get ready for the upcoming week.

Elizabeth had tears in her eyes; this was unfair. Their lives were a byproduct of the choices made by her parents. She was thrown into the role of mom without any warning, training, or say-so in the matter. She had long since let go of resentment toward her parents; she supposed that was because of her grandparents' influence. But never had she been faced with a decision or situation that challenged not only her role of mom but also her belief that she was no longer angry with her parents. Nathan appearing and every decision she had been faced with since wiping her smoothie off her clothes and skin had brought a renewed sense of frustration that she couldn't have her own non-mom life. And it made her very aware of the fact that her current situation—backed by unresolved anger as it was—needed to be dealt with, and soon.

Thus, the next two weeks before going to see Nathan were awful for Elizabeth. She barely slept, couldn't concentrate, and even had to take a sick day from work because of how she was feeling: heavy, discouraged, frustrated—always frustrated. Elizabeth weighed her options constantly. On the phone with Nathan, she barely talked about how her brothers were doing; she preferred to think about and decide on a solution on her own. She reasoned that if she talked with her brothers, they would ask her to leave Nathan, or at the very least stay as vague and aloof as they had been all along. If she talked to Nathan, he would convince her to keep going, certain Bryce, Mitch, and Danny would eventually come around. No, she would decide on her own. Even though, at the heart of it, she always knew what her decision would be, what her decision had always been.

Finally, the Friday came when Elizabeth was scheduled to leave for Nathan's. A storm was brewing outside. Much like the one in her heart, this one seemed to be threatening and violent. Her mind said two different things: *I can't wait to hug him* and *Don't go; you're just going to break his heart.* She had weighed the decision in her mind what felt like a hundred times. Saying goodbye to Nathan seemed best for the boys, but the devastation she and Nathan were about to feel—that she already had a taste of—was unnerving. Elizabeth was already beginning to experience the sadness of not having Nathan in her life, but she knew the feeling would gain strength after the multiple conversations they were bound to have this weekend. She knew he would try to understand, but that ultimately, he couldn't. How could he? He had a normal life, with adult parents who carried baggage but who for the most part took care of themselves.

Elizabeth wasn't even sure how she was going to say it. Every conversation she practiced in her mind fizzled out due to the weakness of her words. She didn't want it to be like removing a bandage: quick and painless, meant to uncover a healing wound. The wound would be far from healed, even if they settled everything on good terms. Elizabeth knew her decision wouldn't be something Nathan could accept right away. He would want to talk about it, in excruciating detail, and try to convince her that she was making the wrong decision.

Nathan had come into their lives with such energy, determined to fit into the Tenner family. Elizabeth knew that his efforts were not for nothing; the boys had softer hearts and a different, more mature view of their big sister. But they were still moving through feeling uncomfortable, angry, confused, and wondering why Elizabeth needed another man in her life; that had to be exhausting. For each of them, the nagging question of a young boy who could never look up to his parents would never quite go away: *Why aren't I enough?*

In what felt like an instant, the storm outside turned from swirling winds to clouds breaking and the sun shining down on Elizabeth's tense body. She basked in the warmth and decided the break in trepid weather was a good time to leave for the airport. Her stuff was packed; she only had to bring it to the car. None of the boys were home, but they knew she'd be gone by the afternoon. They had hugged her goodbye that morning, seeing in her eyes and actions the heaviness she was feeling.

The Tenner family situation was so delicate; all they all ever wanted was a lasting stability inside the home. Bryce once told Elizabeth that he and the other boys were more stable with her than they ever were with their parents, but Elizabeth could only do so much. With nothing and no one to lean on, Elizabeth knew voids existed, gaps that the boys tripped over once in a while. And then she brought Nathan into the picture, which did anything but fill a void like a man's presence could in a normal, functional family.

The sunshine stuck around long enough for Elizabeth's flight to leave on time. Her stomach was doing flip-flops upon arrival as she walked up the terminal in North Carolina; her steps progressively faster as she saw Nathan standing at the end of the long hallway. Her reunion was everything she needed: a big bear hug and kisses to boot. They walked straight to the beach, Jax in tow, at Elizabeth's request. In the late afternoon sun, Elizabeth and Nathan were lying on the beach in thick sweatshirts, cuddled under a blanket with Jax relaxing just beside them. Elizabeth was enjoying the rhythmic crashing of the waves, but she was distracted. Eventually, she was going to have to say it; eventually, sometime this weekend, she was going to have to break up with Nathan. She knew it should happen sooner rather than later, but Elizabeth kept failing to find an opening in the conversation—until Nathan asked her how the rest of her week had gone. Elizabeth and Nathan hadn't gotten a lot of phone time because of Nathan's work schedule; it was conference week and grades were due, so he wanted to know about the pieces he had missed.

Elizabeth answered his question cautiously with wavering breath, "It … was … okay."

"Just okay?"

Elizabeth looked at Nathan's genuinely concerned expression. She hated what was coming. "It was up and down," she said.

"At work or at home?" asked Nathan, genuinely concerned.

"At home." Elizabeth was barely getting out her words.

"Liz, what's going on?" Elizabeth could tell that Nathan saw something stirring within her, and that it was bothersome.

She dove right in, for lack of any better ideas on how to approach the subject: "Nathan, we have to talk. Since you surprised me a couple of weeks ago, I've had a bunch of conversations with my brothers, and I've been doing *so* much thinking—probably way too much—and I think—"

"It sounds like you're about to break this off," said Nathan with a strong voice that demanded an immediate, truthful answer.

Elizabeth shrugged her right shoulder and opened her mouth to respond, but Nathan kept talking.

"Elizabeth, don't tell me that's what you were going to say." They were both sitting up now, Nathan staring hard into Elizabeth's tired, sad eyes.

She could hear the forceful pleading in Nathan's voice, but she had already made up her mind. "Nathan, listen to me. This is tearing my family apart," she said.

"Liz, listen to *me*. I know it's been hard on you guys as a family, but I really believe we'll come out better on the other side of this if we stick with it."

"You're not there every day, Nathan. It's really hard," she said, her voice almost cracking.

"Of course it is," he said. "The situation is one your family has never dealt with before. But great things are done because people push through tough. They say, 'yeah, this is hard, but I think it'll be worth it.' Characters in the books I read with my students are all about facing difficulties but going ahead anyway, and things always work out. But only because people pushed through."

Elizabeth answered, "But not everything works out like the stories you read."

"But they can, Liz." Nathan was adamant. He tried out three examples of stories where the outcome wouldn't be possible without someone in the book/narrative/real-life situation not letting up until he or she achieved the set-upon goal. Elizabeth listened but rolled her eyes at two of his examples, thinking they were much too dissimilar from her situation—they were fictitious. This was real life. The true example he gave was much too rare, she said.

"I have three brothers at home who are hurting. I have to be realistic. Sometimes things don't work out!"

"Did you ever think that by trying to be realistic, you're actually being cynical? That you're not putting any faith in anything or anyone, including yourself?"

Nathan inhaled and exhaled deeply before continuing. Elizabeth could see he was trying to keep his cool; she knew he didn't like yelling. But he was clearly getting more upset as the conversation wore on. When Nathan continued he said, "You said you've been 'thinking.' Have you been *praying* about it? About us? For us? For your family?"

"Ugh! Nathan! Why does God want to hear from me? I don't trust Him like you do!"

"You've got to start somewhere, Elizabeth. Why not with this relationship, right now?"

"I don't have to start if I don't want to. Praying and believing, it's not an on/off switch," she said defensively, angry that he expected her to just snap her fingers and know how to pray.

"No, but it can be an on-ramp. Pray with me. Come to church with me tomorrow night. You need to enlist God's help here because you're crumbling on your own." Now Nathan's voice was cracking. "We're crumbling."

Elizabeth thought about his last statement. He was right; she was falling apart on her own, and because of that, their relationship was at stake. Her thoughts were again playing ping-pong in her head while Nathan held both her hands, his heart-filled gaze pleading for Elizabeth to agree.

Maybe going to church will help.

How? Nathan's been praying this whole time, and we're still a mess.

Maybe that's because you're not praying.

Why do my prayers matter?

Because it's my heart too. Not just Nathan's.

For a full thirty seconds after her last thought, Elizabeth's mind seemed frozen, caught in between what she saw as rational and irresponsible. But finally, grudgingly, she agreed to go to church with Nathan. "I'm here all weekend, anyway."

"That's the spirit," said Nathan dryly. But it made Elizabeth laugh, so the tension broke slightly. They got ready to walk back to Nathan's house.

"Now, I want you to put all your reservations aside for tonight because we have plans, and there is no room for cranky," said Nathan.

Again Elizabeth laughed; she loved that Nathan could always lighten her load. As he took her bags up to his spare bedroom and got Jax settled with some dinner, Elizabeth kept her thoughts moving. *I'll start praying. I'll see what Nathan's church has to offer. I just want my family to be okay. Nathan ...* Elizabeth choked back tears, lost in her thoughts. *Nathan is my dream come true.*

Nathan's romantic evening turned out to be dinner at a beachside restaurant, a movie downtown, and, much to her surprise, candlelit dessert at Nathan's house. When she saw the setup at his house—which a friend of his had put together while the two were gone to dinner and the movie—Elizabeth said, "What is this? No guy does this."

"For your information, some do. Like me. See, I'm doing it right now," he said.

To add to the candles and wine, Nathan started up some music. Then he took Elizabeth's hand, pulled her close, and swayed so slowly she was barely aware that they were moving. Yet, as romantic as it was, Elizabeth couldn't accept the reality of the moment.

She said, "Nathan, I'm sorry. I don't mean to ruin the moment or whatever, but ... this is the stuff great chick flicks are made of. This is not reality." She was shaking her head as she spoke, pulling back to look into his eyes.

"Hmmm. Again with the reality thing. This is happening in real time, Liz," said Nathan, which made Elizabeth laugh again. "I guess you can tell your friends that you starred in your very own romantic comedy. Me being the romantic and the comedy, because you're being too cynical to be either one. Now, be quiet and enjoy my loving you."

———————

Church was on Saturday afternoon. When they pulled up to a building that looked more like a concert venue than a church, Elizabeth doubted Nathan's plans.

"I thought you said we were going to church?"

"We are; this is it. See? ENC Christian Church." Nathan pointed to the larger-than-life gray stone sign on the front grounds of the building.

"ENC?" asked Elizabeth.

"Eastern North Carolina," he said.

"Oh. This is a huge building," she said, eyeing the massive structure before her. The lawn and parking lots, all three of them, expanded far out from the building, indicating a substantially-sized congregation. On one side sat a glorified pond: not quite small, but not large by any stretch of the imagination. Parking attendants with traffic-directing light sabers stood at various points around the lots because there were at least a couple hundred cars pouring in from two different entrances. The very front entrance was covered with a structural canopy, but bold landscaping lined the rest of the building, of what Elizabeth saw, anyway. There were distinct patches of gardenias, daisies, annuals, and sunflowers, the last of which caught her eye the longest because there, in the middle of more subdued flowers and the hustle of pre-service activity, the sunflowers were tall, strong, and swayed just slightly so that you knew they were real, living things. Elizabeth watched them all the way until she and Nathan reached the side entrance near the glorified pond where a "BEWARE OF ALLIGATORS" sign stole her attention; if anything was going to get Elizabeth to hustle inside a church, it would be the threat of alligators. Nothing like being motivated by one fear to get over another; Elizabeth gladly walked into that building to put a safe barrier between herself and the alligators.

"You're sure this is a church?" Elizabeth sounded unsure of what she was about to walk into.

"I'm sure. We've been in this building for about three years. It's still pretty new."

The large building intimidated Elizabeth. Maybe that's because it didn't look like a traditional church, and as they walked into the lobby, it didn't have a traditional church feel, either. She was grateful for the large number of people; she felt like she could blend in with the crowd. After quickly passing more than a dozen people Nathan knew, Elizabeth let Nathan direct her to where he usually sat: ten rows from the front, center aisle.

Elizabeth saw on a movie screen at the front of the room that there was a countdown going; she supposed it was the time until service started. Almost three minutes for Elizabeth to sit and fidget with her purse, the program—Nathan called it a bulletin—and a Bible that sat under the seat in front of her. She didn't want to make eye contact with anyone there; she was sure they could tell she hadn't been in a church in a long while. Her heart actually jumped for joy when the music started; it meant no more avoiding the couple to her right and families in front of and behind her.

Right away, Elizabeth loved the music. It was upbeat and contemporary, but more than that, it was honest. People were singing with their hands raised, and when Elizabeth looked at Nathan, she could see he was singing with his whole heart. Elizabeth had never seen that look on Nathan's face before; it seemed a transcendent peace.

If it means this much to him, I should give this a fair shot. She looked up at the big video screens with the song lyrics and sang along. Her eyes stayed open and her arms down at her sides unlike the others around her, but at least she was singing.

I'm on my own, so take me
I'm lost in this life, so lead me
Where is there to go?
What is there to do?
I'm on my own, so take me
I'm lost in this life, so lead me

I'm lost in this life, so heal me

The words seemed to hit Elizabeth as she felt her chest thump louder than usual. She needed to be healed and she needed to be led, just as the song described. She felt the same connection to the next two songs the band sang.

The first was meant to be a light-at-the-end-of-the-tunnel parallel. Her favorite lyric was the last verse:

My heart is tired
But you promise rest
I'll hold on
If you keep Your word
I know You will, I know You will

Again, Nathan was singing loudly, and he had his eyes closed. His arms were at his sides, which she appreciated. Others around the room with their hands and arms raised didn't bother her, but she supposed that was because it was at a distance. If the person she came with participated in such a display of emotion, Elizabeth would have felt caught between following his lead or her instinctual timidity inside the church. But, really, Elizabeth was getting too much out of the music to be distracted by watching someone else. She kept her eyes and heart forward, unintentionally leaning forward with interest.

The third and final song caught her interest too; it was another upbeat tune, and the singer's expression showed nothing less than complete joy:

Wherever I am
Your praises I sing
You saved the day
Wherever I am
Your praises I sing
Your promises stand, you saved all of my days

All right, Elizabeth thought. *Let's see how the rest of this goes.*

The pastor seemed to be in his fifties, but he had more energy than the twenty-somethings Elizabeth knew back home. From his introduction, she knew she should pay attention:

"Those were some greats songs, weren't they? Man, I just love starting this thing off with music. And they're perfect for today because we're going to talk about how we can hold onto God to push through difficult circumstances in our lives. Because God is a God of perseverance and strength and grace. And when we hold onto Him, He helps us with those things too. Let's dive in."

For the next forty minutes, Elizabeth listened to the jubilant pastor say everything that had been on her heart over the last few months, since the first visit from Nathan when the boys started distancing themselves from her. The difference between the pastor's words and the thoughts running through her mind was that the pastor intermixed reasons and practical ways to rely on God through those kinds of difficult times; Elizabeth always found excuses for why she didn't need to rely on God. The pastor cited examples from the Bible that went over Elizabeth's head, but they sounded legitimate, and she understood his point.

The end of service was fairly unceremonious compared to the rest of it. The pastor finished talking and before she knew it, the lights were brighter and everyone was standing up and filing out of the auditorium-like space. Though she was thankful not to have the awkwardness of having to talk to someone she didn't know, she had been looking forward to more music. When Nathan nudged her along, she followed him quietly to the car, and stayed that way until after a quick grocery store stop.

"So, what'd you think?" Nathan finally asked her. His words weren't exactly cautious, but Elizabeth knew he had carefully chosen when he would ask the question. A simple question of four words, but it was the answer that had the potential for great consequences. Even so, Elizabeth couldn't help injecting some light play into the conversation.

"Think about what?" she asked.

Nathan rolled his eyes. "The grocery store."

"It was fine. Good selection. Could use a bigger chocolate section, though."

Nathan smiled. "Surprise, surprise. But really, what'd you think?"

"I guess they could use a better deli too."

"Liz," said Nathan dryly. He'd had enough.

Elizabeth winked in Nathan's direction and said, "Remember, you love me."

Nathan smiled again. "That I do. Now, what did you think?"

"Boy you're nosy. I thought … I … hmm, I got a lot out of it." Elizabeth sounded shy about her experience. Even if she took a lot in to think about, it didn't mean she was ready to jump into the baptism pool and completely reverse the way she thought about things. Hesitant to give in too much to Nathan so he wouldn't get overly excited, she kept her cool. Yet, he seemed to have expected her answer.

"I thought you would," he said.

"Yeah, did you pay the pastor to say that stuff?" Her sly smile was full of teasing and affection.

"A nominal fee," Nathan said with a sideways glance and a smile to match. He asked, "Is there anything you'd like to talk about?"

"I guess I just want to let you know that I haven't given up on this working out. Your pastor said a lot of things about trusting God that I've never heard before." She was confident in her words but still looked out the window as she said them.

"Yeah?" asked Nathan with strong optimism.

"Yes. If God can move mountains and, what is it, make roads, like in—" This time she searched for a verse she had copied down on her program. "What is it? A road in the wilderness? … Here it is: 'I will even make a road in the wilderness and rivers in the desert,' Isaiah 43:19, then maybe He can turn this whole thing around."

The look on Nathan's face was one of hope and happiness. Elizabeth was amazed to find no hesitation in Nathan's expression. He was so content, so peaceful. Which, honestly, she still didn't understand. Didn't he get nervous about this not working out? Didn't he worry that she would never come all the way over to the God-side, as she called it? He seemed too calm too often.

"I'm just not worried right now. Sometimes I am, though," Nathan responded. "That you'll choose to walk away, that your brothers will never be comfortable with this, that kind of stuff. Same as you."

"You always sound so sure when we talk," she said skeptically. She racked her brain for even one time when he said or sounded like he might say, "We won't survive this," but it was to no avail. Nathan might have been angry, not understanding, or frustrated, but he never seemed to lose faith. Elizabeth was glad to learn that he thought some of the same things she did. However, she made sure to note the reason she thought it might be a little easier for him.

"I think it helps you that you pray about it," Elizabeth told Nathan.

"You're catching on," he said with another sideways glance.

The rest of the weekend was filled with similar conversations, as it seemed the topic was permanently fixed on Elizabeth's mind and as such, mini spurts of her thoughts and questions made their way out of her mouth. The one reverberating, broken-record statement was the half-dozen times she said, "My heart feels strange."

The last time she made the declaration was on the way to the airport late Sunday morning, to which Nathan replied, "I think it might be finally opening up to something bigger than your family."

Chapter 13

"Life will reveal answers at the pace life wishes to do so. You feel like running, but life is on a stroll. This is how God does things."
~*Donald Miller, Blue Like Jazz*

ELIZABETH PULLED UP TO her house around 4:30 Sunday afternoon. She could smell snow in the air of the late October evening, though it wasn't yet falling. The scent was a familiar one, strong in its reminder that the next season was well on its way. Usually a transition in the weather didn't faze Elizabeth in the least; she had become an expert in survival mode, which meant she just kept moving, no matter the time of year or the chaos going on around her. This year, though, the sense of snow seemed to fill and lift her spirits, bringing with it a feeling of renewal.

She had come away from the weekend at Nathan's with a four-part plan: First, Elizabeth was going to go to church with the boys each Sunday. She would listen intently to the music and the sermons, and talk to the boys about what she heard. Second, Elizabeth would pray every morning. Nathan's pastor said that if a person starts off the day talking to God, it's easier to hear Him throughout the rest of the day. She wasn't sure if that was true, but she was willing to give it a try. Third, she would refuse to argue with her brothers—only calm talking from now on. And last, before she took any of the first three actions, Elizabeth wanted to bring her brothers up to speed on her decisions. And while they didn't greet her in the same loud way they had in the summer after her first trip to North Carolina, Elizabeth could tell they were happy to see her back home. She had barely dropped her bags before they came to hug her. They immediately returned to the tasks they had been busy with before she arrived home: Bryce was setting the table, Mitch was draining pasta, and Danny was stirring sauce on the stove.

"How was your weekend?" asked Bryce, genuinely and without a hint of sadness or resentment.

"It was great, thanks, Bryce." Elizabeth noticed how calm her brothers were acting. It felt strange, but she didn't let it deter her from letting them know she had important things to tell them. This made her brothers look at her with alarm, but Elizabeth left them in suspense while she put her bags upstairs. Her ears echoed with the sound of a heart that was beating harder than usual; in an effort to keep her cool, Elizabeth walked up to her room, changed her clothes, and took a deep breath before walking back down into the kitchen.

"Looks good, guys. Thanks for making dinner," she said, trying to steady herself before sharing her string of revelations.

"No problem," said Danny. "We've been looking forward to you coming home tonight."

"Me too," she said with a smile.

"Can I pray?" asked Bryce when they sat at the table.

"Of course," said Elizabeth, though no differently than she had ever agreed to prayer at the dinner table. She didn't want to give anything away too early; her speech was too planned out. Any misstep and she might forget.

"Dear Heavenly Father, thank you for today. Thank You for bringing Liz home safely, for the food in front of us, and for being forever faithful."

Bryce stopped for a moment; he sounded choked up.

When he started back up, all he said was, "We love you, Lord. Amen."

"Thanks, Bryce," said Elizabeth. "Before I jump in with my stuff, do you guys have anything to tell me?" She sensed there was something the brothers wanted to share, because she had been playing the role of mom for a long time and big sister well before that. Their peaceful demeanor, asking kindly about her weekend, Bryce almost crying during his prayer, all indicated something was to be discussed; she could read them all too well. It didn't surprise her, then, when Bryce launched into a quick rundown of their weekend: a last-minute youth retreat where Bryce was a chaperone. It focused on one single verse: 2 Timothy 1:7: "God has not given us a spirit of fear but of one of power, love, and self-discipline." There was a lot of praying—together and separately, he assured her—and it all surrounded the idea of bringing Nathan into the family. Bryce talked about how they used this verse for many things: sports, sharing their faith, but never had they applied it to their current situation. They didn't need to be afraid, because if God brought Nathan into their lives, He had a reason. It sounded cliché even to Elizabeth, but sometimes clichés were only true statements set to repeat. And stripped to their core, they were still true statements. Finally, he explained how excited they were to have Elizabeth back home. They missed her, he told her.

Bryce's short speech was given at record speed, giving Elizabeth barely any time to process any more than a few key words: fear, love, praying, and excited. From her beginner knowledge of church talk, she gathered that they were feeling at least a little better about Nathan hanging around. And they weren't as mad at her as she had convinced herself that they were. So she tied in her story with Bryce's confessions.

"Before any more time goes by, I need to set a couple of things straight." This time it was she who didn't pause to give the boys time to ask questions or interrupt with their own thoughts.

"First things first. I am sorry for any kind of hurt the situation with me and Nathan has caused you. I really am; you know I hate seeing any of you upset. Second, starting next Sunday, I'll be coming to church with you—every week. And last, there will be no more arguing about me and Nathan. None. There will be normal discussions like those that we've always had when it comes to big decisions in this family.

"I had a really great weekend in North Carolina with Nathan.

But the thing that made it really over-the-top was going to church yesterday. The pastor said a lot of things that … that I think are worth giving a shot." Her demeanor was strong as she blew through her plan, but she was well aware that the tiniest upset could flip her brave exterior right on its head.

Danny asked, "Like what?" She couldn't help but notice he was fairly reserved, almost afraid to ask the question for fear the rug could be pulled out from under him at any moment.

"Like … like sometimes we strangle a situation before we give it to God, and how that's a terrible idea because we like to think we have all the answers, but we don't."

Elizabeth looked around at Bryce, Mitch, and Danny to gauge their responses. Still nothing from any of the three boys, so now she stopped to ask them what they thought. They had no reason—in her mind, anyway—not to trust her, so she let the thoughts sink in.

The boys didn't say anything for a long, quiet moment.

"Guys?" asked Elizabeth, hoping for something.

Bryce cleared his throat and said, "I don't know, Lizzie. All that sounds good."

When Bryce stopped at "good," Elizabeth thought of two things: one, he called her Lizzie; and two, he said "good" in a genuinely kind tone of voice. Plus, she thought his face lit up just a touch.

"Yeah? Good?" Elizabeth said tentatively, hopefully.

Now Mitch spoke. "Yeah. I mean, it sounds *really* good." He paused, clearing his throat. It was obvious there was more he wanted to say, even though his eyes were downcast, she thought she saw a small grin on his young-man face. "You went to church?"

Elizabeth could hear the hope in his anything-but-simple question.

"I did," she said. "And I enjoyed it. Can you believe it?"

This time, all three boys smiled smiles that lit up dim places in Elizabeth's heart.

Danny was the last to respond: "I'm glad you're coming with us. You're gonna love it." He held the same genuine expression and tone with which Bryce responded.

"I hope so," Elizabeth said. "I really do."

The rest of dinner was full of joy and talk-over-each-other chatter. Mitch and Danny received one of their mystery phone calls at the end of it, but combined, they were on the phone for less than five minutes.

When the chores were done, Elizabeth and the boys talked about the upcoming holiday season and their plans. The boys would be in an annual Christmas production at church, and they all decided to go to the Christmas lights show at a local park on Christmas Eve. The conversation was almost over when Danny said, "Hey, we did it again. We planned Christmas before Halloween or Thanksgiving."

Familiar grins filled the table. All four liked Christmas the best of all the major holidays. In Elizabeth's mind, there was little rhyme or reason to their preference, but she wasn't going to complain about it.

Mitch still had English homework to finish, and to Elizabeth's surprise, he asked for her help. He had been so quiet with her lately; Elizabeth wondered just how angry with her Mitch was, and how long he was going to stay that way. A short conversation—combined with what they said at dinner—cleared up her misconception. "It's been a while since you asked me to help you with homework."

"Yeah, sorry about that," he said, looking down at his textbook.

"Anything you want to talk about?" she asked softly, placing her hand in a motherly manner on the back of his head.

"No. Just, glad to have you home." He paused. "Hey, how come you're finally coming to church with us? Do you believe in God now?"

"Aw, Mitch. I never stopped believing in God. I just … have been mad at Him for a long time." She gave him a hug around the neck from behind.

"Because of Mom and Dad and how you got stuck with us?" Once again, if Elizabeth could send a big "Forget You" sign to her parents, she would.

"I didn't get *stuck*. I love you boys. But yes, because of Mom and Dad leaving, and Grandma and Grandpa dying. But you know, I'm starting to think that it's time to give that up."

"Yeah, maybe," he said, smiling even though his eyes didn't meet hers. He was unusually vulnerable tonight, she thought. Maybe it was leftover from the weekend.

"Maybe," she said.

Elizabeth got into bed later than usual Sunday night; doing laundry, talking briefly to Nathan, and unpacking took a surprisingly long time. Doing housework always took more time than she thought it would. Yet, she took her sweet time because, for the first time in a long while, she felt peaceful. She had no desire to rush through all her tasks; instead, she relished the peaceful feeling and let it bleed into her daily activities. Later that night, she lay in bed, exhausted but happy. It had been a great weekend. The time with Nathan was special, and Sunday evening with her brothers was more than she had hoped for.

Elizabeth thought about the new additions of church and prayer to her life. Her choices didn't sound like big changes, but thinking about adding prayer to her day and church to her week still left an awkward feeling in the pit of Elizabeth's stomach. Nathan promised she would feel more comfortable after a while; she hoped he was right. This seemed to her to be her last hope for keeping everything she wanted: Nathan and her brothers, everyone comfortable with one another's presence.

Monday morning, Elizabeth woke to her alarm clock at the usual early hour. She got out of bed, walking tiredly to her dresser as she usually did. Her phone was stored there as it charged every night; if there was one habit Americans her age were tied to, it was checking their phone neurotically. Elizabeth often felt this was the only thing she had in common with other twenty-somethings, even though she knew there was no way she checked it as often as others. And besides, this morning something on her dresser stuck out like a neon sign, preventing her from checking her phone: the sticky note she wrote the night before demanded her attention: PRAY THIS MORNING.

"Oh yeah," said Elizabeth to her empty room.

The change she thought minimal just last night now seemed fairly daunting; praying scared her. Yet, true to her committed self, Elizabeth turned herself over to the task. Unsure of whether she should sit, stand, or kneel, she chose to sit on a chair facing the window where the sun spilled over her. It was warming and soothed her nerves a bit. She far-reachingly equated it to sitting on the beach, which is truthfully what Elizabeth thought of every single time she basked in the sun. But here, she folded her hands, closed her eyes, and bowed her head, just like she saw Nathan and the boys do whenever they prayed.

"Good morning, God. This feels kind of strange to me, but you probably knew that," she paused briefly. "Today I want to pray for a great day, no fighting with my brothers, and patience in the situation with Nathan. That's what he says I need, anyway. And, I pray for a great day for everyone else. Nathan, Bryce, Mitch, and Danny. Thank you. Amen." Her words were soft, hesitant, sometimes barely there. Almost like a first-time sky-diver walking up to the plane, knowing this could offer something powerful, but being deathly afraid to climb inside. But she made it through a whole prayer.

Elizabeth opened her eyes, unfolded her hands, and raised her head—all in one slow motion.

"That wasn't so bad," she said aloud. "Now, for the rest of the day."

Elizabeth's work week started in a routine, humdrum fashion and for that, she was grateful. Prayer was enough change, especially for a Monday; predictability at work was appreciated. But of course, Nathan checked in Monday night to see how Elizabeth's first morning of prayer went.

"It was okay," she said. "Kind of awkward, but you said that would change, right?"

"I think it will," Nathan told her. "Just keep talking, Liz. Just keep talking to Him."

"I will. How was your day?" Elizabeth was eager to move on to the next subject.

"It was good. I had a good day," said Nathan, but he sounded better than good—almost giddy, even.

"Did something special happen today?" she asked, confused by his sudden glee.

"Mmmm, no. Why?" asked Nathan, still sounding especially happy.

"You sound funny."

"I'm happy, Liz. Just happy," he said. He didn't explain further, but Elizabeth assumed it was because she was "finally"—her brothers' words, not hers—praying. She didn't think it was anything too great: her prayer was simple, to the point, and nothing grand like she heard Nathan's pastor utter in church the day before. But, she supposed, if he had been waiting for Elizabeth to start praying, and he himself finds prayer an integral part of his day, it would be natural for him to express delight at Elizabeth's attempt at it.

She carried a light heart with her the rest of the week and into the weekend—until Saturday night when she laid in bed. She was thinking of a slew of topics, as she knew most people did when they lay down. Getting into bed is a completely separate activity than going to sleep. Nathan often teased that her brain was like falling dominoes: one finished thought always laid into another one. Yet, even if the items weren't related, Elizabeth could always dictate the trail. Tonight her trail started with thinking about the accident she saw on the way to the grocery store earlier that day, to being thankful that her car was in good shape, to needing to get her in-dash CD player fixed, to her favorite band, to the concert she and Bryce went to last year, to Nathan's church looking like a concert hall, to going to church the next morning.

Church! She was suddenly alarmed by the fact that, in less than twelve hours, she was going to be sitting in a seat at her brothers' church, the one filled with people her brothers had known for years, people who knew their entire family history. People who would be staring at her because she was the saint/heathen sister who took care of her brothers but never came to church.

In the euphoric state Elizabeth had basked in this past week, she had all but forgotten about the first Sunday on which she would make good on her promise to go to church with her brothers. She had remembered to pray every day; she had even glanced at a Bible Bryce had brought her, and she kept calm in every conversation with her brothers as promised.

I wonder why the boys didn't say anything tonight, thought Elizabeth.

"They probably didn't want to scare me off," she said into the darkness.

But Elizabeth knew that she had to go to church in the morning, never mind the butterflies that were moving in her stomach. Never mind the excuses that were flooding her head. She would go with an open mind and an open heart—as best she could, anyway. A little bit scared, but open. Because she hoped this would help bridge the gap that still existed between her and her brothers. They were an oven compared to just a few weeks ago, but they still acted cold to her on a semi-regular basis. Elizabeth wanted them to know they were still a family, just as the four of them always had been. And that she was willing to make extra efforts to reach out to them, connect with them, and keep their family together. Eventually, she fell into a deep sleep and so woke up Sunday morning rested and ready to face the one thing she had avoided for so many years until just last week.

Elizabeth said her daily prayer and got ready like she would any other day, despite the strong-winged butterflies that had again made their home in her stomach. She headed downstairs just before nine, fifteen minutes before the Tenners were set to leave for the 9:45 service. In the kitchen, her brothers were already eating breakfast. She could hear them talking, so she tiptoed quietly to the edge of the stairs to eavesdrop.

"What's the sermon on today?" asked Danny.

Mitch answered, "Remember? We're still in the middle of the Flying High series. Last week was about what keeps us from feeling free. I think this week is all about how to experience freedom."

"That'll be great for Liz to hear," said Danny.

"I agree," interjected Bryce. "Are you two staying in the sanctuary today?"

"Mitch, are we?" asked Danny.

"Yeah, I think we should. So Liz doesn't feel too uncomfortable."

The room turned silent..

Maybe they're nodding, she thought.

Elizabeth went back upstairs quietly, deciding to come back down again loudly so they wouldn't suspect her eavesdropping.

Bryce drove to church since he knew the way better than Elizabeth. She was paying attention to the mood in the car, which was surprisingly casual. Her brothers seemed to want to distract Elizabeth from her own nerves, and it was working. They discussed upcoming school events and the holiday production all three boys would be in for Christmas, and they wondered aloud how soon it would snow. It wasn't until Bryce pulled the car up to the church that Elizabeth let her nerves get the best of her; she retreated almost immediately.

The structure was large—huge, actually—just like Nathan's church. The building in front of her looked brand new and again more like a small concert venue than a church. Like Nathan's, a large graystone sign read RockPointe Christian Church. The outside landscaping wasn't quite as grand as at ENC, but Nathan's church had a lake and warmer weather to work with. This one had flower beds along the whole front of the building, though bare with the coming winter, and a magnificent oak tree with a few stray leaves just a couple hundred yards from the entrance. Elizabeth didn't realize she was staring until one of her brothers said her name.

"Liz? Are you all right?" asked Mitch.

She snapped to attention.

"What? Oh. Yeah. I'm fine. Fine. I'm surprised at how big this is. I thought you went to the smaller campus near our house where you guys play soccer sometimes," she said. Her speech was choppy, nervous.

"You mean a small church where you think everyone knows our business?" asked Bryce, directly but kindly. He even held a smirk on his face long enough for Elizabeth to see it. She looked Bryce in the eye, startled at his insight. But it was Mitch who answered her question. "We go there about half the time, but on communion weekends, we like to come to the big campus. It's a little less than a year old, so it's a really nice building."

Elizabeth, Bryce, Mitch, and Danny walked into the lobby—atrium, really—where the boys were greeted by people of all ages. The high-ceilinged, warmly lit space was filled with people milling around in between an info center, a music counter, a resource center, a bookstore, couches, and big, comfy chairs. Feeling like she was in an event center as opposed to a church, nothing yet put her off or scared her. They walked straight to the sanctuary, and immediately, Elizabeth liked what she saw. The big room was sort of chilly but still inviting and peaceful. She liked the colors of the walls, the flags around the perimeter hanging from the ceiling, the soft lighting, and the smiling pastor walking around greeting people. The only way Elizabeth knew this guy was a pastor was from a woman introducing him to another man a few rows ahead of where the Tenners sat. If Elizabeth hadn't heard the woman say "Pastor Tim," Elizabeth never would have guessed he was the pastor; he seemed like an ordinary guy. He wasn't dressed in a fancy suit, but rather jeans, moccasin-type shoes, and a plain black t-shirt.

Why did I think he'd be so different? Elizabeth thought.

The service started, and Elizabeth was soon clapping to the music, which she liked very much.

This is a good start.

When the sermon began, Elizabeth felt comfortable enough, but as it went on, she became progressively anxious. The pastor was talking about the freedom that comes with having a relationship with Christ. Prayer and church were one thing, but another new relationship was a bear of its own. Elizabeth was having a hard time enjoying the message as much as she enjoyed her time at Nathan's church because of the magnitude with which he carried his words to the audience. Still, she listened every step of the way, saving her reservations and questions for later.

On the way out of church, Pastor Tim stood at the door to shake hands and give hugs. Elizabeth got a handshake with a "thanks for coming," until he saw she was with her brothers.

"Oh, hey! You're Elizabeth! I'm Tim Messing, senior pastor. It's great to meet you," said the smiling, energetic man.

"Thank you, it's great to be here," said Elizabeth, politely exaggerating with the word *great*.

"Hey, if you need anything, just let us know, okay?" said Tim. He turned to Bryce, Mitch, and Danny and said, "How're you boys doing? Treating your sister right?"

"Yes, sir," they all answered at once with smiles on their faces.

Are they always this happy in church, or is this a show? Just because I'm here?

Tim directed his attention back to Elizabeth. "Elizabeth, you raised some wonderful boys. They are kind, respectful, honest, and full of energy. We love having them here every week."

Elizabeth was taken aback. Not quite surprised the pastor felt this way about her brothers, but it was such a kind, direct, and unexpected statement. Her eyes watered some as she responded with her thanks to the pastor.

"I hope to see you back here soon," he said genuinely, giving her a gentle pat on the shoulder that lingered in a sincerely welcoming manner.

"Thank you." She didn't know what else to say, but that seemed sufficient. The boys talked business-as-usual on the way to the car and only asked what she thought when they were on their way home.

"It was ... unexpected," said Elizabeth slowly.

"What does that mean?" asked Danny.

Elizabeth didn't want her thoughts to come out negatively when they were put into words, so she said, "Well, it was bigger than I expected. Friendlier than I expected."

"Friendlier? Did you like it?" asked Mitch, confused at Elizabeth's minimal evaluation. She could tell he was irritated by her ambiguous response.

Elizabeth took a short breath, carefully thinking about her answer. She weighed telling the truth about how uncomfortable she was and that she didn't love it as she had Nathan's church. Deciding to ask for permission to discuss it later that day, the boys just sat back in their seats, Danny and Mitch taking deep breaths and Bryce slightly hanging his head. The ride home was less carefree than their ride to church.

Nathan happened to call Elizabeth's cell phone just as she and the boys were pulling into the driveway. Everyone had their own plans—study, video games, reading—so the Tenners agreed to re-convene for dinner. Elizabeth called Nathan back as soon as she could without rushing anything the boys had to say before they started their own things.

"So, how was church?" asked Nathan, genuinely interested in Elizabeth's morning experience.

"It was okay," she answered honestly.

"Just okay, huh?"

Elizabeth couldn't tell yet if this news disappointed Nathan.

"I mean, it was okay. It's a big church, just like yours. I just felt sort of awkward," she added.

"Did you feel like everyone was looking at you?" he asked.

"Yes! Like I had a sign on me that said 'NEW AT THIS.'"

Nathan laughed lightly, apparently not too concerned with her less-than-favorable experience at her brothers' church. "That probably distracted you from soaking in the whole experience, then."

"Probably," agreed Elizabeth. She paused as she bit nervously on her fingernails. She continued, "I think my brothers were kind of disappointed that I didn't love it."

"Just make sure they know that you're going again next week, even if you feel uncomfortable," Nathan reassured her.

His comforting words sunk in, but she expressed concern that the situation wasn't easier today than it was a week ago before she started praying every day. Again, Nathan chuckled; he said, "It's only been a week. God isn't a magic pill. Give it time."

Elizabeth let out a dramatic sigh and said, "Yeah, yeah."

After hanging up with Nathan an hour later, Elizabeth walked around the house to see what her brothers were up to. Mitch was practicing guitar with his headphones over his ears; the setup had been a gift from a youth leader at church. He was in a zone; Elizabeth left him alone. Danny was doing his homework at the dinner table. Sometimes he asked for help, but right now he looked absorbed in his assignment. Bryce was standing still out on their deck. Elizabeth wondered what he was thinking about but didn't want to disturb him, either; he, too, looked as if he were intently concentrating on something. She made her way up to her room, where she prayed for the fourth time that day—once in the morning before church and twice at church. It was becoming slightly more natural, and even though it wasn't the morning, Elizabeth felt the urge to talk to God. She assumed it was okay to talk to God at any time of the day, but still she addressed that thought in her prayer:

"Hi, God. I hope it's okay that I'm coming to you for a fourth time like this. I just want to ask … please keep helping me with my brothers. I want us to be okay so bad that it hurts."

She stopped there, choked up enough to where she couldn't go any further in her prayer. She didn't want to cry; she didn't particularly care for crying. It was a sign of weakness in her mind, since her mom cried a theatrical blubbering every time she knew she had let down Elizabeth's grandparents. It was an action that Elizabeth felt her mom carried out because she was trying to gain sympathy, not because she actually felt guilty or broken about any of the foolish decisions she always made. As a result, Elizabeth cried tears of grief when her grandparents died, and since then had really only shed tears of pride for her brothers. When her mom died, Elizabeth cried a few tears, but she decided they were more in remembrance of her grandparents. Elizabeth knew she had three boys to continue caring for; tears would have only slowed her down. But suddenly, the strong-willed, steel-hearted Elizabeth was filled with such strong emotion that tears were soaking her face, and she couldn't stop them.

I haven't cried like this in years'. What the heck is this?

But the tears kept coming. All she could think of was her brothers and the desire to make everything work—her and Nathan; Nathan and her brothers; her, Nathan, and her brothers. For almost an hour, Elizabeth stayed in the chair beside her bed with her knees up to her chest, crying months' (if not years') worth of pent-up tears. Images of her grandparents, then her brothers, parents, and the churches flashed before her like a highlight reel. Nothing slowed her tears;

anything that flashed through her mind pricked her heart like a needle, letting one more valve of sadness leak out until it seemed to be bone dry. Eventually, she fell asleep, waking an hour later to the sound of her brothers' screams downstairs. She shook herself awake, jostled her head to shake the fogginess, and then headed down to see what the commotion was.

"Get it, Mitch!"

"I'm trying, Bry. Chill out!"

Video games, of course. Elizabeth just smiled and watched her three favorite guys bond over games she didn't understand. So much shooting and blood, and her brothers always—every single time—came away from the game frustrated with each other. Thankfully, the real-life tension never lasted more than five minutes, so by now Elizabeth regarded it as a way of life for the Tenner household. She had long ago stopped trying to restore order following a video game. Tonight, after a few minutes of watching her brothers, she went into the kitchen to start dinner. A Sunday favorite: salad, pasta, and garlic bread.

At the dinner table, Elizabeth brought up the topic of church as Nathan suggested. Ways to broach the subject slipped through her mind during the whole time she prepared the meal. She knew honesty to be the best approach but wanted to keep the peace too. She started, "Hey, guys, about church this morning."

The boys all stopped what little noise they were making, and all heads turned toward Elizabeth as though they had been waiting for this moment since the four of them had stepped out of church earlier that day. If anything was going to make her forget her rehearsed words, it was that.

"Wow, you really want to know what I'm about to say. Okay, well, I'm sorry I couldn't give you a full answer earlier about how I felt about church. The truth is, it was kind of awkward for me. Like everyone was looking at me because I'm new and your sister, and I thought most of them might know our story."

Bryce nodded.

"Did you like the sermon?" asked Mitch eagerly. In this moment, Elizabeth hated that she had made the boys wait all day to ask their questions. They cared so much, and it came from such a pure place. This knowledge didn't make it any easier to continue being honest in this conversation. Still, they deserved her full engagement in her promise to go to church with them each week. Being dishonest about her experiences wouldn't help the situation in the least, so she almost had no choice but to speak the truth.

"Honestly, I think I was so distracted from feeling awkward that I didn't let much else sink in."

Danny and Mitch nodded slowly as Bryce asked, "What does that mean?"

"It means …" began Elizabeth. "It means it was an awkward first time, but I'll make an effort to make it better next time."

"Next time? You're coming back?" asked Danny, eyebrows raised and eyes wide.

Elizabeth laughed. "Of course! I gave you guys my word. Every week." Elizabeth hit her hand to the table to emphasize her point.

The boys looked only partially relieved. Elizabeth was confused until Danny said, "Even the weeks Nathan is here?"

"Yes," said Elizabeth, slowly and drawn out. "Why wouldn't I? Nathan will be so happy to go; he's wanted to go with you guys since his first visit."

"Really?" asked Bryce, sounding pleasantly surprised.

"Yes. I told you guys he was hoping I would go to church," answered Elizabeth, getting frustrated. *Maybe this is one of the reasons this has been so difficult: you haven't been listening to me.*

"Why didn't he come when he was here before?" asked Danny.

"Because, Danny, your big sister can be stubborn," said Elizabeth. "Imagine that."

The boys smiled.

The rest of the night was enjoyable—easy, light laughter, and relaxed conversation. Elizabeth hoped the rest of the new week would be the same; it was still the case that one day's progress with her brothers didn't always predict their next day's attitudes. Elizabeth thought about praying again, but decided not to bother God with the same request she'd already made that day. Plus, she didn't want to fall into another crying fit. Even though her tears felt completely dried out, she didn't trust herself to keep her emotions at bay if she made herself so vulnerable so soon after her earlier episode. Instead, Elizabeth got ready for bed and drifted easily off to sleep, thoughts of herself and Nathan snuggling bringing her into sweet dreams.

Chapter 14

"There are no guarantees. From the viewpoint of fear, none are strong enough. From the viewpoint of love, none are necessary."
~Emmanuel

THE FOLLOWING WEEK, HALLOWEEN came and went as just another Wednesday night. The boys handed out candy while watching scary movies, just as they had for the past two years after Danny decided he was too old to trick-or-treat. Elizabeth thought he was too young to stop such a youthful activity, but he was determined, saying that most of his friends had stopped, and he didn't want to be the "loser going with his brothers or sister." Elizabeth stayed busy with chores, not fazed by the movies her brothers were watching. Her mind instead reflected on the past week: seven full days of committed daily prayer and the first of many weekly church attendances. She couldn't say the prayer had been bad for her daily life; the biggest difference Elizabeth noticed was a joyful feeling in the morning before and after she prayed. Before she understood what the sentiment was, Elizabeth asked Nathan what it might be; he told her it was probably peace because she was in God's presence. What that meant, Elizabeth wasn't entirely sure. Yet, the feeling was one she wanted every day, and prayer seemed to bring it.

Maybe I just need to pay more attention. To myself and to God.

However, the peace was the only change Elizabeth could see in her life; everything else seemed to stay the same. Despite their good weekend, her brothers still felt far away, she still felt guilty for having a romantic relationship that caused such a disconnect in her family, and she still thought she might have to give up Nathan. Elizabeth hadn't yet talked about this with him. Instead, it was something she constantly thought and prayed about. She thought back to the first weekend Nathan came to visit her family and how much of an emotional roller coaster it had been. She thought about how far everyone had come; she was going to church. *Church.* Maybe it was time to talk to Nathan; she wasn't getting far on her own. Wasn't that Nathan's biggest argument for Elizabeth going to church? She was crumbling on her own and needed a leg to stand on, and Nathan said God could be that support? Maybe for this, Nathan could see something she couldn't, and maybe the situation was better than she had thus far determined it to be. Deciding to have that talk with Nathan on Friday when he came to visit, she jumped back to the present where she and her brothers were sitting comfortably in the living room with a somewhat new tradition. And she quite enjoyed the quality, albeit quiet, time.

The first Friday of November was a pleasant one with a bright sun shining freely without a trace of cloud cover. Some leaves were still on the trees, which, despite the scent of snow in the crisp fall air, gave the illusion that winter wasn't about to sneak up on everyone like it did every year. Fall was hanging around for at least a little while.

Elizabeth made breakfast for the boys because it was the morning before the weekend Nathan was coming into town. She thought she could score some brownie points that would carry over through the weekend if she baked; food always eased at least some of the tension whenever it existed in the Tenner house. Which, as of late, had been running rampant compared to the last few years. After their mother died, the Tenner siblings experienced a semblance of serenity. Elizabeth had already been in a routine of caring for her brothers, and their mother dying only eased the burden: one less child for Elizabeth to worry about.

In response to her Thursday night reminder that Nathan would be in town beginning Friday, the boys just nodded nonchalantly with words of "We know," and "Okay." It was this kind of response that confused Elizabeth. They weren't upset, and they weren't excited; they seemed to be somewhere in the middle, but she couldn't figure out where.

Her brothers' feelings fought for her attention all day Friday, along with the anticipation of seeing Nathan. Thankfully, the day flew by and before she knew it, Elizabeth was standing in Nathan's embrace while they waited for the garlic bread to come out of the oven.

"It feels like forever since I've seen you," said Nathan, peppering her neck with light kisses.

Elizabeth laughed and said, "It's only been three weeks."

"I know. Too long," said Nathan, now rocking Elizabeth back and forth in his arms.

Elizabeth leaned into Nathan's chest, savoring the warmth of another body so close to hers. After a few seconds of silence, she said, "So, I want you to pay attention to my brothers tonight. I can't really tell if it's getting better."

"Really?" Nathan sounded surprised. "On the phone you said you thought everything was fine. Or was that one of those 'fine' answers that really means 'crappy'?"

She swatted his arm. "Sometimes it feels fine. But I really want an outside opinion."

"I'm not really an outsider. I care as much as you care," said Nathan sincerely.

Her moist eyes let him know she appreciated his attitude. But she made sure he understood that she believed he might see things she didn't, since Elizabeth was with the boys every day and Nathan wasn't.

Nathan nodded slowly and waited a moment before answering. When he responded, he said, soberly, "Okay, as long as you do a favor for me."

"Oh boy," said Elizabeth. She pushed back from Nathan to reveal her playful smile.

"C'mon. Hear me out," he said. He looked to the ceiling

before tightening his grip, and Elizabeth thought she saw him take the faintest deep breath before he said, "I will give you honest feedback about what I see between you and your brothers, and then we will talk about me coming here for Thanksgiving."

Elizabeth thought she felt her heart stop, even if for a moment. Thanksgiving was a topic Elizabeth expected to talk about this weekend, if only because the holiday was on its way, and she realized that it was a natural progression for couples who are as serious about each other as she and Nathan were to start spending holidays together. Still, she felt surprised at the timing of Nathan's request. In the midst of expressing concern over whether or not her brothers were adjusting to the idea of her and Nathan's relationship, Nathan raised the subject of spending a major holiday together.

Elizabeth had two courses of thought: in her fairy-tale mind, Elizabeth imagined Nathan being with her family for Thanksgiving and everyone being enthusiastic about it; in her cynical mind, the one that immediately jumped to the worst-case scenario, Elizabeth dreaded the holiday because she knew if Nathan was with Elizabeth's family, the boys might be withdrawn. But if Nathan stayed home in North Carolina or went back to California, it might put a strain on his and Elizabeth's relationship.

Another lose-lose situation, she thought.

Elizabeth's thoughts played out on her face as they usually did, and Nathan asked her, "Are you worried about your brothers?"

"Do you even have to ask?" She gave him a look of exasperation.

"True. Well, let's see how tonight goes. Okay?" Nathan sounded encouraging and hopeful.

Elizabeth knew that was the only thing they could do, just wait and see. She couldn't force her brothers to accept as much of this situation as she so desperately wanted them to, but she knew they were trying for her. She still felt like she was spending a lot of energy between her brothers and Nathan, but she wasn't as exhausted as she had felt in the beginning.

Maybe this is *working*, she thought.

Elizabeth's hopes were confirmed throughout dinner, dessert, and the board game everyone played together after the ice cream cake. When everyone sat down for dinner, Danny asked Nathan if Nathan would like to pray, and then all three boys thanked Nathan for the prayer. Lively conversation continued into the cheesecake with talk about school, unusual news stories, and crazy weather stories.

Elizabeth got confused when, after dessert, Bryce asked Nathan if they could talk outside. Mitch and Danny looked nervously at each other and then at Bryce.

When Bryce and Nathan were gone, Elizabeth asked, "What's going on, guys?" sounding as unsure as she felt.

But all Elizabeth got out of Mitch and Danny were shoulder shrugs. To make matters worse for Elizabeth's imagination, neither Bryce nor Nathan looked any different when they came inside not two minutes later. Elizabeth hesitated to ask what was going on because her intuition told her it was something sensitive. Yet, for the whole time they played Wits and Wagers, not one of them—her brothers or Nathan—gave an indication that anything was out of the ordinary. It wasn't until Elizabeth and Nathan were finally alone and saying their goodnights that Elizabeth had the chance to ask what Bryce said to Nathan outside.

"I was wondering how long it was going to take after the boys were out of earshot for you to ask me that question." Nathan looked at his watch. "Hmm—twelve seconds. I was way off; I figured two."

Elizabeth threw a couch pillow at Nathan's head; he turned so it hit him in the back.

"Okay, okay," Nathan gave in. "If you're going to get violent, I'll talk! Bryce simply said that he was glad I was here and that each of the boys is making a concerted effort with me tonight."

"Oh," said Elizabeth. She thought for a moment before continuing: "So they were okay with you tonight, or they were just acting?"

"Honestly, I think a little of both," he said with his mouth slightly upturned. Elizabeth was disappointed until Nathan kept talking. He said, "Elizabeth, this is a good thing; before, they'd just clam up. At least they're trying, even if it is just halfway."

Elizabeth had her arms folded and her head down for a moment, but it came up gradually as she slowly agreed with Nathan that halfway was better than nothing. "You're right, some is better than none." She paused. "It just feels like it's taken forever to get even this far."

Nathan nodded and agreed. "It does feel that way. But keep the faith, Liz. Keep the faith. We're getting there."

Saturday was a low-key day. Nothing special was planned for Nathan's visit, so when Mitch and Danny were called about a touch football game with their youth group, the boys asked if they could go.

Elizabeth hadn't even answered before Mitch added, "Bryce and Nathan can play too, and you can come watch, Liz. Please?"

Elizabeth had a fleeting thought that Mitch had included Nathan just so he could go, but Elizabeth chose instead to take Nathan's constant advice to stop being so cynical and believe that Mitch genuinely wanted to include Nathan. So, off to church they went for a touch football game and an impromptu pizza party afterwards. Elizabeth spent her time not watching the game but rather watching her brothers interact with Nathan, and talking to other women who were watching their boyfriends, husbands, and sons. It was normal conversation, but Elizabeth was surprised at how effortlessly it flowed and how at ease everyone seemed. Elizabeth's previous thoughts on people at church—especially women—were that they were nothing like her, they would never understand her, and she wouldn't get along with any of them. About a dozen people proved her wrong Saturday, including Katie and Bri, two women to whom she took a particular liking. Elizabeth readily admitted her change of heart to Nathan and her brothers on their way home Saturday night when Danny asked her if she had fun. The men in Elizabeth's life were happy to hear her experience was a positive one, especially Sunday morning when Elizabeth seemed more than ready for church. She was the second one ready behind Bryce.

Sitting in the sanctuary surrounded by her brothers—Danny and Mitch stayed again in the sanctuary for service—gave Elizabeth an extraordinary feeling in her heart, as though it were a bucket filling up and about to overflow. Her fullness increased when the pastor talked about things that bring us joy, and, after a quick dip, it increased yet again during the car ride home when Danny asked an important question.

He started the conversation by saying, "Hey, Liz, we have a question for you, but I don't want to ask you in front of Nathan."

Immediately defensive, Elizabeth said, "Danny, that was kind of rude. Can't you wait until we get home?"

"No, I really can't wait," said Danny with a serious expression.

Elizabeth's eyes widened as she gave Nathan a pleading look and mouthed, "I'm so sorry." She turned to Danny and said, "I don't see any way for you to ask me now without Nathan hearing. You're going to have to wait," she said sternly.

"Can I whisper it in your ear?" asked Danny, still very serious.

Elizabeth sighed with a sense of resignation and said, "I suppose."

Within seconds, Elizabeth's face lit up. Nathan looked confused, so she waived her hand as if to say, "Don't worry!" and said to Mitch, "Go ahead."

Mitch smiled, face turned toward Nathan, and asked, "Would you like to come to our house for Thanksgiving?"

Nathan let out a nervous laugh and then broke into a wide smile. He said, "Of course I would! Of course. But why did that have to be a secret?"

Danny grinned and said, "To mess with Lizzie."

Everyone was in great spirits when Elizabeth took Nathan to the airport. On the way, he said to her, "So I guess we answered your question about the boys being okay."

"I guess we did," she said, still with some reservation. "We're not exactly where I want to be; it's still kind of up and down. But I suppose we're getting there."

"That a girl," said Nathan with a wink.

"So I'll see you in two-and-a-half weeks?" she asked when they were saying goodbye.

"I guess so," said Nathan, lamenting that it was too long.

Their hug and kisses lasted long enough that a security guard had to shoo Elizabeth out of the drop-off lane in front of the terminal. Only slightly embarrassed, they still managed to share a briefly intimate kiss before Elizabeth got back into her car and drove away.

Smiling all the way home, Elizabeth thought about the time just a few months ago when she drove to work in a fit of anger because she didn't think her brothers would ever be okay with her and Nathan's relationship. It felt like yesterday and forever-ago at the same time. Now here they were, more than five months later, and things might be turning out the way she'd hoped.

The one thing that made Elizabeth unsure of the stability of her brothers' feelings were some of the arguments they all were still having: Danny getting mad that Elizabeth was on the phone almost every night; Mitch and Bryce arguing over another bad test score Mitch got on a history test—he had never gotten a bad test score before this school year; Danny and Bryce getting into an argument over Danny being late getting home from a friend's house. Elizabeth listened to each argument closely, and her brothers' irritations mostly seemed to be blown out of proportion and sometimes unjustified. These were the times Elizabeth thought their attitudes masked something deeper, something either they didn't recognize or weren't sharing with her. Nathan tried to convince her that she was making too big a deal of some things, that nothing will ever be perfect, and that "we should rejoice in our victories," such as the boys inviting Nathan for Thanksgiving. A simple life lesson, but one Elizabeth had trouble holding on to.

"What victories? Did you not just hear all those arguments that have happened in the last two weeks since you left? Danny still isn't letting me help him with his math homework; he still seems so mad at me when you're not around."

"You think him getting mad and your brothers fighting sums everything up? Are you telling me they never fought before I came along? And, correct me if I'm wrong, but didn't Danny say that he wants to start doing his math on his own? And, again, correct me if I'm wrong, but didn't your brothers—not you—invite me for Thanksgiving?"

Elizabeth didn't say anything. She was silenced by Nathan's common sense.

"Liz?" he said almost impatiently.

"Yeah?"

"You have *got* to start having more faith in your brothers. They're adapting. And I think if your attitude went from fearful to hopeful, they'd adapt faster."

Elizabeth felt guilty after Nathan's words. She had slipped back into having a bad attitude after a week or two of letting her new-found peace takeover. She knew this could be boiled down to one word: expectation. She had expected going to church and praying to change her heart automatically, but it was still taking time. Time Elizabeth felt they didn't have.

Chapter 15

"Lend me a heart replete with thankfulness."
~Shakespeare

A LL OF A SUDDEN, the week of Thanksgiving arrived. Elizabeth was about four weeks into her church and prayer commitments. Finally—*finally*—she was able to see some movement. She took Nathan's advice and stopped paying such close attention to every single word her brothers said or each move they made; she relaxed in church and gave up being paranoid that others were watching her; and she was open with Bryce, Mitch, and Danny about how much she cared for Nathan, how Nathan loved her too, and how desperately—though she used a different word—she wanted the relationship to work out. To her surprise, her brothers claimed they knew how badly Elizabeth wanted everything to work out. Their claims were confirmed when, after Elizabeth's vulnerable confession to each of them, Bryce, Mitch, Danny, and Elizabeth fell into their familiar pre-Nathan cadence: no walking on eggshells, complete and mostly tactful honesty, and genuine concern for each other manifested in kind conversation. Even the fact that Nathan was coming into town in just a few short hours did nothing to hinder the boys' spirits. In fact, it was Elizabeth—again—setting them on edge with her ever-present pre-Nathan jitters.

The snow hadn't yet begun to fall, but the frosty spurts of breath when anyone spoke outside said the air was surely cold enough to warrant at least some snowflakes. The trees were all bare, the ground was frozen, and cars demanded a good five-minute warm-up before being driven. Nathan was coming into town Tuesday night and staying until Sunday afternoon, his longest visit to date. Elizabeth was filled with more anxiety than every other visit combined. She was afraid that if they didn't figure this out soon, come up with a cadence for Nathan being in their lives, then he might not be able to stay. Thus, her demeanor the four days before Nathan arrived mirrored her jitters from his first visit back in August. She over-cleaned the house, over-bought the groceries, and was on edge during dinner Tuesday.

"Liz, you really need to relax," said Bryce. "You're driving us crazy. Again." Mitch and Danny nodded readily in agreement.

"Seriously, Liz. What are you so nervous about?" asked Mitch as he reached for another piece of sushi. Elizabeth had served this meal the Tuesday before Thanksgiving for the last six years because Wednesday is when the cooking started. This take-out choice was easy, light, and always a hit.

"This is the first time it's ever been us plus one for a major holiday," said Elizabeth, whining just a little bit.

"We've gone to other peoples' houses for Thanksgiving before. Plus, I thought you really wanted Nathan here," said Bryce, sounding exasperated at having to convince Elizabeth that he and his brothers really wanted her boyfriend at their table for the holiday. He added for good measure, "That is why *we* invited him."

She winced at his *we* emphasis. Shouldn't she be over-the-moon at her brothers' willingness to add Nathan to their holiday table? Doesn't that hint at the boys' acceptance of the situation? Still, her nerves weren't settling down just yet. "This just feels different. I really want it to go well," she confessed. Everyone knew how she felt, how badly she wanted all parties involved to feel loved, respected, and content, and quite honestly, she continued to feel vulnerable since opening herself to prayer and church.

Bryce, Mitch, and Danny were all silent, but they looked at each other. As always, Elizabeth wished she could read their minds. Her intuition often let her know her brothers' mood or whether one of them had more to say, but it rarely, if ever, gave her an inclination toward the secret, non-spoken language the three brothers shared. Finally, Bryce shook his head and told her, "Just chill out, Liz. Just relax. It'll be fine."

"You promise?" asked Elizabeth with raised eyebrows as she looked down toward the table, fiddling nervously with her napkin in her hands.

"Yes," answered Bryce, "we promise." He made no effort to mask his exasperation, but Nathan's pending visit was no small thing.

Nathan had taken a cab to the house from the airport, and so he got there after eleven Tuesday night. A warm smile met him in the driveway even though it was a down-to-your-bones kind of cold. She had waited all day—all week—to see Nathan's smile and to be enveloped in his embrace.

"Hey, you," said Nathan in a low voice that Elizabeth found irresistible.

He pulled Elizabeth into a hug. After a long moment, he pulled back to give her a bag of chocolate that she hadn't seen in her rush to hug him. He certainly knew his way around Elizabeth's heart: a big bear hug and chocolate.

The two talked while gathering Nathan's stuff from the ground where he left it in his rush to hold Elizabeth. Beside his usual duffel bag and briefcase was an extra small suitcase, since he was staying two days longer than every other visit. That alone split Elizabeth's mind in half: two extra days of snuggling, good conversation, and great kisses, but also two extra days of worrying about everyone's feelings but her own.

Maybe I can chill out this time and concentrate on the good stuff.
Yeah, maybe.

She quieted her mind on the short walk inside the house, where Bryce was the only one to greet Nathan because the other two had already gone to bed. He was reading in the living room but got up when he heard Elizabeth and Nathan come through the front door.

"Hey, Nathan," said Bryce, shaking Nathan's hand. "Let me take those for you." Bryce took Nathan's bags and put them on the bottom stair.

"Hey, Bryce. Thanks. How ya doin'? Ready for the holidays?"

"Kind of. It's always so busy at work. I like the money, but it's pretty tiring," he said, yawning.

"I bet. In college I worked at a grocery store, and from Thanksgiving to New Year's, it was nothing but nonstop insanity."

"Pretty much," said Bryce, just before another wide yawn came upon him. "I guess that's my cue. I work a double tomorrow, anyway."

"Get some rest, Bryce," said Elizabeth. Already some of her anxiety was squashed by the easy interaction she had just witnessed.

I guess I do need to just relax. Thank you, God.

"Goodnight, guys," said Bryce.

After Bryce was safely downstairs, Nathan pulled Elizabeth into the living room and kissed her much longer than the peck he had given her out in the driveway. Elizabeth savored his kisses as she reciprocated every ounce of affection Nathan showed her. A few minutes passed before Nathan pulled back and said "Hello" again, with a wide smile.

"Hi there," said Elizabeth with an equally large smile and mischief underneath her words.

"So," Nathan began, "I'm really excited to be here for five whole days."

Elizabeth could see that Nathan couldn't hide his feelings if he tried; his face was all but glowing, even in the dim light of the living room. "If that kiss is any indication, I guess you are," said Elizabeth, a coy expression coloring her flushed face. She was still reeling from their brief-but-wonderful intimacy a moment ago. "I've been looking forward to it too. One of these times you're going to have bring Jax with you, though."

"I know. I miss him too," Nathan said. "But, more importantly, you haven't been nervous about me being here not only for five days, but also for a major holiday?" Now his eyes and mouth were flat, Nathan's way of letting Elizabeth know he knew the answer to his own question but couldn't resist asking it anyway. Nathan asked his question so naturally, she sighed a knowing sigh, audibly.

People know me better than I think they do.

"No, of course not," but she quickly reneged, "Well, okay, yes. But I feel a little better than I did yesterday."

"Good." And that was that. He let it go, moving on to wondering about weekend details. "What's the plan? What do the Tenners do for Thanksgiving?"

In the two weeks leading up to this visit, Elizabeth had given him a scattered account of a typical Thanksgiving but had been too nervous to give a wholly detailed explanation. Now the couple was cuddling on the couch. Elizabeth was in her comfort zone and could tell Nathan how most every year she cooked the desserts on Wednesday, and the boys usually picked at that stuff all day. "Which is fine. It's one of our many traditions, if you will." She told him how the boys' plans always vary; sometimes they stay home, and sometimes they go out together. It never mattered, because they were always home by nightfall. It wasn't until the middle of Elizabeth's holiday weekend explanation that she became serious.

"There is only one rule for this weekend: you may not ask, at any given time, 'what are you making?' It's not allowed. And for Wednesday night din—"

"Not allowed? You have rules in your kitchen?" Nathan was amused enough to interrupt her mid-sentence.

"Absolutely. The boys used to ask what I was making, I'd answer, and they'd make comments about it. So I made the rule. Every time they asked, they lost one turn picking a movie. The first year, they asked so many times that they had to watch seven chick flicks in a row."

"No mercy, huh?"

"They haven't asked since," said Elizabeth, shrugging her shoulders, clearly satisfied with her Thanksgiving Eve caveat.

Nathan inquired again about what her brothers would do on Wednesday but wasn't too worried when Elizabeth had no idea aside from Bryce's double work shift. He said, "I'm sure we'll figure something out. They invited me, so at least I know they want me here." His open smile was genuine and did more to relieve her frazzled nerves.

The clock read a late-night hour, but Nathan and Elizabeth

stayed up for a while longer. They talked about past and future holidays, and, as always, faith and church. Elizabeth had been going to church every Sunday now for a little more than a month, beginning with her visit to Nathan's church, and had been praying daily for that long too. She and Nathan hadn't talked about it very much over the phone because Elizabeth preferred face-to-face talk when it came to what she called high-stakes topics, especially faith. Since the first day, Elizabeth had enjoyed her daily prayer time and had come to rely on it to fuel her inner peace for the day. The times when she read her Bible—a couple times a week before going to bed—were growing on her too. At first, she looked at it as a textbook, something she had to read in order to understand and pass some kind of Belief Test. But in time, Elizabeth had come to read it as words filled with hope and practical applications for her life. She told this to Nathan late Tuesday night.

"I'm really enjoying the Psalms and Philippians. I remember one phrase—verse, sorry—one verse said, 'Be anxious for nothing, but in everything by prayer and' … Oh, I can't remember. 'By prayer and …'"

Nathan added, "'Petition, with thanksgiving, let your requests be known to God—'"

Elizabeth finished, "'And the peace of God, which surpasses all understanding, will guard your hearts and minds through Christ Jesus.'[1] I really liked that because I like the part about peace. His peace surpasses my understanding. I like thinking about something bigger than myself. I like not thinking I have to do it all."

"I'm glad you're paying attention and getting something out of the time you're putting in," said Nathan.

"What do you mean?" she asked. Sometimes his insight seemed to smack her right in her defensive side.

Nathan was used to this—he told her so—and thus answered calmly, "I'm just glad you've kept an open mind and heart to this stuff. If you'd read and prayed but kept your heart closed, I think it would just bounce off of you, and we wouldn't be having this conversation."

Elizabeth's eyes filled with tears at his comment.

"And, by the look in your eyes, I can tell it's working. You're more sensitive than you used to be." He quickly added, "In a good way, of course."

"I suppose," she said, agreeing with Nathan but knowing that there was still a portion of the puzzle that she hadn't been able to fit together, and until she could do so, that missing piece would keep her from experiencing the full joy Nathan always talked about. Her frustration was once again reflected on her face.

"What's going on in that mind of yours?" asked Nathan, confused by how the moment had gone from joyful to heavy in a matter of seconds.

"I was thinking," she started slowly, careful to express herself honestly but clearly, "that no matter how great this feels—my having even a little bit of faith and us sharing the experience—until I know my brothers have no heartache regarding you and me, I will not feel free."

The moment wasn't quite awkward, but it was as close as could be. She let out a sigh, and Nathan let out a deep breath. It always came down to that, didn't it? How her brothers felt about their relationship.

Nathan rubbed his hands over his face and said, "I don't know what to say, Liz. It's not like we haven't talked about this."

"I know," was all she could say. Variations of this conversation had been hashed out so many times, there was nothing new to discuss. All it seemed anyone could do was wait, and then wait some more.

Nathan again breathed deeply; he looked so vulnerable, she noticed. Elizabeth could see his heart trying to settle itself as his face showed understanding on its last nerve. "This resistance of yours gets exhausting."

"I know that too," was Elizabeth's only answer. What else could she offer? She couldn't just let go of eleven years of pseudo-motherhood. But she owed Nathan the effort, that she knew. If for no other reason than she had given him her word that she would try to have a better attitude. He had come into their lives with no warning, yes. But she encouraged his presence, she kept him around. The least she could do was have an attitude consistent with those actions.

A few moments' silence passed before Elizabeth asked if they could get some sleep for now and try to enjoy the holiday weekend as a family. "We'll see where we are on Sunday." Even though she nervously choked out the operative phrase in that statement—see where we are—she could see Nathan light up from the inside out.

"That—" Nathan kissed Elizabeth lightly, "sounds like a plan."

After a goodnight kiss that was as lengthy as their second hello kiss, Elizabeth headed upstairs to her bedroom, and Nathan set up camp in the living room. Even with uncertainty floating around in her heart, and her mind racing a thousand thoughts a minute, Elizabeth couldn't help but fall asleep with a smile on her face, knowing that a man whom she loved and who loved her was asleep just underneath her floor. This had been an unrealized dream up until the past summer when Nathan accidentally allowed a slobbery dog to spill orange-pink sticky smoothie all over her, thus inducing the beginning of the deepest relationship Elizabeth had ever experienced outside of her brothers. Yet, true to form, Elizabeth fell into a restless sleep as a result of being torn down the middle between loads of "maybe" statements and complete contentment.

Wednesday passed in a way Elizabeth didn't expect. It turned out Mitch and Danny had made plans to play a touch football game with some families from church. Elizabeth felt herself getting anxious until Danny said the magic words: "You're coming, right, Nathan? You'll be bored staying here all day. Liz just cooks and doesn't even let you know what she's making. She doesn't even like anyone in the kitchen!"

"Danny," stated Elizabeth, "you're being dramatic." His words might have embarrassed her—had she not been so overjoyed that Danny assumed Nathan would be coming with him to the sudden invitation of a touch football game.

"Whatever, Liz, it's true. C'mon, Nathan, get your stuff," he said.

Nathan looked at Elizabeth with an expression that seemed to say, "What choice do I have?" She could tell Nathan was happy about this "forced" time he would spend with her brothers. He didn't seem nervous, but she guessed that was just for show, or maybe not since he seemed to have so much more faith in her brothers' ability to adapt and accept him as part of the family. Either way, she would find out later. For now, she would bake her desserts, hoping the boys were playing nice.

Nathan drove Bryce's car; Bryce had gotten a ride to work that morning. As it turned out, Elizabeth was short one stick of butter. Forty-five minutes after the boys left, she did too. Humming along to the radio, she realized she would be around the corner from where the boys were playing their touch football game with people from church. Curiosity grabbed hold. Elizabeth wanted to see how everyone was doing. Were the boys letting Nathan play? Were they having fun together? Was it awkward?

Elizabeth wasn't sure what she expected. Nathan would probably tell her she was foolishly expecting the worst. But when she saw what she saw, her eyes welled up with tears, and naturally, ever so quietly, she whispered, "Thank you, God."

Danny had just scored and had run to Mitch and Nathan for high fives. Elizabeth saw Nathan give Danny a pat on the back, and all three were laughing and smiling as if they were three brothers, not two brothers and a man trying to fit into their life. Nothing seemed out of place, nobody seemed left out or left to feel unwanted. It struck Elizabeth like an unforeseen June bug smacking her on the forehead; for months, she had been looking down, fearing the worst and not looking to anywhere or anyone for help. She wasn't paying attention to what was *really* going on in front of her, but only to what she expected to see. Now, the situation seemed to hit her hard enough to cause her to look up and watch where she was going. She saw a situation she had almost written off, a man she had almost cast away, brothers she had underestimated. Finally, smiling and satisfied, Elizabeth drove home and finished her baking, all with an honest grin created out of nothing less than bliss. She enjoyed the boy-less house by putting on her iPod and dancing around as she baked. A true measure of a happy woman is uninhibited dancing in the kitchen, which Elizabeth did until Nathan walked in. Or at least until she saw Nathan standing at the doorway of the kitchen, not even trying to hide a smirk as he watched her unreserved side fill the room.

"I guess the church was open after the game, but it was a teens-only thing. The boys are getting a ride from the Donovans."

"The Donovans?" asked Elizabeth. Now it was her turn for a smirk.

"Yes, why is that funny?"

"It's not funny. You just ... you sounded like ..." Elizabeth became suddenly serious.

"What?" asked Nathan urgently.

"You sounded like you've always been here. Like it was the most natural thing in the world for you to be here and my brothers to be hanging out with the Donovans. It just sounded so ... family-like."

Nathan's smile was one of pleasant realization as he said, "It did, didn't it?" He proceeded to fill in Elizabeth on his day: how their team won, how well her brothers and he got along, how they opened up to Nathan some about what Elizabeth had meant to them over the years. Elizabeth ended up having tears in her eyes as Nathan detailed the day, which was becoming something of a normal occurrence for her. Never before had Elizabeth cried or come close to crying as often as she recently had. She thought it silly; Nathan assured her it was because she was opening her heart. His exact words were "You're finally letting it flow. It's not rusted shut anymore." Her brothers, on the other hand, when they witnessed her tears, just looked at her strangely, wondering why their sister, who almost never shed a single tear, was suddenly bubbling up like an ever-running faucet.

When the sentimentality of the moment passed, Nathan, in all seriousness, asked Elizabeth what she was currently making in the kitchen. Elizabeth raised her eyebrows; Nathan stared right back, asking what the big deal was. Yet, almost as soon as he saw Elizabeth's face, his own facial expression indicated that he'd just realized his mistake. He quickly tried to recover. "I meant, what's for dinner?"

"Nice try. You lose one chance to pick a movie," she said with a ha-ha smile on her face.

"Man! I knew better," said Nathan. He hung his head in mock defeat.

"You did. I warned you fair and square. I knew I'd get you. Now, give me a hand and order some food," she said, still smiling. "All we've got are desserts."

"Sure," he said.

———————————

Thursday morning was typical of past Thanksgivings in the Tenner household. Elizabeth worked in the kitchen, and her brothers watched the parade while they played poker, using coin change as betting money. Elizabeth's grandfather used to keep four cans in his closet, one for each coin value. Once he and their grandmother passed away, Elizabeth continued the organized tradition as a way of remembering her grandparents. Since they were the only role models she ever truly had, she kept as many of their ways incorporated into her daily life as she could. And every Thanksgiving, while Elizabeth cooked in the kitchen, the Tenners' coffee table looked the same: stacked with varying piles of quarters, dimes, nickels, and pennies, as her brothers good-naturedly played cards. Nobody ever kept the change, but sometimes they played Winner Eats First or Winner Gets the First Slice of Pie.

The biggest variable this year in the Tenners' holiday was Nathan's presence in the kitchen with Elizabeth. When she encouraged him to hang out with the boys in the living room, Nathan refused, insisting he was with the boys the whole day before. This morning he wanted to spend time with her. Elizabeth blushed and kindly accepted.

They brushed and basted and mixed and poured for almost five hours until they could finally say, "Time to eat." Elizabeth paid close attention to how she and Nathan worked together in the kitchen. They had cooked together before, but this was not any old day. Not only was it a major holiday, but it was very familiar territory for Elizabeth. Traditions held strong ground in her home, and

Nathan's being there could either severely disrupt the stability of such traditions, or the holiday could be made better by the presence of a man who deeply cared for this family. Plus, Elizabeth had been cooking alone in that kitchen for more than a decade; she had worried Nathan's presence would make her feel crowded. Instead, they moved together and around each other easily, another indication that they fit together well.

When the group sat down to eat, Nathan asked if they did anything special for grace on Thanksgiving, knowing that at any moment a quirky Tenner ritual could make an entrance.

Mitch answered, "Not for saying grace, but we have a game we play."

"Why am I not surprised?" asked Nathan, shaking his head. "What's the game?"

Danny answered, "Well, we roll a dice and however many it lands on, we count that many to the right. Whoever that lands on, we have to tell why we're grateful for that person in our life over the past year."

"Hmm. I've never heard of that before," said Nathan.

"Just one more game Liz made up when we were little that we never stopped playing," said Bryce nonchalantly.

Nathan looked to Elizabeth with noticeable admiration.

"It's not that big of a deal," she said. "Our folks weren't around, and after Grandma and Grandpa died, I had to think of ways to keep the holidays happy."

"Who goes first?" asked Nathan.

"The first person to roll four," answered Elizabeth.

"Why four?" asked Nathan.

"Because there are four people in our family," she said, although she became immediately quiet as her brothers looked from her to Nathan, wondering if that was going to hurt Nathan's feelings.

Nathan casually carried on the conversation with another question: "Who rolls first?"

"Liz," all three brothers answered at the same time. Because she's the oldest and made up the game, they explained. Though Danny suggested—while Elizabeth rolled a two—a reevaluation of that rule; it may be someone else's turn to go first one of these years.

"Ha ha! *You* can't go first." Danny made fun of her because Elizabeth had gotten a four the last three years in a row.

"Whatever," said Elizabeth with a fake air of annoyance. Then she said, "You're up, Mitch," because he was to the left of her. He rolled a one.

"Ooh, maybe next year, bro," said Bryce. Everyone was laughing when Bryce rolled; they kept laughing when he got a six.

"Ooh, maybe next year, bro," said Mitch, mocking Bryce in a brotherly way.

The next person around the table was Nathan. Everyone seemed to realize it at the same time because all were suddenly subdued and silent. Nobody said 'yea' or 'nay' to him playing their game; in the past any guest would play, but Nathan was a high-stakes addition to the table. Elizabeth and her brothers, and even Nathan, knew this was a test run for possible future years of Nathan sitting at the Tenner holiday table.

Elizabeth looked like she wanted to say "Roll" but wasn't sure how her brothers would feel. She almost felt like it wasn't her call to make. At the same time, Danny was looking down at his plate, and Mitch and Bryce were looking from each other to Danny to Elizabeth and back at each other. Finally, after what felt like a long-suffering hour, Bryce said, "Go ahead, Nathan. Roll."

Danny's head snapped up, and Elizabeth asked, "Are you sure?"

Bryce looked at Mitch and nodded. He said, "Yeah, absolutely. Roll."

As predictable as it was, Nathan rolled a four. He asked for a reminder as to which way to count around the table. The answer was to the right since the dice rolling went to the left.

Nathan counted: one, Bryce; two, Mitch; three, Elizabeth; and four, Danny. What Elizabeth would thank Nathan for later would be not only Nathan's words but also how quickly Nathan answered. He said, "Danny, I am grateful that you invited me to play touch football yesterday. I had a blast. Thank you."

Danny looked mildly uncomfortable but was polite and said, "Thank you, Nathan."

Elizabeth didn't let it sit too long. She said, "Okay, Danny, you're up."

Danny rolled: a four.

"Weird. Another four," he said. "That's one, two, three, four. That's you, Lizzie. Let's see … I am grateful that you make my lunch every day. My favorite part is the note you put in there," he paused for a moment before continuing, "You're the best, Lizzie."

Elizabeth had tears in her eyes—*Again!* she thought to herself—which she tried, unsuccessfully, to hide. She cleared her throat and said, "Okay, who's next?"

"You are," said Mitch. He added in Nathan's direction, "We always make her cry at least a little bit. The *one* time out of the whole year we are guaranteed to see tears in Elizabeth's eyes."

"That's not true," Elizabeth said in a very unconvincing manner. She thought it ironic that Mitch emphasized *one*: In years past, he would have been right, but lately her eyes were practically an irrigation system without an off switch.

She continued, "Okay, I go again," she rolled a four. "Where are all these fours coming from? That's one, two, three, Mitch. Hmmm …" Elizabeth pretended to think hard about her words before she said, "Mitch, I am grateful that at fifteen years old, you still hang out with your family. You're an awesome kid—young man, sorry."

Mitch smiled wide. Then he rolled a three, which went around to Nathan. A tense smile formed again on Elizabeth's face, but that changed when Mitch gave his answer. He said, "Nathan, I am grateful that you are the reason for Elizabeth's permanent smile. We've gotten many more cheesecakes because Liz bakes when she's happy. So, kudos, man. Thanks!"

They all laughed, but Nathan's smile was smeared on his face. It was evident he loved this game and this family.

Suddenly Bryce broke through the laughter by waving his hands over the table. He said, "Hey, nobody said anything about me!"

"You know what that means," said Elizabeth matter-of-factly.

"I don't," said Nathan. "What does it mean?"

"It means," she said, "that Bryce rolls, and that person says something about him. Go ahead, Bryce."

"Here goes." He rolled what he wished he had rolled in the first place. "Sure, now I get a four."

He counted four to Nathan and said, "You're on, man."

Again, Nathan didn't hesitate when he said, "Bryce, I am grateful that you stayed in church with your brothers. You are a great role model for Mitch and Danny, and a great help to your sister. Thank you."

Obviously touched by Nathan's sentiment, Bryce nodded and cleared his throat three times before saying, "Thank you." He paused shortly. "Now, who's hungry?" Even though emotions were shared freely in the Tenner household, Nathan wasn't part of that. Not yet, anyway. Yet Nathan seemed unfazed by Bryce's cut-off of what may have been a seminal moment. Instead, Danny said grace, and Thanksgiving dinner at the Tenner dinner table was a sight to see. At one point, Elizabeth sat back and watched while Nathan and her brothers talked and laughed. She was in awe; she felt content, joyful.

I do need to relax, she thought. *Everything seems to be going fine; every*one *seems fine.*

There were only three brief moments the entire weekend when she could tell someone was uncomfortable. In each situation, Nathan and Elizabeth were showing physical affection to one another, and at different times, each brother seemed uneasy. Elizabeth only brought this to Nathan's attention on the way to the airport that Sunday afternoon; she didn't want to spoil his time with her family.

In response to Elizabeth's concern, Nathan said, "I think that's an okay kind of uncomfortable, though. How are they going to get used to it if they don't see it?"

"I don't know. I just hate seeing any kind of confusion or discomfort on their faces, especially if I'm the reason for it," she said.

"I know, Liz. But you've got to realize that some kinds of discomfort are okay. Some things they really will get over," he said to encourage her. "Just keep concentrating on the good."

Elizabeth only nodded in agreement.

Nathan added, "How about we give them more chances to get

used to the physical affection? Say, in about a month?"

"I thought we already decided you'd skip Christmas but come for Valentine's Day?" She wasn't agitated at his question because she had come to expect Nathan to make what she believed were overly bold requests of her and her brothers when it came to his visits.

Nathan made a "hmmm" noise and said, "I don't know, Liz. I was thinking I'd come for Christmas."

Elizabeth shook her head and told Nathan, "We talked about that. It's too big of a holiday. Plus, what about seeing your family back in California?"

"What if I told you," said Nathan, pausing to build anticipation, "that your brothers invited me?"

"I'd say, are you sure you weren't daydreaming?"

But when Nathan smiled, she had to reconsider. Which she did, but only for a moment. "No way." Nathan kept smiling. "I don't believe you." Still, Nathan remained where he was. Finally: "My brothers asked you up for Christmas?"

"Yep, this morning after church," he said happily.

Elizabeth was silent, but she had a doubting smile on her face.

Nathan asked, "Is that a yes? I can come for Christmas?"

Elizabeth swatted him on the arm and said, "Smart aleck. What about your family?"

"They're actually coming out to see me early next year, so I'll see them then. They know I really want to come to New York, and they're okay with it," he said.

"If you say so," she said in a singsong voice.

"I do say so. And I'm telling you, Liz, trust your brothers more. I think they're really coming around more so than you think."

Elizabeth nodded, thinking about Nathan's words and her other thoughts from the weekend. Thoughts on how the weekend went better than she expected, and how much fun everyone seemed to have. On her drive home, Elizabeth thought solely of her brothers and how far they'd really come. From just a few months ago, Danny's crying outburst at the table and the argument she and Bryce had when she found out they were talking about her behind her back. She remembered feeling so betrayed, furious even. But now, Elizabeth was blown away by the fact that her brothers, without even talking to her about it, invited Nathan, her love, to their home for Christmas. She surged with pride for them and decided she'd call everyone together when she got home from the airport.

The boys didn't seem too surprised at the impromptu meeting. Bryce said when they sat down, "We figured Nathan would tell you on the way to the airport, and that you'd have something to say about it when you got back."

"You're all telling me," said Elizabeth with a smile and a finger waving, "that you're completely okay with Nathan being here on Christmas? The biggest holiday in this house? The one where we have more traditions than the rest of the year combined? Exchanging gifts with us? Decorating cookies with us? Eating Christmas dinner with us?"

The boys looked at each other as though deciding who would answer their big sister. It was Mitch, but all he said was, "Yep." No explanation, simple as that.

"Anything you want to add? Like a reason or something?" she asked, still confused.

Mitch and Danny looked at Bryce, so Bryce answered: "Look, Liz. We tried like you asked us, because we knew you would give him up if we asked you to. Truth is, we like having him around. It's a little weird once in a while, but overall, it's not too bad."

All she could do was put her hand on her heart while she swallowed fresh tears. A few managed to spill out onto her cheek, silently, but there nonetheless. She thanked them through the clearing of her thick throat, and asked to talk to Bryce alone. Mitch and Danny never minded being excluded from what they called brother/sister mom/dad talks; they gladly walked downstairs to their room.

When the younger boys were out of earshot, Elizabeth asked Bryce when this shift in attitude came about.

"I think it's a combination of things," said Bryce.

"Of what things?" asked Elizabeth, almost suspiciously, still reeling from her brothers having invited Nathan to their house at Christmas. *Christmas.*

Bryce answered, as always, quite candidly: "Well, you not

backing down right away, Nathan making a huge effort, and our youth pastors at church."

"What do your youth pastors have to do with anything?" Now she was even more confused.

"Are you kidding? Derek and Steven checked in with Mitch and Danny almost every week when this whole thing started. They've talked them through stuff the boys needed outside perspectives on."

"Derek and Steven? I thought Greg was your youth pastor?"

"He moved up to the twenty-something's," said Bryce.

She shook her head quickly, as though that was a detail she didn't care about. Not at this moment. "This is great news," said Elizabeth, wrapping her arms around her brother. And that's when it hit her: "Hey! Is that what all those phone calls for Mitch and Danny were about?"

Bryce laughed lightly and said yes. Again lost for words, all Elizabeth could do was nod. Her heart felt still, her mind drawn a blank, as she tried to pinpoint when this shift happened. In the back of her fuzzy mind, she knew Nathan would tell her that God was working in the background of the situation, that just because Elizabeth didn't see every step of improvement didn't mean nothing was happening.

"God's finally listening," she said, almost to herself but loud enough so that Bryce clearly heard her.

He responded in kind, nonchalantly and without missing a beat, "No, Liz, I think you're finally listening." He walked away, leaving Elizabeth to marvel at how mature and kind-hearted her brothers were. All the kicking and screaming each of them did when it came to bringing Nathan into the family had subsided. Each seemed to have made peace with their part of the equation; she could see it on everyone's face and in everyone's behavior, including her own.

How'd I get this lucky?

She quickly added out loud, "Thank you, God."

Chapter 16

"What we really need to teach ourselves is to stay until the end.
Finish what we start. Work it out."

THIS YEAR'S HOLIDAY SEASON seemed especially pleasant for Elizabeth. She relished the cold weather because it felt refreshing; she cherished the holiday decorations she and her brothers put up in the house; and she found no stress in the long lines at the store when Christmas shopping for her brothers and Nathan.

Just ten days away, Christmas was the Tenners' favorite time of the year, and it showed. Handcrafted decorations lined the doorframes and shelf surfaces, the Christmas tree was small but lit to the hilt with colorful lights, and there was a snowman mailbox outside and a mailbox for Santa inside, both fashioned by Mitch and Danny, respectively, as school projects. The boys always spent a lot of time at church for the annual production, and Elizabeth never minded the serenity of the house. It glowed in the holiday lights, and Elizabeth liked almost nothing more than reading by the tree, drinking freshly brewed cinnamon tea. This was often a time of reflection for Elizabeth, as she thought about the past year, wondering how in the world everyone survived another three-hundred-sixty-five days. She would think about what to get her brothers for Christmas, wonder how the coming year would be, and dream of ways to make their lives better, easier. Even though, really, their lives were fine before Nathan entered the picture. Stability in their house didn't mean a mom and dad; it meant banding together and loving each other fully, knowing there wasn't anything that could break their bond. But this year, Elizabeth had the luxury of relishing in something else: her relationship with Nathan. It had been one to toss her into the throes of making the difficult decision to push her brothers forward in a situation they had no desire to be in. Yet, look what had happened. Never before had Elizabeth experienced such a deep-seated peace, such an honest sense of belonging as she did when surrounded by her favorite boys. With Bryce, Mitch, Danny, and Nathan, life seemed as it should be. As it should have always been. As it should always be. Only traces of her cynicism remained, and with it, she hoped against hope that her brothers' feelings of acceptance—ready acceptance—toward Nathan were true and permanent.

Another one of Elizabeth's treasured Christmas activities was walking patiently through a nearby mall, looking for potential presents for her brothers. Her family never had a lot of money, so there was always a price limit for gifts, but Elizabeth rarely stayed under budget, especially when she started her career after college. She couldn't help it; Elizabeth delighted in seeing her brothers' faces when they opened their gifts Christmas morning. Even though no more than two gifts each were ever exchanged, the morning was always special. When her brothers were younger—even just five years ago—they made Elizabeth homemade gifts or took a goofy picture of themselves and framed it for her. Elizabeth's all-time favorite gift from her brothers was a picture where they dressed up like three characters from *The Princess Bride*—one of all the siblings' favorite movies—with materials from their church's drama resources and took a humorous picture.

Again, Elizabeth thought to herself, *How'd I get so lucky?* In the middle of the store, her inner dialogue started, one side of her heart fighting the other over reason and faith.

It's not luck, Liz. You worked hard to keep those boys straight.

I know, but church helped too. I think that's something I can no longer deny. I can only imagine where we'd be without their help.

I can't believe I'm thinking these things. Wasn't it just six months ago that I was ranting dead-set against the church?

God changes hearts, huh?

There I go again. Stop being so cheesy, just pick out some presents.

Elizabeth tried shutting off her wandering thoughts so she could enjoy the Christmas music and finish shopping. She found a new football on sale for Danny, a video game for Mitch, and a new school bag for Bryce. Their other gift would be a gift card each.

Now for Nathan's gift.

She and Nathan had also decided on a price cap for their gifts to each other, but Elizabeth had trouble finding something appropriate. She picked up books and put them back down. She did the same with clothes, electronics, movies, and with items from what felt like every department in every store.

Finally, after hitting each store in the mall at least once—and some twice—she settled on a new Bible with his name engraved in the cover. It wasn't two weeks ago that Nathan had complained about needing a new Bible. She remembered seeing it at Thanksgiving; it was all written in and highlighted, pages were torn, and the back binding was coming undone. She saw this as a thoughtful, meaningful gift.

At home, Elizabeth spent time making three kinds of Christmas cookies: shortbread cutouts with different color frostings—some without frosting, saved for a Christmas day tradition; chocolate snowballs with icing, the boys' favorite; and gingerbread men that Elizabeth and the boys traditionally dipped into hot chocolate on Christmas Eve while they watched their favorite Christmas movies. Rituals like these were all the more reason for Elizabeth and the boys to enjoy Christmas so much. With the amount of instability the four had experienced in their short lives, the traditions Elizabeth was able to establish made a big difference for her and her brothers. It gave them something certain that they could look forward to at different times throughout the year.

To go along with the sliver of skepticism she still had in her heart, Elizabeth watched her brothers each night for an indication that they felt this Christmas might be different from the last since Nathan would be joining them. Yet, she could see no such sign that her brothers felt any less holiday cheer this year compared to years past. They laughed and talked easily, each excited for their school breaks. They briefly discussed gifts, but only to tell each other that they'd all be really excited. Danny requested a Christmas movie more than once after dinner or dessert was finished. One particular night, he asked for his favorite, a TV movie about a misplaced reindeer. It was one Danny asked for that the rest of them inwardly cringed at every year. But Danny loved it, and after all, he sat through movies that he didn't care for, either. It was on television as dinner was ending a few nights before Nathan was to arrive. Cookies in hand, Elizabeth, Bryce, Mitch, and Danny enjoyed the movie together by the glow of their Christmas tree and lighted manger scene sitting under their television. Just that one night with her brothers would have been enough to fill Elizabeth with holiday spirit, but she seemed to keep finding a reason every day to be joyful: Christmas music on the radio, great grades for Bryce's first semester, an easy day at work, wrapping presents. From the simple to the sentimental, the reoccurring feeling for Elizabeth was joy.

Nathan arrived at Elizabeth's house late on the twenty-third; inclement weather kept his flight from being on time, which Elizabeth half expected because what was Christmas in New York without some squally weather? He was so tired when he pulled in the driveway in his rental car; he told Elizabeth that aside from a sweet kiss from her, he wanted nothing more than to fall asleep in a comfortable place. Elizabeth had no time to confess to him that she was still kind of nervous about him being there for Christmas, but she had no choice. Nathan's eyes were closing before he hit the pillow.

Maybe that's a good thing: less time to verbally fret about it.

The next morning, on Christmas Eve day, Elizabeth saw to it that Nathan and the boys woke up to the smell of sweet cinnamon rolls, a tradition started by Elizabeth's grandmother. Christmas Eve was always a lounge-around day for Elizabeth and her brothers, and this year was no exception. A few times in the past, the siblings had been invited to other families' houses, but they usually preferred to stay home. The Christmas production at church would be performed the next day, and participants always had Christmas Eve off to spend with their families. Sometimes movies were watched, games were played, and new batches of cookies made if too many of them had been eaten the previous week. But today was different, and not just because Nathan made it five rather than four people. Bryce, Mitch, and Danny completely surprised Elizabeth and said they were going to build a snowman outside.

"You realize you're all over the age of six, right?" Elizabeth teased.

Danny answered, "Whatever, Liz. You'll see how awesome our snowman turns out to be. Then you will be jealous that you didn't help us."

Elizabeth laughed, but four hours later—just in time for dinner—Bryce, Mitch, and Danny had indeed built a tall yet plump, jolly-looking snowman. Elizabeth left Nathan inside while she ran outside with her camera to capture the boys and their creation. This was a moment she wanted to remember, because after all of the out-of-the-ordinary things the Tenner boys had experienced in the previous six months, here they were, embracing a child-like spirit and building a snowman.

After the boys were changed and warmed up, dinner was served. Elizabeth liked to switch up the menu each year; she wanted the boys to expect at least one surprise aside from their gifts, amid the volume of traditions celebrated during the month of December. This year the table was covered with roasted chicken, a baked pasta dish, Italian garlic bread, salad, and carrots. The only complaint was from Mitch about the salad: "Too healthy, Liz."

Elizabeth made him eat some anyway.

Once stomachs were full and plates were cleared, the Tenners plus Nathan parked in the living room with cookies, tea, and hot cocoa, ready to watch three Christmas movies.

Nathan commented at the end of the evening how great the day was. He said, "You all moved like well-oiled machines today. I could tell even the order of events was a tradition not to be messed with."

"You know, I started them as much for me as for the boys," said Elizabeth. "Our parents certainly weren't going to give us any."

Nathan nodded. He asked, "What about your grandparents?"

She said, "They started a lot of them, but I added more after they died. We needed stability and comfort, you know?" Her strong-willed approach to life was evident in everything she did, everything she said. Nathan said he was proud to be with her and thanked her for letting him be a part of everything. He waved his hands around in a large circle, as though to indicate the entire house. Not just the holiday activities, but the doing-life stuff, like making dinner together and then eating as a family, going to church, letting him choose a movie. These little things mattered, to Nathan and to Elizabeth.

Elizabeth was moved; she didn't know what to say. Nathan left her with a kiss on her forehead so she could sit in the moment as long as she needed. Her emotions were on a hair trigger, and it seemed anything she found touching or endearing made her have to catch her breath. It was added weight to an already-weighty weekend, but in a good way.

Later that night after everyone said their goodnights and headed to bed in high anticipation of the morning, Elizabeth sat by herself in her room. She was alone with every bit of hope and heartache, every bit of faith and fury she had felt since Nathan walked into her life. It all seemed to culminate tonight, when she and her brothers shared an evening that had always been precious to only them, with a man who, without a shadow of a doubt, wanted to be involved in the rest of the Tenner family Christmases. It was time to pray, she decided. She had gotten used to the feeling of prayer over the last several weeks, and tonight was one of those nights that warranted an extra conversation with God. She knelt in front of her bed, slowly folded her hands, and with a wavering voice began to talk to Him.

"Hi, God." She paused, checking to see if tears were coming. None so far, so she continued. "God, thank you for today. Thank You for ... everything. For the boys, for Nathan. For how much they love me. For how much I love them." She paused again, still waiting for the tears, then finished. "Thank you for how much You love. How much You love them, how much You love me. Goodnight."

With a sense of having just laid her restless heart completely in someone else's able hands, Elizabeth fell soundly asleep; she was ready for Christmas morning.

Elizabeth woke to the usual sounds and smells the next morning; Bryce, Mitch, and Danny were making—or had finished making, she couldn't tell—breakfast for the family and Nathan to enjoy. They did this every year, but just like every other tradition, this one never got old. She walked downstairs and to her delight saw Nathan in the kitchen with her brothers, getting the dishes ready with food and the glasses filled with orange juice. The boys were cleaning up, so she assumed they had just finished preparing the meal. Elizabeth had been standing in the doorway for a good two minutes before anyone saw her. Nathan was the first one.

"Good morning, babe," he said as he walked over to give Elizabeth a light kiss. She had learned to enjoy small breath mints on weekends with Nathan, so the moment was minty too.

"Hey, Liz. Finally! Ready for breakfast?" asked Danny. He was the one who could never wait to get the morning activities started. Not just because of the church production, but because he was the most enthusiastic about the gift exchange.

"Of course, of course. Need any help?" she asked.

"Nope, we're good," said Mitch. "We'll meet you in the living room. You too, Nathan."

Elizabeth and Nathan walked into the living room, where they shared a longer kiss before Nathan said, "Good morning, again."

"Good morning," said Elizabeth. "And merry Christmas."

"Merry Christmas to you," said Nathan with a sincerely serene smile. As if there was no place in the whole world he'd rather be than standing right in that spot, about to eat breakfast with Elizabeth and her brothers.

Could this be any better?

"Merry Christmas, Liz," said Bryce as he, Mitch, and Danny walked in with breakfast.

Like every other year, they ate breakfast on the floor in the living room. Nobody could remember when that tradition had started, but it was theirs, and nobody ever tried to change it. Sometimes they rushed through breakfast; other times, it was more leisurely. This morning, it was the former, and Danny was the one pushing everyone to finish. Always excited about Christmas morning, he seemed to have extra pep this morning. But Elizabeth noticed Mitch and Bryce giving some kind of eye contact to each other that, as always, seemed all too mysterious and sneaky. To rile Danny up, Elizabeth pretended to slow down, but only for a second before Danny gave her the stink-eye.

"Danny, what's the big deal?" said Elizabeth.

"I'm really excited about your present," he said, wide, bright eyes backing up his words.

Yet, no matter how zealous Danny was, he still had to wait: Elizabeth always liked to give her gifts first. She always pulled the "I'm the oldest" card and won every time. Just like dice rolling at Thanksgiving, Danny always suggested a reevaluation of that rule.

The boys said they loved their presents, and so did Nathan. Finally, it was Elizabeth's turn to receive from her brothers. "I'm so anxious to know what this is. You guys are acting more excited than usual," said Elizabeth.

They only smiled.

Danny handed Elizabeth a large, thin rectangular box of medium weight and said, "Here," with a giddy, goofy smile on his face. Mitch took a deep breath, and Bryce leaned forward casually.

"What the heck is this?" Elizabeth unwrapped the box with fervor, anxious to know what her brothers were so excited about. She was confused when she saw on the cover that it contained a six-frame décor piece. It was attractive, but a home décor item was hardly something her brothers would express enthusiasm over. She thanked them, but Bryce wasn't satisfied.

"Open it!" he said eagerly.

Elizabeth obliged, and when enough of the gift was out of the box, she realized what it was and barely caught her breath.

The deep brown frames were arranged in two rows, connected

by a decorative horizontal bar in the middle and held together by a similar bar above the top three frames. The top three frames held separate pictures of Bryce, Mitch, and Danny. The photos were professionally done, and each brother looked more grown up than they usually did in their day-to-day lives. But what really struck Elizabeth was the bottom set of frames. Under each boy's picture was a hand-written letter. She read them aloud, her tears starting at the beginning of Bryce's:

Lizzie,

> *The past 6 months have been especially difficult for our family. But I thank you from the bottom of my heart for trusting God to make room in our family for Nathan. I've been learning from you for a long time, Lizzie, and now is no exception. You're the **best** sister, ever.*
>
> > *I love you.*
> > *Bryce*

He had run his pen noticeably over "best" so that it was bolded. This was her favorite part of the letter, because from the repetitive motions he must have made with his pen, there was plenty of time to think about what he was writing. And he must really mean it if he bolded that one word.

Next, Mitch's:

Dear Liz,

> *This gift is meant to be a reminder of how much we love and appreciate you. You do more for us than you ever have to, and I don't even want to think about where we'd be without you. You're one of my heroes, Lizzie.*
>
> > *I love you.*
> > *Mitch*

No bold in this letter, but still Elizabeth felt like she couldn't handle any more emotion. She cherished Mitch's sentiment because she felt the same way. No matter how often she wanted a non-mom life, Elizabeth had no idea where she would be without her brothers.

She was already crying, but happy tears on her face were now a familiar and welcomed sensation. Danny's letter was last, and he had been the one waiting so eagerly for her to open the gift in the first place, so she knew there was no stopping. Reading aloud, her voice wavered the entire time:

Hi Lizzie,

> *Thank you for never leaving our side. Thank you for finally coming to church. Thank you for making our lunches and washing our clothes. Thank you for finding a guy like Nathan who not only loves God but really loves us too. You're the greatest, Liz. I love you!*

> *Love,*
> *Danny*

Elizabeth was speechless, mainly because she had tears running down her face. She kept going back to the greeting of Danny's letter: "Hi Lizzie," the endearing name he called her when he was expressing a deeper-than-normal sense of brotherly love. She could hear his voice through the letter, and for that she knew she would be moved each time she glanced at this gift. A few more sniffles escaped as she silently re-read the letters. She could hardly believe what she was seeing: a transformation of hearts, in the best way possible. What used to seem impossible, now felt gloriously possible. Confident in her brothers' full acceptance of Nathan's presence in their family, she was deeply moved to a place in her heart that, until recently, she had no idea existed. It breathed new life into her; it gave her reasons to dream and courage to love.

FOUR YEARS LATER

"Most of all, best of all, it lives in our hearts."
~Les Miserables

O N A SUMMER DAY similar to the one almost five years ago
when Nathan and Elizabeth met, the couple was set to marry
in a small ceremony at Nathan's old church in North Carolina. He
had moved up to New York with Jax—much to Danny's liking—
more than two years ago, but the town where the two kindled
their relationship held special meaning. It was home of their first
encounter, their first kiss, their first taste of life with one another.
The officiating pastor was Pastor Tim, the man charged with bap-
tizing Elizabeth more than a year ago. He had been part of the boys'
lives for enough time that Elizabeth finally took the time to get
to know him, the youth pastors, and other people in her brothers'
church. This had been the last bit of the puzzle to cause Elizabeth
worry: feeling at home in a church. The boys assured Elizabeth
that her faith was her own, meaning she could come to that point
whenever she was ready. In true Elizabeth fashion, she worried for
weeks about whether or not this was hurting her brothers' feelings, if her brothers would feel betrayed that she didn't feel settled
right away, and even if she was making the right decision in following her newfound sense of faith. After what felt like countless
conversations, Bryce, Mitch, and Danny finally asked her to stop
asking them so many questions. She was driving them crazy with
her nerves. Again.

Pastor Tim had also taken a special liking to Nathan. By the time Nathan moved to New York, he had already visited RockPointe more than a dozen times. Tim had walked Elizabeth and Nathan through pre-wedding conversations and decisions, Elizabeth needing to move methodically through the process. Some days, the change was still too much for her. Those days were fewer and farther between as time went on, but they were frustrating, nonetheless. Nathan was split on his attitude toward her continued hesitancy: half the time he was patient, half the time he was maddened by her resistance to change.

But today was not one of those days. The sun shone alone in a deep blue sky, joined only by a bird here and there. The church grounds held a gazebo, beside which stood the pastor, Nathan, and the wedding party. Standing up for Nathan were three friends from New York. All three were from church, and one was a co-worker at the school where he taught. Standing up for Elizabeth were her three brothers and Katie and Bri, two women she met from church four years ago. Through their constant outreach and patient friendship courting, they both taught Elizabeth a lot about faith and relationships. She was glad to have them stand by her.

Bryce, Mitch, and Danny had one other role in the ceremony: they would walk Elizabeth down the aisle and give her away. In Elizabeth's mind, there was no other way for the ceremony to start, considering the boys had been the most important men in her life for most of her thirty years.

When the music started, Elizabeth watched from behind her curtain; she couldn't believe that almost one hundred people had come to support her and Nathan's forever union. People from church and work, New York, North Carolina, and California. She had finally met Nathan's family three-and-a-half years ago when they traveled to the East Coast to visit Nathan. It wasn't earth shattering, but everyone got along okay, which is what mattered most to Nathan. He wanted no drama. He had had enough of that growing up, he said.

Elizabeth had not been paying attention to the ceremony,

and suddenly the music changed. Her heart did a flip-flop as seventeen-year-old Danny asked, "Are you ready?"

She most certainly was. This was a moment that just five years ago seemed so far into the future; it wasn't even a smidgen of a thought, a blip on her radar. Not even a *maybe* had crossed her mind. Elizabeth had been certain that a relationship of any kind—let alone one this deep, one this permanent—would be ten, even fifteen years away, well after the boys were out of the house. And yet here she was, being proven wrong for the umpteenth time in the past five years.

The walk down the flower-strewn aisle was intentionally slow, and Elizabeth tried to soak in every moment. The guests were watching her every move as she held onto her smiling brothers. Mitch was holding her hand; Bryce and Danny were each holding an arm. They were quite the sight, the Tenner siblings. But everything was as it should be.

At the altar, her brothers answered the "Who gives Elizabeth to Nathan?" question with an affirmative "We do." Then her young men stood to the side in their handsome tuxedos, watching their family grow by one.

The pastor kept the ceremony short and sweet upon Nathan and Elizabeth's request, but still, when Elizabeth heard "You may now kiss the bride," she couldn't believe it was the end. She and Nathan shared a tender moment to the cheers and hollers of their friends and family.

The reception was on site, starting almost immediately following the ceremony. Toasts were made, dinner was served, the cake was cut, and Nathan and Elizabeth shared their first dance. The day went by in a blur, but Elizabeth made sure to hold onto every memory she could: being walked down the aisle by her brothers, forgetting part of her vows, accidentally saying "wife" instead of "husband" after "I take you as my lawfully wedded ...," watching others dance, seeing the sun set beyond the church.

In the middle of the insanity, Elizabeth kept thinking about how fortunate she was. All the gifts she had been given, she realized, were given by a God who loved her deeply and wanted nothing more than for her to know that and feel free in His love and in the life He'd given her.

Elizabeth held Nathan's hand as they walked around to mingle, and she compared her thoughts on God from five years ago to her thoughts on God today. Certainly, she believed more in His divinity and intervention strategies, but she also chose to trust His people more. She chose to trust the church by keeping her commitment to going every week and getting to know other people. She chose to trust her brothers in new ways, especially in regard to her and Nathan's relationship. She also knew that her far-from-perfect family would always face challenges, but her confidence in their ability to handle them was magnified.

Elizabeth Tenner (now Elizabeth Monroe) would be the last person to say that the five years since she met Nathan were easy or altogether enjoyable. Her heart was pushed and pulled, broken and pieced together repeatedly, in ways she had never before experienced. But for all the drama and grief Elizabeth's life held in her first twenty-two years of life, nothing could have prepared her for the movement in her heart that she underwent since knowing Nathan.

But above all, Elizabeth had learned a wider definition of love, a definition that covered her and her brothers, her and Nathan, Nathan and her brothers, and most of all, best of all, it covered her and God.

Acknowledgements

K. Lucas, I am thinking of you as I write this.

It's hard to fit all the gratitude I have in my heart into 1 page of 11-point font. My life is full – God has given me incredibly loving and supportive parents (including my step-mom); a brother that makes me laugh like no one else; faithful and genuine friends; a Mac Daddy small group that never ceases to amaze me or make me smile; family that overwhelms me with their kindness and congratulations through each of my adventures; and a husband who is a consistent example of Love. I only hope that my daily life reflects the love and appreciation I have for each one of you.

For this book specifically, Thank you to: Katlyn, Jim & Aunt Bonnie for being my first editors.

My first readers for your love, pride, excitement, and insight.

Savannah Morning News for being my first professional outlet for writing on a regular basis.

P&G team: you had no idea I was writing this when I was working with you, but your friendships gave me an irreplaceable gift of hope at just the right time.

Sam Lowry & everyone at Ambassador International for taking chances on first-time authors like me and being so helpful throughout this entire process.

And Greg, for being the biggest part of a life I love. (Time flies like an arrow. Fruit flies like a banana).

Footnotes

Chapter 6
    1: You Still Hold Me, Savannah Christian Church, Live Praise: We Want to See Jesus, 2008

Chapter 9
    1: Matthew 11:28
    2: Galatians 5:1
    3: 1 Corinthians 10:23
    4: Proverbs 3:5

Chapter 10
    1: Proverbs 27:17

Chapter 15
    1: Philippians 4:6

Discussion Questions

1. Which character do you identify with the most? In personality? In your attitude toward faith?

2. It took Elizabeth months to go to church after initially meeting Nathan, but that was years after failed attempts on her brothers' efforts. What might have been different had Elizabeth listened to her brothers weeks, months, or even years earlier? Have you or someone you know ever been on either side of that equation: refusing to go to church, or trying to convince someone to go? What was your experience?

3. Elizabeth's faith is a slow growth process. It is put into motion by Nathan's presence in her life, as Nathan opens her eyes to the possibility of peace in her heart. She starts to think that maybe she doesn't have to do her life alone. Describe a time in your life when you were stubborn toward something that would ease a burden, but it took someone or something bold to open your eyes and heart to it.

4. How did Elizabeth's past play into her stubbornness toward the church? How does your life story influence your daily life? Your big and small decisions?

5. Nathan was mostly patient with Elizabeth's journey; only once in a while did his frustration come out. How might

their relationship have been different had Nathan been less patient with Elizabeth? Have you ever experienced a relationship where you were waiting for someone to come around to something? How did you handle it?

6. The dynamic of Elizabeth's relationship with her brothers shifted when they had to make room for Nathan in the family. What was it like before Nathan? How did it change? How do relationships change through time and circumstance?

7. Elizabeth's brothers could have done a lot worse as they grew up, but the biggest headache they gave Elizabeth were attitude problems and the occasional fight at school. Homes without stable parents have high potential for turning out children who are reckless and irresponsible due to the instability of the family of origin. What helped Bryce, Mitch, and Danny stay so focused and out of trouble? Did one factor have more of an impact than another?

8. What was most important to Elizabeth as she tried to draw Nathan into her family? Did she focus too much on one piece of the puzzle? Have you ever experienced a similar situation of facing obstacles in a relationship? What did you focus on to make it better? Looking back, were there things you could have done differently?

9. At the start of the story (and for most of the years before), Elizabeth was not a crier. Now, in the middle of everything happening in her life, she sheds tears quite easily. Why do you think that is? Can you relate that to an experience in your life?

10. Bryce makes it clear that the brothers' changes are not by their own efforts, but that both prayer and Elizabeth's willingness to pray help the situation. Do you think it was one

thing or several things that worked on Elizabeth's heart? Did she have control over her heart softening? Think of a time when your heart was hardened toward something. How long did it take to break down your walls? Talk about your experience.

For more information about
ELISA POMPILI
&
MAKING ROOM
please visit:

elisapompili.wordpress.com
ecpompili@gmail.com
@ecpompili
www.facebook.com/elisapompili

For more information about
AMBASSADOR INTERNATIONAL
please visit:

www.ambassador-international.com
@AmbassadorIntl
www.facebook.com/AmbassadorIntl